Dr. Joe

AND THE SNOWMAN

Dr. Joe
AND THE SNOWMAN

STEVE RIEDEL

Published by Tate Publishing & Enterprises, LLC
127 E. Trade Center Terrace | Mustang, Oklahoma 73064 USA
1.888.361.9473 | www.tatepublishing.com

Tate Publishing is committed to excellence in the publishing industry. The company reflects the philosophy established by the founders, based on Psalm 68:11,
"The Lord gave the word and great was the company of those who published it."

Book design copyright © 2011 by Tate Publishing, LLC. All rights reserved.
Cover design by Kenna Davis
Interior design by Nathan Harmony

Published in the United States of America

ISBN: 978-1-61346-115-0
1. Fiction / Romance / Suspense
2. Fiction / Psychological
11.05.03

Dedication

This book is dedicated to all those who have survived physical and sexual abuse, especially those abused by perpetrators holding positions of authority and trust.

Acknowledgments

I want to begin by acknowledging everyone who works in the "helping professions." Each and every day, substance abuse counselors, school counselors, social workers, ministers, teachers, and psychologists hear disturbing life histories that weigh heavily on the heart. It is my hope that through this story, the reader will grow in appreciation for the work that such trained professionals do.

Because stories can be thieves, robbers of time, a special thank you goes to my wife, Marietta, for enduring another novel. Through all of the work, you have not only understood, you have encouraged and guided. Please know that you are appreciated beyond description or measure. I also want to express highest regard for my editor, Hannah Tranberg. Hannah, as *A Homestead Holiday* is warm and cozy, this story is at times cold and discomforting. Thank you for venturing into both fictional worlds with me. Also, thank you for your endless patience and for helping me find the better writer within. Finally, I wish to express my appreciation to the entire Tate Publishing team for their continuing support of my work.

Prologue

My name is Bob Michael, and if we were together, I would reach out, shake your hand, and say, "Welcome to Dakota City." However, since a handshake is out of the question, let me begin by telling you that Dakota City, my new home town, is a picturesque little community located in eastern South Dakota. The town is nestled on a knoll and sits just a short stroll from the north shore of a large shallow lake. The other three sides of town are surrounded by wide-open farmland, which stretches as far as the eye can see. The nearest neighboring community is twenty-eight miles away, and the nearest city of any size is what we call "a good piece down the road." Only twenty blocks square, Dakota City is dissected precisely in half by Main Street. Main Street is bordered by two rows of tall, silver, metal streetlights. On a clear summer night, these sixteen lights, eight on each side of the street, glow like a radiant dome and mark our small place on what was once vast rolling prairie. On a cold winter night, the lights reflect brightly off the snow and their yellow beams point high into the unobstructed sky, offering comfort for nervous travelers who might be more than thirty miles away.

There's only one highway passing through town, and sadly, more people travel the outbound direction than the inbound. I say sadly because Dakota City is a good place to live, and good people live here. We recruit and welcome newcomers. Yet we can be slow at truly accepting them into our tight-knit social circle...unless love should happen to intervene. In this story, the people of Dakota City are blessed with a newcomer: Dr. Joseph Doyle, PhD. Dr. Joe, like me, came to town hoping for a fresh start in life.

Even as "newcomers," it did not take long for either of us to discover that the people of Dakota City constitute what is, in the truest sense of the word, a *community*. Because there are so few of us living here, when one person grieves, everyone grieves. When one celebrates, all celebrate. Folks are always willing to help a neighbor, but they also make a practice of minding their own business. More often than not, our cars and homes are unlocked, and it can be said that we trust each other, maybe to a fault. Because crime is so low, many assume watchful *vigilance* to be unnecessary; some go so far as to consider it offensive. It was this assumption that once allowed Dakota City to be the home of an evil man, a man who lived hidden within a position of sacred trust until the snowman got involved.

Dr. Joe and the Snowman

Ifirst heard the story of Dr. Joe and the snowman from Dr. Art Bowen and several of his friends the day I moved to town. We were sitting in Kelsey's Restaurant sharing an endless cup of coffee when I asked about rumors of some rather unusual local events—events that I later came to discover played a big role in my coming to town. Of course, I never had the opportunity to meet the snowman, but Art, after twenty-eight years of being the only clinical psychologist at the Dakota City Mental Health Program, knew him all too well. I guess you could say Dr. Art and the snowman were competitors. I know it sounds strange for a psychologist to be in competition with a snowman, but this was no ordinary snowman.

"Who's this snowman fellow I've been hearing so much about, Art?"

After a thoughtful pause, Art answered. "Who is the snowman? Who *is* the snowman? The snowman is a charlatan, that's who he is. Yes, that's correct; it's a great big fake."

"What do you mean by a fake?"

"Well, the snowman isn't even made of real snow. It's a big piece of cheap fiberglass. South Dakota is a strange place, Bob. If something can be reproduced with fiberglass, we've done it. Drive around here long enough, and you'll find fiberglass buffalo, fiberglass pheasants, fiberglass dinosaurs, fiberglass cattle, fiberglass cowboys, and fiberglass Indians. We even have parks filled with fiberglass imitations of cartoon characters."

"Are you telling me that the infamous snowman is nothing more than a piece of plastic playground equipment?"

"Yes, at least that was the case at first. But what started as a simple playground attraction meant to play Christmas carols in City Park transformed into something far more complex than a mere fiberglass shell."

"Transformed?"

"The darn thing took on a life of its own when the park maintenance crew installed lights in it. Once it glowed from the inside out, it acquired a … a certain magnetism. That was fifteen years ago. When it was new, the snowman gave off a soft white glow. As it faded with age, its hue turned to what I call jaundice yellow."

I couldn't help but hear a sense of angry frustration in Dr. Art's voice when he spoke of the snowman. "You said it's big. How big?"

"Big enough that a large man could crawl into it and sit. I suspect there's a small stool inside it too. The bulbous monster has two arms that look like brooms. One of his arms is directed forward and downward until it touches the ground. The second arm extends outward from his shoulder and bends around. You know, as if he were wrapping his arm around you in support. Some say this arm gives the snowman a friendly look. I think he looks cocky. Anyway, all year long, the snowman stands in the park where he leans against his broom and radiates self-confidence. He wears a black stove-pipe hat that's tipped slightly to the left. His face gazes down even on a tall man, and it seems to ooze with empathy."

Art stopped to calm down and take a deep breath. "The dang thing has an orange, carrot-shaped nose, and in the daylight, its eyes are coal black. But at night, when the snowman's lights come on, those same eyes glow with a deep and inviting blue. At fall's first chill, the sheriff goes out after dark and ties a warm red scarf around its neck as if the thing actually has feelings!"

"That's a kind gesture," I said.

Dr. Art gave me an annoyed sigh that made his envy perfectly clear. "The story gets worse," he said. "Every year on the first of November, someone, *and nobody knows for sure who,* crawls into the contraption and turns on the lights. That, in my opinion, is when the serious trouble begins. Folks come from all over, and get this, they stand outside in the cold disclosing their personal problems to the snowman. And the snowman, well…he patiently stands there with his outreached arm, counseling all of those who should be *my patients.*"

"I don't understand. How does a fiberglass snowman communicate with real people?"

"I forgot to tell you about his mouth, didn't I? His big mouth is wide open and frozen stiff in a warm empathetic smile. At the center of this smile are the salvaged remains of a two-way communication device taken from the ticket booth in the old gymnasium. At first, the speakers were only used to play Christmas songs for people while they strolled in the park. But about ten years ago, whoever climbed in and turned on the lights started to hand out advice through those same speakers—speakers so muffled that one voice is virtually indistinguishable from another."

"So people can talk to the snowman without any concern about confidentiality, can't they?"

"That's right." Now a tone of resentment consumed Art's voice. "There's a lot of stigma attached to talking with a psychologist in a small town like this."

"So rather than come to you, they talk to a big piece of plast' that happens to have a personality."

"Exactly. Many of my friends and neighbors even go so far as to personalize the thing and call it 'Snowman,' but I do my best to call it 'the snowman.' It doesn't deserve any personal regard in my book."

By now, it was quite clear that Art would rather not talk about the snowman at all, but in this case, doing so was a necessity. The sage old psychologist continued on in a litany about his nemesis. "I can guarantee you something else too..."

Since Art had paused to invite my return question, I asked, "What's that?"

"I'll guarantee you that the snowman is not licensed to practice psychology, but that's what he does."

The longer Art vented about the snowman, the more spiteful he became. "As ridiculous and ugly as the snowman is, I'll give him credit for one thing. He has a way with people. He always has, right from the start. In the summer, little kids gather around him, join hands, and play Ring around the Rosy. In the winter, they form a horseshoe in front of him and sing Christmas carols with him."

"So he's one of those guys with natural charisma?"

Art nodded his head. "Oh, and one more thing, he set up his practice a mere thirty yards outside my office window by the big blue spruce tree just behind the courthouse."

"The snowman sounds like some pretty tough competition."

Art nodded again with a sad frown on his face. "Tough is an understatement. The truth is the snowman was driving me toward an early retirement, but the commissioner put the brakes on that plan."

"How does the commissioner fit into the picture?"

As it turns out, the commissioner was the town's only elected city official, and as such, he served as both mayor and commissioner of public safety. He was also Art's boss. Approximately two and one half years ago, Art had marched into the commissioner's office, head-strong and ready to resign. The commissioner saw the announcement stamped on Art's face and in his determined stride. "Don't tell me you're going to take that early retirement package the union is offering?" the commissioner asked.

Art answered without hesitation. "That's right, Commissioner. I'm ready to head out to pasture. I'm burnt out, and the perch fishing is good. It's time for me to call it quits."

"Have you written a letter of resignation?"

Art pulled a letter from his shirt pocket, opened it, and blew on the ink. "Yes, I have." Then he handed the farewell letter to the commissioner.

Art was expecting to hear, "Thanks for all the years of hard work." But instead, the commissioner gave him a thoughtful smile. "I'll have to give this to Susan and have her look things over."

Susan was the courthouse receptionist, and Art knew her to be a stickler for details, so he was not excited about having the attractive redhead reviewing the paperwork. He scratched his right ear and grabbed a handful of his distinguished gray hair. "I don't believe this. I'm giving you two months' notice. What's to look over?"

"You know how government works, Art. Things like this need to be checked out. I'll have Susan review the fine print, and you can stop back in a few days."

When Art came back a week later, Susan was on guard with orders to prevent access to the commissioner's door. "Hi, Art." Susan's confident voice stopped Art in his tracks. He looked beyond her engaging brown eyes and toward the commissioner's door.

"Hi, Susan. Have you printed my first retirement check yet?"

Susan rolled her eyes. "Dream on."

Susan sounded all too serious. "Is the commissioner in?" Art asked.

"Yes, but he's busy. Can I help you?"

"No, I need to see him about my retirement." Making an assertive advance, Art took two steps toward the commissioner's door.

Susan, determined to do her job, stood up and stepped between Art and her boss's door. "That reminds me, Art. The commissioner said I should give you a message."

"And what's that?"

"He said the fine print on the federal grant requires you to recruit a replacement before quitting."

"What? You're kidding me, right?"

"No, Art, I'm not kidding. I read that boring grant cover to cover for you, and there's only one escape clause."

"What's the clause?"

"You aren't going to like it."

Art looked toward the floor and in his growing impatience scuffed his right foot on the floor. He looked at Susan again. "What is it?"

Susan picked up the official-looking bundle of paper and read. "Now listen carefully, Art. It says, 'unless you are deceased,' and we can both tell that's not the case—"

Art couldn't believe his ears. "Does this mean—"

"Yes, it means no retirement checks until you've fulfilled your obligations."

"Susan—"

"Look, Art, I'm in no mood to argue, and I have instructions to follow."

"Is the commissioner free yet?"

"No, and he's not going to be free." Susan dramatically highlighted the contract clause with a chartreuse marker and showed him the bold highlight at the bottom of the page. There, Art could see his own signature defiantly precluding a retirement party for Dr. Art Bowen, PhD. In an attempt to quit, Art had accomplished nothing but to cause more work for himself. Now, he faced the dubious task of finding his own replacement.

The Best Man for the Job

Indeed, the task of recruiting a duly licensed psychologist complete with a PhD in clinical psychology *and* a license to practice would be a challenge. Art started his search by placing position announcements in several newspapers and on a popular Internet job-search site. Over the course of time, a few applications drifted in, and Art invited the handful of candidates who didn't have criminal records to Dakota City for interviews. After several months, Art's cordial and welcoming efforts netted nothing but failure—failure that was reflected in his meticulous interview notes.

Recruit 1. Question: What are winters like around here? My answer: Temperatures can dip to minus thirty degrees Fahrenheit, which is tolerable, unless there's a wind-chill. Recruit Response: Not the type of climate I'm looking for. Signed: Dr. Art Bowen.

Recruit 3. Question: Do you have a lot of mosquitoes around here in the summer? My answer: A few, but the media has hyped West Nile Virus *way* out of proportion. Recruit response: I'm considering a job with less risk in South America. Signed: Dr. Art Bowen.

Recruit 5. Question: Doesn't that duck slough outside your office window stink? My answer: Not as bad as the hog confinement north of town. Recruit Response: No thanks, environmental issues. Signed: Dr. Art Bowen.

Since applicants did not rate Dakota City, population 3,567, as among America's best places to live, Art faced one rejection after another. Struggling to stay optimistic, he kept his hometown's finer qualities in mind.

- The cost of living is low
- Fishing is good—when the water is high
- Pheasant hunting is great, and we can't keep the whitetail deer off the roads
- Most people are friendly
- There is very little crime
- The one school that we have is good.

These qualities were the source of what little hope Art could muster during his relentless search for his own replacement. Fortunately though, optimism has its rewards. Just before reaching the point of surrender, Art received a telephone call from Dr. Larry Longview, a colleague from northeastern Minnesota. "I have a live one for you, Art...a bright young man not too long out of graduate school," Dr. Larry said.

"What can you tell me about him?" Art asked.

"Well, he has his PhD, he's licensed, and he graduated third in a class of forty."

After Art's countless and failed recruitment experiences, he was suspicious. "So far so good, but what aren't you telling me?"

"Nothing, so long as you can overlook his probationary status."

"Great, he has a criminal record! I knew there had to be a catch. What did he do?"

"He's not a criminal. His license to practice psychology is probationary." Dr. Larry paused to clear his throat and picked up the pace of his speech. "As far as what he did, he had an affair with a married patient."

"I don't know, Larry. I have some concerns."

"I'm telling you, Art, he's a talented young man. If he only could work in a rural environment where things are less stressful—"

"Hey, watch what you are saying. Practicing psychology in a rural town is not as easy as you think. The commissioner would have my hide if I brought that kind of trouble to town."

"Come on, Art. Take a look at the kid. I was on his graduate committee, and I think you'll like him. He was a good high school athlete too."

Art thought for a moment. "Let me guess. If he was from your neck of the woods, I'll bet he was a hockey player? That's even worse."

"Did you hear what I said earlier? I said third in his class."

"What was his game like?"

"Physical. He was one of those explosive wings that could come out of nowhere and find the net."

"A wing, huh? That means he's a bit on the cocky side and the girls loved him. Am I right?"

"Back then, yes. However, the guy I saw pleading his case in front of the ethics committee was a different man than the one I watched on the ice. This relationship thing has shaken his confidence."

"You'll vouch for him?"

"Yes, I'm trying to help him out. I sort of suggested he relocate until his probationary status blows over."

"Okay. So he's on probation, he's unemployed, and he needs to relocate. May I assume that he's broke?"

"Definitely, and I'd be willing to bet that there are past-due college loans and a big car payment knocking on his door to boot."

"With vulnerabilities like that, I might get the guy to come. I'll give him a call."

A few moments later Dr. Joe's phone rang. "Dr. Doyle, this is Dr. Art Bowen, and I would like to talk to you about a great job opportunity."

"Where's this opportunity located?"

"Eastern South Dakota."

"That's in the middle of nowhere, right?"

"Well, it's over four hundred miles from where you are. Is that a problem?"

"I'm a little short on cash right now, so I can't afford to drive over for an interview."

This was music to Art's ears. If he went to northern Minnesota for the interview, they would be less likely to get caught up in details about life in small-town America. "No problem, I'll come to you. I have always wanted to see your neck of the woods anyway. When could we meet?"

A few days later, Art knocked on Joe's door. "Hello, I'm Dr. Bowen," Art said, reaching out and shaking Dr. Joe's hand.

Dr. Joe smiled at Art and motioned him forward. "Come in. The place isn't much, and I've been selling my furniture one piece at a time to make ends meet. I still have a kitchen table and a couple of chairs, though. Would you like to sit down?"

After visiting at Joe's kitchen table for twenty minutes, Art figured it was time to test Joe's honesty. "So what's your story, Joe?"

"It's a rather complicated one."

"As is mine. How about you fill me in on the details?"

"It all started when I accepted Mrs. Terry Ann Schaffer as a patient. What can I say…" Joe paused. "Twenty-five, working on a divorce, lovely green eyes, a head full of sandy blonde hair cut to chin length in one of those little hairdos with bounce. Speaking of bounce—"

"I get the picture."

"Terry swore she was finished with her husband, and one thing led to another. And me, I was foolish enough to think she might be *the one*."

"So you really fell for her?"

"You could say that. Anyway, the next thing I know, Terry Ann is back with her hubby, and I'm standing in front of the ethics board."

"Do you mean they didn't take your license?"

"No, I still have it, but I'm on probation for five years," Joe admitted.

"Probation is not an issue in this situation. Did the board take any other disciplinary action?"

"I had to take a professional ethics course again."

"Have you done that?"

"Yes, I took it on the Internet. Got an A. Look, Art, I appreciate you coming all the way over here to talk with me, but from what I have heard, South Dakota is a pretty desolate place."

"Can I be frank with you, Joe?" Art waited for Joe to nod in affirmation. He extended his arms and motioned around Joe's kitchen. "Dakota City may be small, but it's not as desolate as your apartment. Look, Joe, the pay is competitive, and the cost of living is low. Do you have anything better in the works?"

Joe's head dropped. "No," he admitted.

Before the morning passed, Joe and Art shook hands, sealing a gentlemen's agreement. Joe would come to Dakota City, and Art would relinquish his job. Art was pleased with the interview. Even though Dr. Joe had himself in a bind, he impressed Art as a determined young man, strong of spirit and committed to helping others. Of course, Art also had a secondary impression. While Dr. Joe might not be the type to go looking for trouble, trouble was bound to come looking for him.

During the drive back home, Art analyzed the interview, and there was one only thing that surprised him about their entire discussion. Joe had but one question about life in Dakota City. Pointing at a pair of skates and a hockey stick that stood in the corner by his apartment door, Joe asked, "Do you have ice?" As the miles passed, Art started to feel a little guilty about his answer. He knew in his heart that Joe was asking about an indoor ice arena, and he also knew Dakota City's only ice would be on the shallow lake bordering the south end of town. Of course, the lake wouldn't freeze over until the middle of November, which was usually a few days after the snowman opened for business. Since Art did not want a minute detail to stand between Dr. Joe and a second chance, he had simply told Joe, "Yes, we have ice."

The Long Hand of the Law

O n October 11, the day Joe was scheduled to arrive, Art went to his office in the county courthouse fifteen minutes early hoping for a private moment to reflect on his long career. He opened the window blinds and even though the rising orange sun cast a fiery glow onto the lake, all Art could see was the snowman. As if mesmerized by his nemesis, the aging psychologist was oblivious to the large waves crashing against the red rock rip-rap at lake's edge. He was equally oblivious to Sheriff Tom Oster who walked through his office door. Since Tom stood six foot four inches tall and weighed two hundred and ninety-five pounds, this was no small oversight. "Bidding the competition a fond farewell?" Tom asked.

Art looked into the forty-five-year-old sheriff's round, happy face. "That's not funny, Tom. You know how I feel about that monster. It doesn't have an education, nor is it licensed to practice psychology. And yet you protect it!"

"There are four doors into those tunnels, Art. I can't keep my eyes on all of them."

"I wouldn't be surprised if you handed the snowman, whoever he is, a key to every one of those doors. You don't even try to catch him, and you know it."

The bulky sheriff grabbed his wide black belt and pulled up his sagging tan pants. Tapping his flashlight with his index finger, he thought for a moment. "I report to the voters—"

"Yes, yes, I know. You've told me a hundred times 'the voters want the snowman's privacy respected.'"

Tom was eager to change the subject. "Say, isn't this the day your replacement is supposed to arrive?"

"Yes, I'm expecting him anytime after nine."

Tom chuckled. "I'm surprised he hasn't canceled." On most days, Tom, the former center on the Dakota City high school football team, would go out of his way to avoid conflict. But today was special. As far as Tom knew, this was his best friend's last day of work, and some teasing was in order.

Art was annoyed. "This is nothing to joke about, Tom."

"Relax. He'll be rolling into town any minute now."

Art would not passively sit and wait for his replacement to come "rolling into town." Rather, Art had plans to put his usually easygoing friend to work. "You've got me on your calendar for the morning, don't you, Tom?"

"You're penciled in, but—"

"Don't even think about canceling on me. Look, Tom, I don't want to leave anything to chance. Dr. Joe is my last and only hope."

"You worry too much."

"You're not going to back out on me, are you?"

Tom sipped his coffee and pondered the question. "Do you really want me to set up a stakeout north of town and follow him in?"

"You're darn right I do. I've witnessed more than one flight reaction in my lifetime, and I am not going to have a panic attack ruin this deal. Not when I'm this close to retirement," Art said, showing Tom a half inch of space between his thumb and index finger.

"This plan of yours feels like entrapment to me."

"Come on. You can't bail out now. I've been counting on you. You know how recruiting young professionals to Dakota City goes. It's next to impossible. They drive down Main Street, take a look around, turn their backsides at us, and drive away faster than they came."

"I guess I can't deny that. We haven't had a dentist for over five years."

"You said you would do this, Tom. All I'm asking is that you make sure he gets here so I can spend some quality time with him. You know, until he gets a good feel for the place."

"You mean until he has signed papers at Susan's office. Why are you so worried, Art?"

Art didn't want to create a negative impression about Dr. Joe before he was even in town, so he did his best to evade Tom's question. "The kid is a bit impulsive."

"Did you say 'kid'?"

"He's twenty-seven."

"Wet behind the ears, huh?"

"Tom, look at the time. It's getting late. Get out there and close down the road back to Minnesota. You know, just in case he panics. You're good at that sort of thing."

By now, Tom had heard enough to pique his curiosity. "Just how low did you have to dig in the barrel to come up with this guy, Art?"

"Okay, Tom, I'll fill you in a bit. He's only made one major mistake that I'm aware of. Look, Dr. Joe is a bright, well-trained, psychologist, and I'm convinced he has a lot of potential. Did I mention that he's licensed to boot?"

"What major mistake? No, don't answer that. Let me guess, a woman. Am I right?"

"Come on; give the man a break. He's a nice guy."

"Nice guy or someone who's going to upset all the women in the apple cart around here?"

"Oh, I'm sure the ladies will like him, but he's on the back side of a bad relationship. I doubt he'll be too eager to get into a mess like that for a while. Look, Tom, do me the favor. Get out there so when Dr. Joe gets close to town he doesn't turn tail and run."

"Okay, Art, but only under two conditions."

"What?"

"One, I get to take that forty-two-inch flat screen TV you have in your office home over the holidays so I can use it to watch the bowl games."

"I was going to set that up at home," Art protested.

"You can get by with your thirty-two inch."

"What's the other condition?"

"Convince the new guy that the mental health office is responsible for buying and making the morning coffee for the next six months. If you don't, I keep the TV until the All-Star Game next summer."

"How am I going to sell him that line of hooey?"

"I don't know. That's your problem."

"Okay, but I get to use your fishing boat one day a week until there's ice on the lake."

"It's a deal," Tom agreed.

Suspended Anxiety

Tom pondered the favor he was about to do for his friend and shook his head one more time. "I can't believe I'm going along with this strategy of yours, Art." Standing up from his chair, he walked over to the coffee pot, filled his travel mug, and walked toward the office door.

Art got up and followed Tom outdoors to his green and white SUV. "I'll wait in my office. Give me a call as soon as you see him. By the way, he drives a fancy, red convertible. It'll be easy to recognize."

Tom got into the SUV and pushed the button to let the electric window down so he could finish the conversation with Art. "A convertible. You don't say? This guy is trouble. I can feel it." After giving Art a disgusted look and shaking his head, he drove out of the courthouse cul-de-sac and proceeded three miles north of town to a pyramid-shaped mound of gravel. This large pile of gravel with tumble weeds growing on top made a perfect place for him to hide sight unseen. Since the pile was located along the only highway coming into town, Dr. Joe had to pass by it. Tom looked at his wrist watch. "Ten minutes before ten," he mumbled to himself. "I'm going to miss coffee." Needing to kill time, he sat back in his seat and watched the pheasant hunters get ready for action at the Big Dog Hunting Lodge.

A half mile away, the hunters were spreading out in a long line across a field of chest-high switch grass. They paused just barely within Tom's sight and waited for legal shooting time. During this lull in action, Sheriff Tom's phone rang. He checked his caller ID, and, just as he expected, it was Art. "Have you seen anything yet?" Art asked.

"The boys out at Big Dog are setting up to make a pheasant drive toward the road. Other than that, I haven't seen a thing."

"Remember, give me a call on my cell phone as soon as you see him." Art hung up and set his cell phone to ring with the 'Hallelujah Chorus.' Then he settled back into his soft office chair. With Tom on watch and ready to keep Joe from making an escape, he could relax. Art turned on the TV news and caught up with current events.

Hallelujah! Art's phone rang.

"Your relief is in sight, Art, but he just broke his windshield."

"So much for relaxing. Is he all right?"

"Don't worry. I've already called for the ambulance. By the looks of things, he'll need a few days of sick leave before coming to work," Tom taunted.

"He doesn't have any sick leave," Art countered. "What really happened?"

"One of the pheasants took a shot in the heart. You know one of those kills where the bird flies a good distance, goes fifteen yards straight up into the sky, and then drops like a rock off a skyscraper. Well, the bird came down over the road. Your boy smashed into it and cracked his windshield. Look, Art, there's already a problem. He flew by the gravel pile doing ninety miles an hour."

"Why did you have your radar on?"

"I needed a legitimate reason to be out here. He slowed down to eighty-five after smacking into that pheasant. Did you hear me, Art? I said he was doing ninety miles an hour in a sixty-five zone. To make matters worse, the boys at the club saw him. I have no choice but to pull him over and give him a ticket."

"Tom, the kid is broke. He hasn't had a job for a while."

"Oh really, I wonder why? Look, I can't just throw the book out the window because you're desperate to retire. I need to set the tone with this guy right from the start."

"Tom, so help me, if you scare the kid off—"

Tom turned on his siren and followed Dr. Joe until he pulled over to the side of the road. He continued his conversation with Art as he sat behind Joe with his patrol lights flashing. "Relax, Art, all we need to do is adjust our plan a bit. I'll issue a warning ticket and tell him there's a ten dollar nuisance fee for getting picked up. Then I'll tell him to pay the fee down at the courthouse. He'll buy the line of B.S., and the ticket will bring him right to your lap."

"Tom, don't you—"

"Call Susan and tip her off to what we're doing. You can get the ten bucks from her later and figure out a sly way to get it back to him. Bye, I've got to go."

"Tom, if you screw this up for me—" but Tom had already hung up.

Now, sweat was forming on Art's brow, and some of it dripped onto his round wire-rim glasses. For a long moment, he did nothing but cling tight to his cell phone.

Hallelujah! Art answered his phone again. "Did you pick him up?" he asked Tom.

"Of course."

"Did he turn around and leave?"

"No, he's coming into town."

"Where's he now?"

"He's just passing the 'Dakota City-One Mile' sign. My guess is that he'll be coming right to the courthouse. You can put the beer on ice and dust off the fishing poles. The way I see it, you're as good as retired."

"Thanks, Tom." Art hurried out the courthouse front doors. From here he would be able to savor the sight of Dr. Joe driving into town. As he watched, Dr. Joe's red convertible, shiny, little, and clean, rolled into town. The sports car was noticeable enough among the dirty, mud-caked pickups and SUVs that lined the street, but the bloody windshield made Joe's entrance downright conspicuous. Conspicuous was not what Art had been hoping for! He quickly wiped the sweat from his brow and cleaned his glasses. This was a pinnacle moment, a moment that Art wanted to savor. He watched every rotation of Dr. Doyle's tires as they turned over Main Street. As the convertible slowly came his way, Art watched as Joe surveyed his new surroundings.

There's a New Kid in Town

As Joe drove ever closer, Art realized that he was not the only person in town who was tense. Joe was sitting in his car with elbows locked and hands gripping the steering wheel. The backward pressure pushed his strong shoulders deep into the driver's seat, and his muscular arms looked as if they might force the car's small steering wheel into the dashboard. An unmistakable head full of sandy-blond hair, nervous smile, and handsome face gave Art a welcome sense of relief. Joe drove into the large cul-de-sac and parked in front of the courthouse. His compassionate blue eyes reached out to Art in a friendly hello.

Art had noticed the compassion in Joe's eyes when they met in his apartment. Certainly, these were eyes that reflected an empathetic and caring man. Not that Art was completely deceived. These sparkling eyes also contained just a touch of deviance. Still, the bottom line was this: Dr. Joe would not be in Dakota City if it were not for the kindness emanating from his striking blue eyes. Joe opened the car door and made his first cautious footprint on Dakota City pavement. If he had known the impact he would have on this small, rural community, he might have stepped even more cautiously. Art walked over to greet his new recruit. Shaking Joe's hand, Art said, "Welcome to Dakota City. It's nice to see you again."

"Thanks."

Art looked at Joe's face and noticed a defining blemish that he had missed in Joe's dim-lit apartment; a thin scar about one inch long under his chin. Art brushed his own chin with his index finger and then pointed at the scar. "Did you pick that up since we met?"

Joe shook his head and shrugged his shoulders. "No, I've had that since high school."

"What happened?"

"It's an old hockey wound. A cheap check from behind says it best."

"I've watched some hockey, and usually—"

"Okay, there may have been some minor retaliation involved," Joe quickly conceded.

"Minor retaliation or a gloves-off fight?"

Joe chuckled but said nothing.

Art tried to interpret the chuckle. While he didn't know for sure that Joe had been in a fight, he no longer had any doubt; Joe, like other hockey players he had known, occasionally ventured onto thin ice. Art let the subject of the scar drop. There were matters more important than a hockey skirmish on his mind. Right now, his major concern was whether or not Joe had learned his lesson about mixing personal and professional affairs.

Doing It Right This Time

I f taking a chance on love can be considered a mistake, then Art knew that Dr. Joseph Doyle had committed a big blunder. He also knew that throwing a mistake of this magnitude in a man's face was no way to welcome a person to town. So Art simply gave Joe a stern look and asked, "Are you ready to go to work?"

"I know what you're thinking, Art, and I *am* going to do things right this time. I promise."

"Thanks for saying that. I'm sure you'll do your best."

"I'll admit it straight out. This ethics thing has shaken my confidence. I feel like I'm in the penalty box."

Art pointed at the wadded-up warning ticket in Dr. Joe's shirt pocket. "I see you met Sheriff Oster. Did he give you a fine?"

"No, just something he called a nuisance fee."

Art smiled. "I'll show you where to pay that later."

Joe knew that having had a run-in with Sheriff Tom before he even got into town called to question the likelihood of his future good conduct. "I'm serious, Art. I'm going to do things right."

"You'll do fine, but remember, things can get complicated in a business as complex as ours."

"Actually, I thought the ethics committee was going to kick me off the ice for good."

"You must have made a persuasive argument on your own behalf." Of course, Art had the advantage of knowing that Joe's misguided venture at love had nearly ruined his career and that it was a kind-hearted colleague who had actually saved his skin. Maybe working in Dakota City would give him a chance to rebuild his life.

"Where's the ice, Art?"

"Ah …" Art paused. "The lake hasn't frozen over yet."

"Art, did you lie to me?"

"No. You asked if we had ice, and I said, 'Yes.' Come on, Joe. Let's not allow little details to stand between you and a second chance."

Art put his hand on Joe's shoulder and promptly guided him around the backside of the courthouse so he could get a better look at the landscape. "Joe, this is City Park, and, as you can see, our fine town is nestled right next to Cottonwood Lake. There'll be ice before you even get acquainted around here. Once the ice is thick enough, the city blades off the snow and puts out two goals."

"Oh man, did I fall for a line of—"

"Let me show you your office. You can keep skates in there and go down to the ice right from the back door of the courthouse."

City Park was plotted in a triangular shape behind the courthouse. It extended more than three hundred yards south and down a knoll where it met with the lake's edge. The massive park also stretched out both east and west of the red stone building for almost the entire width of the town. Art hesitated for a moment so Joe could take in the beautiful view. Strategically placed evergreen trees had been planted in clusters of three and four throughout the park to decorate the acres of plush green lawn. The lake's shoreline was rimmed with gigantic cottonwood trees that not only overhung the water but also draped over the land offering shade to those sitting on shore. Park benches and picnic tables were scattered everywhere. "Joe, you can enjoy this view every day. Wait until the snow geese migrate. When they sit on the water, the lake turns white. It's spectacular."

"It's a nice view. I'll give you that."

"Let's take a quick glimpse from your office window," Art said, opening the courthouse door. The men stepped inside where they were surrounded by white marble columns, walls, and floors. Joe stood in place while his eyes adjusted to the change in light, and eventually the black horsehair lines than ran through the marble came into focus. Art, being accustomed to the change in light, forged ahead toward the mental health office, which was located in the backside of the building and tucked away in the far southwest corner. Joe scurried to catch up.

As their footsteps clicked the hard marble floor, Joe noticed that a stairwell rose from a basement into the hallway. The stairwell was guarded by an exterior wall on one side and a waist-high marble banister on the other. A chain drooped across the stairwell's entrance, and a tin sign hung in the middle of the chain. The sign's message was perfectly clear. "Do Not Enter." Any place marked as having forbidden access captured Joe's curiosity. "What's down there?" he asked Art.

Art did not want to answer this question. He knew that this stairwell led to the entrance of a tunnel. It was one of three tunnels that formed a small, underground labyrinth which was originally designed to keep the sprinkling system from freezing and to provide access for plumbing repair. All three tunnels departed from a pump house and entered into the courthouse where they rose through three stairwells, one of which Joe had just noticed near the mental health office. The second stairwell came into the courthouse by the jail and the third by the judge's chambers. Art knew that these tunnels provided access to the snowman and served to protect the snowman's secret identity. Art hurried Joe along with two quick waves of the arm and said, "Nothing but a musty old tunnel." A few rapid steps later, he unlocked the mental health office door and directed Joe's attention to the window. "Just look at that view."

Art was sincerely proud of the view from his office window, but there were, in his opinion, two visual encumbrances. One encumbrance was the backside of the graffiti-marred, brick pump house situated near the lake. Although an eyesore, the pump house served as the heart for the elaborate underground sprinkling system that kept the park's plush lawn green late into the season. Two sidewalks arched out from the pump house and extended well out into the park. One of these sidewalks arched out three hundred yards to the west and connected to the west side of the courthouse. The other arched out three hundred yards to the east and connected to the east side of the building. A third sidewalk ran in a straight line from the pump house halfway back to the courthouse. At the halfway point, this sidewalk expanded into a circle of concrete and then continued straight on to connect with the backside of the courthouse. The second visual encumbrance, the snowman, sat smack-dab in the middle of this concrete circle.

While Art stared at the snowman, Joe enjoyed the view. "When does that duck slough freeze over?"

Joe's question awakened Art from his near trance. "Huh—what did you ask? Oh ... I'm sorry. We usually have some ice around the middle of November."

"I can't believe this. No rink."

"Like I said, Joe, don't let a minor miscommunication stand between you and a second chance."

Looking over Town

A rt was eager to get the paperwork done. "We better get back to the lobby and see if we can find Susan," he said. Susan, however, had stepped away from her desk. Needing a way to keep Joe distracted until she returned, Art said, "Let's step back outside and look the town over.

Joe nodded, and the men walked back outdoors.

Acutely aware that Joe had looked the town over as he drove down Main Street, Art asked, "What do you think of the place?"

Joe gave Art a cautious grin. "Oppositional and defiant, that's what I think."

Joe's answer caught Art by surprise. "That's an interesting observation." Art took a scrutinizing look around town. He studied the courthouse. The Sioux County Courthouse was a large red stone building that housed both county and city government offices. Prior to the construction of this shared facility, an enormous pile of fill dirt had been hauled in and formed into an elevated plateau. Situated high on this plateau, the courthouse resembled a medieval castle perched above a kingdom. The building's central structure contained the courtroom and the judge's chambers. A dome-capped rotunda rose high into the sky. Less lofty wings extended both east and west from the rotunda. The west wing accommodated several governmental offices and the mental health office. The east wing contained the sheriff's office and a small jail.

Main Street allowed for two-way traffic. Were it not for the paved cul-de-sac that wrapped in front of the courthouse, the two-lane roadway would have been on a collision course with the rock-solid building. A large black cannon with a waist-high pyramid of cannon balls was strategically placed in the middle of the cul-de-sac. The cannon's long barrel was aimed directly at oncoming vehicles and appeared ready to unleash fury upon anyone so bold as to make trouble.

Many of the local businesses and the religious institutions were on opposite sides of the street and seemed to face each other in competition. "The car dealers go head to head at the far end of Main— imports to the left and domestics to the right," Art said. "Then we have Lake City Food sitting across from what used to be Dakota City Grocery. As you can see, Lake City won the battle for groceries. The owner of Dakota City Grocery just reopened as D.C. Appliances."

"The churches each consume two full blocks. That's St. Peter's Church of the Holy Roman Authority on the west side of the street. The Bethlehem Redeemer Church of Grace is on the east side. I'm sure you noticed the convenience gas stop across from the vacant lot. Then there's Kelsey's Restaurant on the west side of the street. My brother-in-law, Roger, started the business in 1967, and my sister turned it over to her daughters a couple of years back when Roger died of a heart attack. Across from Kelsey's is Ruth's Donut and Sandwich Shop. City Bar sits across from the Farmhand Steakhouse and Lounge. Last, we have the bank on the west side of the street and the hardware store on the east. That's about it for Main Street, Joe. We aren't big, but we are friendly."

"What about me? Do I have any competition?"

"Aside from me, you're the only licensed psychologist in town," Art said, dodging another question about the snowman.

Joe carefully scanned the length of Main Street one more time and looked all the way to the far end of town. As his eyes followed the street back, they made an abrupt stop in the vicinity of the churches. First, Joe took an extended look at St. Peter's Church. It was constructed of dark-brown brick and had six small stained glass windows on the courthouse side. A towering steeple climbed into the heavens and was capped with a white cross that, today, stood out against the bright turquoise sky. A sturdy brick rectory sat next to the church. A dormitory for "The Brides of Rome" sat behind the rectory. "A convent?" Joe asked.

"You could call it that."

Joe's head snapped toward the Bethlehem Redeemer Church. Bethlehem was a newer church built with light-tan brick. It had large stained glass windows encased with dark-brown trim. Rather than imitating their neighbors, the Redeemer congregation opted for a lofty square bell tower that was topped off with a large wooden cross. A new parsonage was located immediately to the north of the church, and a small, older parsonage sat to the south.

"Which church do you go to, Art?"

The question surprised Art. For some reason, Joe didn't strike him as the type to show an interest in the community's churches. "I'm a member at Redeemer, but you won't find me there much unless you count funerals and weddings. Why do you ask?"

Joe had his reasons for asking the question. First, religion, like the scar on his chin, was an old hockey wound. His obsession with high school hockey had competed with regular church attendance and caused conflict between father and son. However, in this case, there was also something undefined; something more sinister and alive than an old family feud. "I just want to know more about them," Joe said.

Art gave a dismissive chuckle, not realizing that Dr. Joe was very serious about this inquiry. "You can learn pretty much all you need to know by reading their signs."

St. Peter's promotional sign was encased in glass and was surrounded by a brick housing. The black lettering on the flat white-board background had read the same for over twenty years:

Blessings from the Holy Father
Celebrate with us at 10:30 a.m. every Sunday.
Father Mac Riley

The Bethlehem Redeemer sign was a brand new six-foot-by-six-foot electric digital sign, and it had been the talk of the town during the week before Joe arrived. The conspicuous sign came complete with colored lights and a digital scrolling feature. Joe studied the sign from a distance.

"The pastor at Redeemer is a zealous one, and five will get you ten that by three o'clock this afternoon his new sign will read: 'Newcomers Welcome -Worship at 10:45 a.m. - Pastor Derrick Dalton Officiating - Small House for Rent," Art said dismissively.

Joe's tone of voice grew more serious. "Do you believe in gut reactions, Art?"

"I'm a psychologist, Joe. What do you think? Of course I believe in gut reactions, although I'm more inclined to call them 'cognitive insights.' Why? Is something wrong?"

"I don't know. I just felt something in my gut as I drove by the churches on the way into town."

"Something like what?"

"Something like a giant ice cube lying in the bottom of my stomach and slowly thawing its way through me."

"You come with a new soul and a wallet, Joe. You're bound to feel recruiting pressure until you declare your faith and pledge an allegiance. Maybe that's what you felt."

All about Susan

Art had just finished Joe's tour of Dakota City when his cell phone rang "Hallelujah."

"Hello," Art said. It was Susan.

"Art, the commissioner had me look at that grant again. It requires you to work with the new guy for a full week."

"Stop trying to be funny, Susan."

"I'm not joking, Art."

"No way! Tell the commissioner I can't do that."

"Dr. Art, if you want to complain, you'll have to take it up with the commissioner yourself."

"Come on; enough of this. You're kidding me, right?"

"No. I am not kidding you. I'm only following my instructions."

"Where is he?"

"The commissioner's not available. Oh, and Art, there's one more thing."

"What's that?"

"Whatever a service gap is, the commissioner doesn't want one. He also mumbled something about you not being down by the lake until the new guy knows what's going on."

"Dang it. Will we both get paid?"

"Yes, you'll both get paid. I asked about that. The health insurance coverage transfers to Dr. Joe though."

"Man—"

"I took the liberty of checking out the insurance situation for you. Your existing policy carries you for thirty days. Once you're officially retired, the union's insurance policy takes effect."

"Are you sure about all of this?"

Annoyed by Art's questioning her correctness, Susan snapped at him. "Would you like to come to my office and look at the fine print for yourself? I have it all highlighted."

Art sighed in frustration. "I'm sure you do. Good-bye."

Susan's directive meant that Art could not simply toss his keys to Joe and give him a cell phone number to use in the case of an emergency. In fact, the directive placed Art on unfamiliar ground. He'd never had an employee to train before. With that realization in mind, Art slapped his cell phone shut and began to weigh certain questions—questions like, *Should I tell Joe about my real workload? Should I tell him about that ridiculous snowman? Should I maybe warn Joe about the Kelsey twins?*

"That sounded like directives from above," Joe said, calling Art back from distraction.

"Not exactly. That was Susan."

"Who's Susan?"

"That's an interesting question, and Susan is an interesting person."

"Why do you say that?"

"Let me put it this way. Susan has a rather unique role around here. She's the courthouse receptionist and the commissioner's assistant. Since the commissioner is a firm believer in delegation, he delegates *a lot* of his work to her."

"I'm not sure I understand."

"She covers the phone in the courthouse, and the commissioner counts on her to keep things running smoothly. That makes her a big cog in the wheel."

"So if I'm hearing you right, the shared secretary is my boss by default?"

"I don't know if I would put it that way."

"I don't have any clerical help, do I, Art?"

"Golly, did I forget to mention that?" Art ducked Joe's frustrated glance by turning his eyes away. The lack of office support would not be an issue unless Dr. Joe's caseload somehow miraculously grew to be bigger than his own. So, in Art's mind, there was no real harm in the oversight.

"Is it safe to assume that the one secretary I do have is trouble?" Joe asked, knowing full well that Susan had been barking out directives.

"I can't say that she has caused me any real trouble. Let me put it this way. You need to know two things about Susan. She's big on following orders, and she's a stickler for details."

"So the 'b' word applies?"

"No, that's not a fair judgment. She's actually quite pleasant day in and day out. It would be more accurate to say 'obsessed with following instructions,' and if the commissioner puts her on a project, she's a bulldog."

"What's her personal history?"

"That's a tough question. Susan is not one to tell you who she is. She was born and raised right here in Dakota City, and she's worked in the courthouse with us for over three years now. I watched her grow up, and I know her parents. After all that, I can't say I feel as if I really know her."

"So why's she so guarded?"

"You would maybe do better forming your own impression."

"Come on, Art, loosen up a bit. Fill me in on what's going on around here."

"I'm only going to talk impressions, mind you, so don't repeat a word I say. Confidentiality is crucial in a small town like this."

"I'm good at keeping my mouth shut, Art."

"I'm convinced that Susan's rather structured personality is a consequence of growing up with the Trapper."

"Who's the Trapper?"

"Susan's father. We call him Trapper."

"Her dad's a fur trapper?"

"Yes, he was employed by the state as an animal control officer until he retired three years ago. Trapper made a living catching and killing skunks, coyotes, beavers, or any other critter that managed to cause a complaint."

"Trapper has done his share of killing then?"

"Let me put it this way, Trapper is very good at what he does. He's removed muskrats from the women's bathroom stool twice at Ruth's Doughnut Shop. That earned him quite a few points with the women around here."

"How do muskrats get into the—"

"They swim up the sewer line and somehow squeeze themselves through the hole in the toilet bowl. Pop! The next thing you know, they're making waves. Before Trapper came along, the sheriff had to deal with things like that."

"I'd like to meet him sometime. He sounds interesting."

"You're bound to meet Trapper before the day is out. But if not, you'll recognize him at first sight. He's about six feet tall and has a red beard that's mixed with hints of gray. This time of the year, he's bound to be walking down by the lake wearing a camouflage ball cap, hip waders, and a folding military spade strapped on his belt. One more thing, if it's early in the morning, he'll be carrying a twenty-two caliber rifle with him. Don't let the gun scare you."

"He carries a rifle in town?" Joe asked in disbelief.

"The commissioner gives him a special permit for that. Trapper's on a part-time contract to control damage caused by beaver. The darn things swim up the river and into the lake. The next thing you know, they are cutting down our big cottonwood trees. It's Trapper's job to protect the trees from the beaver."

"I'd like to hear more about Susan's relationship with her dad."

"As I was saying, Trapper is good at what he does, and he is also very conscientious. Every animal he catches with a prime fur is skinned out. Their hides are stretched, dried, and then sold—even the skunks. During Susan's high school years, Trapper put her to work in his garage skinning critters and fleshing hides late into the night. I think it was his idea of family involvement. I called it a misguided way to keep an eye on an attractive daughter. Anyway, I'd argue that social isolation, skinning wild animals down to bloody carcasses, and fleshing hides is bound to have an impact on a young woman's personality structure."

"I haven't heard the whole story yet, have I?"

"I doubt I know the whole story myself, but I can tell you that Trapper once lived on the rougher side of life. In his younger years, he was a guide out at the Big Dog. Now, let me try to say this next part nicely. A man can get pretty much anything he wants from the women they invite to the lodge during pheasant season. As things turned out, Trapper got a wife."

"Let me guess, she returned to her old ways and abandoned dad and daughter?"

"No. Millie's been a faithful wife, a devoted mother, and, in my opinion, an upright citizen. She played piano at our church for years, but aside from church activities, the family lived a pretty secluded lifestyle."

"A little blood and guts and some social isolation doesn't seem that far out of the ordinary in this case."

"The isolation was maybe more than I've conveyed."

"How so?"

"Many folks around here refused to forget Millie's history. Even today, if she were to walk into Kelsey's, heads would turn, and the whispering would begin. 'Did you know she was a prostitute?' But all of that is about to come to an end," Art said as his voice trailed off into sadness.

"What do you mean?"

"Millie's on her deathbed over at the assisted living center dying from lung cancer."

"I'm sorry to hear that."

Art looked down at the ground in regret. "Let me tell you something. There are no sharper tongues than those that dwell in small-town mouths. And, Joe, sharp comments cut deep. In my opinion, Trapper turned all that hurtful whispering about Millie onto Susan by becoming overprotective. No sports. No cheerleading. No dressing up. No dating. Her only social outlets were going to school and to the youth group activities at Redeemer Church. Susan had a proper spiritual foundation. I can assure you of that."

"Interesting. Did you say she's attractive?"

"Yes, and she can skin a coyote faster than her dad, so be careful. Consider this part of your training. Either you work for her or she works for you part time, and remember—"

"Relax, Art, I'm not going to sleep with the help. Like I said, I'm going to do things right this time. Anyway, you're taking me all wrong. I was merely wondering if Susan had chances to date. If that was the case, it would have made her situation even more difficult in my view."

"She had plenty of chances. To make matters worse, all through high school, Trapper conducted an ongoing and rather public investigation into her integrity. He made rounds asking all of us the same question: 'What do you hear about my girl?' We'd all say, 'Nothing but good,' and he'd say, 'I want to make sure it stays that way. No girl of mine is going to be running loose on the streets.'"

"He did go overboard, didn't he?"

"I'm sure Susan knew what he was doing, and she had to be embarrassed to death."

"Did she ever have a flight-or-fight reaction—you know, try to break away?"

"She did, in her own way. During her senior year in high school she hung around with a jerk named Gary. He was a couple of years older than she and nothing but trouble—an angry and violent sort with a long history. Sheriff Tom knew him all too well, and I've done more than one drug and alcohol evaluation on him. Anyway, when Susan showed up bruised and beaten, the sheriff wanted to nab the punk. He tried to get Susan to corroborate, but she refused. I informally probed into the circumstances surrounding a black eye. We talked down by the lake, and, man, was she mum. She wouldn't say a word. I'll bet the two of them felt the pressure and took off for parts unknown."

"So they completely left town? How long were they gone?"

"He never did come back. Susan was gone for over two years. One afternoon about four years ago, she just showed up out of the blue and came to the courthouse looking for work. I assume she got tired of the bum and left him."

"Nobody knows where they went?"

"Not even Trapper, and he has a keen eye when it comes to tracking things down. I'm telling you, Joe, if a critter puts its paws to the earth and moves as much as a speck of dirt around here, Trapper knows about it."

"So daughter is better at hiding than dad is at catching—intriguing."

"There is another strange twist to the story, too."

"What's that?"

"Susan still disappears at least once a year. She saves her vacation time like a scrooge, gives the commissioner a leave slip, and then falls off the map for two weeks. Trapper has an edge about him every minute she's gone, too."

"The more I hear about the Trapper, the more I want to meet him."

"He'd make for an intriguing case study, I'll grant you that. But just so you know, you're not likely to engage Trapper in much conversation. He's more inclined to ask questions than answer them."

Making It Official

Art put his arm on Dr. Joe's shoulder and gave him a firm and friendly turn toward the front doors of the courthouse. "Time is wasting. Let's get you officially signed in." Joe's hand was just reaching for the door handle when Sheriff Tom's siren did a low, slow *whew*. It was the kind of *whew* that falls in pitch and dies just before resonating into a repetitive pattern of *whew, whew, whew*. Art knew what the short siren meant. Tom wanted to visit.

"Dang it, hold up a minute," Art said.

"What's wrong?"

"Another delay." Tom pulled up behind Dr. Joe's car and stepped from his SUV onto the cul-de-sac.

"I thought you'd be at the lake by now, Art," Tom said with a playful laugh.

The laugh told Art that Tom's sole point of business was to hassle him. "Tom, I've got things to do. Can we make this snappy? Joe needs to get on the payroll."

Tom was in no hurry and found Art's brush-off annoying. "It sounds like you can still escape if you want, Joe."

"Thanks for the advice, Sheriff, but I need a paycheck."

"Well, if you plan to hang around, I better explain the parking regulations." Tom pointed at Joe's car. "Art should have told you this by now, but employees can't park in the cul-de-sac. The first eight places on either side of Main Street are reserved for us. You'll need to park down there from here on out."

"No problem, Sheriff."

"Since you're halfway between being a regular citizen and an employee, I'll forgive the parking violation."

The sheriff was starting to get under Joe's skin. "Gee, thanks. Say, Sheriff, the boys out at that Big Dog Hunting Lodge get a little carried away with their bird hunting, don't they?"

"I'd have to agree with you on that point. There's more that goes on out there than I care to tolerate. But since the club is on private property, I can only do so much."

"They shoot pretty close to the road if you ask me. They dropped a bird right on my car."

"That bird you smashed into was shot legally—long before the safety zone. It just happened to die in the wrong place...one of those things we call an 'act of God' around here. Of course, if you had been driving the speed—"

"Accidents happen," Art said, cutting into the building tension. "Joe, the sheriff's office is just down the hall from yours, and I'm sure he'll be sending some work your way. The point is, the two of you need to be well acquainted."

Joe fumbled with the warning ticket in his shirt pocket. "I don't think getting to know the sheriff will be a problem."

Tom ignored Joe's subtle dig and surprised him with a devious wink. "Art and I would've done a lot more work together over the years if it weren't for the snowman. The snowman—"

Art cleared his throat and shot Tom a dirty look, cutting him off midsentence. Badge or no badge, he would not allow Tom to ridicule him about the snowman, especially not before Joe signed on the dotted line. "Tom, I don't have time for joking around, not this morning. Did you want something?"

Tom didn't want to put too much strain on their friendship, so he let the subject of the snowman drop. "Susan called me, and she wants to see you both at her desk pronto. She was all worked up about getting Joe officially signed in."

"We better get in there then," Art said.

As Joe turned toward the courthouse doors, Tom pointed to Joe's shirt pocket. "Joe, don't forget to pay that ten dollar nuisance fee. It automatically goes up to twenty bucks after a week."

"Gee, thanks again, Sheriff. Maybe I can do you a favor sometime."

The tension was mounting again so Art put his hand on Joe's back and budged him along. "If Susan's upset, we better get into the courthouse."

"Art, I'm going to coffee. Are you going to bring Joe down and introduce him at the table when that paperwork is done?"

"We'll be along in a few minutes."

Susan's desk was strategically located in the middle of the large open rotunda so she could see anyone who walked in. As the men approached, Susan was visiting with her best friend, Vickie. "Hi, Art," Susan said.

Art smiled. "Ladies, I'd like you to meet my replacement, Dr. Joe Doyle. Joe, this is Susan, and this is Vickie. Vickie is our register of deeds."

"Welcome to town, Joe," Vickie said with a warm smile as she stood up and excused herself. "I'll be running along. I'm sure you folks have work to do."

Susan stood up from behind a massive antique oak desk, and her bright hazel eyes met Joe's without so much as a hint of intimidation. Her five-foot-eleven-inch frame leaned forward to shake his hand. Her long red hair flowed gracefully around her face and brushed her shoulders. Joe scanned her shapely athletic frame and stern, down-to-business face. *Three, maybe four years younger than me,* Joe thought as he inhaled the enticing fragrance of her hair. Joe reached out and took Susan's hand. She greeted him with a firm grip, a grip that said "all woman" but not in a delicate sort of way.

"It's a pleasure to meet you, Susan. I understand you're the Zamboni around here."

Since Susan didn't know hockey, she stood there with a confused look on her face. Joe realized that she missed the point of his analogy and clarified. "Art told me you're the person who keeps things running smoothly around here."

Susan recognized superficial flattery when she saw it. "I doubt that's true. But it'll be good to have someone around here with a bit of tact for a change." Susan let go of Joe's hand. "It's nice to meet you, Dr. Joe."

"Please, just call me Joe."

"My, look at the clock; it'll be noon before we know it. Susan, do you have those papers ready to sign?"

Susan nodded. "They're right here on the desk. Joe, all you need to do is sign by the red tabs and here on this W-2 form. I put you down for no dependents. Let me know if you want to change that."

Joe took the ball-point pen Susan offered him, looked high toward one of the large ceiling fans in the rotunda, and closed his eyes for a moment. *I'll probably regret doing this.* Then, he signed the three lines Susan had marked with tabs. Joe looked at Art. "That makes it official." For Joe, the signature meant he was on a countdown to payday.

For Art, Joe's signature meant liberation. His mind said, *Yahoo*, and his legs made an instinctive bend as if to jump in celebration. Struggling to contain himself, he smiled in relief. "Joe, we both have cause to celebrate. Let's catch up with Tom down at Kelsey's."

Falling Again

K elsey's Restaurant, one of the largest buildings on Main
Street, was impossible to miss. Formerly an implement
dealership, the building had been updated several years
ago with cedar siding, two storefront picture windows, and three
additional picture windows on each side wall. A single glass door
invited customers in and also served as a community bulletin board.
The busy restaurant was the favorite community hangout for several
good reasons, only one of which was the food, and was located just
over a block from the courthouse.

"Joe, it's time to get you down to the table," Art said. The table
was a special meeting place tucked into an out-of-the way corner in
Kelsey's. Almost everyone was welcome at the big round table, but
usually it was the common meeting ground for Sheriff Tom, Judge
Waters, Father Riley, and Art. Trapper had also fallen into this con-
federacy of friends ever since Millie had moved into the assisted living
center. Then, there was Pastor Dalton. Pastor Dalton was considered
an habitual intruder because he was prone to budge in, beg coffee, and
dominate the conversation. He was tolerated more out of respect for

his calling than for his companionship. Anyway, this select group of men, including Pastor Dalton, got together during the morning — Monday through Friday—to have coffee and to analyze Dakota City's current affairs. Art wanted to bring Joe into the group.

The psychologists walked to Kelsey's and, once again, Art opened the front door and motioned for Joe to enter first. Joe stepped in the entryway, and his eyes were immediately captured by the attractive hostess standing behind the cash register. Billie Kelsey, still carrying a hint of summer tan and glowing with vitality, smiled. Her dark-brown hair, deep-brown eyes, and slender frame stopped Joe dead in his tracks. In fact, he stopped so abruptly that Art smashed into him from behind. Joe went into a nosedive. On his way down, he made a frantic grab for the counter, taking a glass tip jar along with him. The jar shattered on the tile floor, and all eyes turned Joe's way. Broken glass and money flew everywhere. Joe hit the floor face first. Embarrassed, he stayed low as if the clumsy fall had not happened, at least until a quarter, which was two inches from his nose, stopped rotating.

Billie rushed from behind the counter and squatted low in front of her new customer's face. "Are you okay?"

Drawn upward by the concern in her voice, Joe started to push himself from the floor. When he looked up, he couldn't avoid catching a quick but incomplete glimpse of Billie's breasts. *Flawless,* Joe thought, as he tried to force his wandering eyes away from the uninvited view.

While Billie's customary work clothes, a blue jean skirt and white button-down blouse, were not in any way flaunting fashion, she was quick to realize that bending down had compromised her modesty. She promptly stood up in a graceful move that drew Joe's attention to her legs. His eyes followed Billie's sleek, smooth legs upward and upward. *Perfection.* Once again, Joe's mind fought with his wandering eyes, but this battle was lost.

"What are you looking at down there?" Billie chastised.

By now, Joe had pushed himself onto his hands and knees. He snapped his head sideways and made an awkward attempt to collect the money that lay strewn all over the floor. "Ah ... the money I spilled." First, Joe frantically snatched up dollar bills, and then he grabbed at what loose change he could gather without crawling around like an infant.

"I'm quite certain that the money you're looking for didn't roll up my skirt."

"I'm sorry. I couldn't help myself. You have great legs," Joe said in a last-ditch effort to save face.

For a moment, Billie's eyes sizzled, and Joe felt them pressing him back toward the floor. Recognizing Joe's sincere plea for forgiveness, Billie looked at him and gave a friendly laugh. "Get up. You look ridiculous down there," she said, tossing her hair in playful disgust.

The toss of hair enticed Joe off the floor. Billie had his attention, and she knew it. "Men," she said, taking the money from Joe's hand. "Be careful. Don't cut yourself on the broken glass when you get up." Now she looked at Art. "So who in the he ... ck is this, Uncle Art?" Billie said, catching herself just before using a cuss word. "Don't tell me he's your replacement."

Art shrugged his shoulders. "Yes, Billie, this is my replacement, Dr. Joseph Doyle."

Joe took Billie's hand as if to shake it, and the two of them continued to hold hands just long enough to make Art uncomfortable. "It's nice to meet you, Billie—"

"Kelsey. Billie Kelsey," Art said, interrupting the extended hand clasp. "Joe, Billie's my niece. She's also the owner of this place."

"Half owner," Billie said in clarification.

Billie's cover-girl face had Joe captured. "Who owns the other half?"

"My twin sister, Bobbi. You'll like her; she has great legs, too."

Joe ignored the feisty remark. "Your place looks great. I'm impressed."

"Thanks. I've always wondered how it looked from the floor."

Joe would only be pushed around so long. He countered Billie's second spirited remark by taking a playful step backward and pretended to stab his chest. "Ouch, that hurts," he said. With the step backward, he bumped into a customer standing directly behind him.

"Maybe you better go sit down before you hurt somebody, Dr. Joe," Billie said.

Meanwhile, Art tried to deny the instant attraction he was witnessing and jabbered on about restaurant operations. "The girls took the place over when their dad passed away two years ago. Billie manages breakfast and lunch. Bobbi covers dinner and the late evening crowd."

"I'm sorry about the broken jar and the mess," Joe said, still focused on Billie and completely ignoring Art's comment.

"That's okay. I have more jars."

"Maybe a tin can would work better. I'm sure I'll be back."

Billie smiled and Art frowned. In his view, the last thing Joe needed right now was a relationship.

Art had considered telling Joe about his nieces but avoided it. In addition to being gorgeous, the twins were playful, mischievous, and mildly flirtatious. They were also nearly indistinguishable. Art was one of the few people in town who could, on occasion, tell one identical twin from the other. This was a feat he accomplished by looking for a slight burn scar on the inside of Bobbi's right calf. She had acquired this small blemish years ago while helping her father make French fries.

Another way that Art could sometimes tell Billie from Bobbi was by simply listening to them. Sadly, both of the twins had an unbecoming propensity to use an occasional swear word. In all fairness to them, this was not something that they did very often. However, when it happened, the bad words seemed quite out of character for their warm and friendly nature. Art had noticed over the years that each twin showed a partiality to certain cuss words. For example, Billie might slip and say something like, "Hell, Art, where have you been all week?" Bobbi, on the other hand, had a tendency to select more crass swear words. Even as minimal as it was, the twins' swearing caused a sundry of problems, not only for them but for others as well. It grieved their mother and Art, as their substitute father, didn't like the cussing either.

Small-Town Dynamics

The longer Billie and Joe traded playful glances, the more Art's tension rose. It was definitely time for him to break up this dangerous combination and get to the table. "Joe, Billie is a busy woman. In addition to working here, she helps Bobbi look after her mom."

"My, my, with two psychologists in town, how will the snowman ever stay in business this year?"

"Not funny," Art said.

"Joe, welcome to town. I need to get another chair so you have a place to sit." As Billie stepped away, she subtly brushed her hair back and gave Joe an inviting smile. Joe returned the smile and lingered hoping to visit longer.

Art caught the smile and rushed Joe toward the table. "Gentlemen, this is Dr. Joseph Doyle."

Fascinated by Billie's graceful movement, Joe saw her struggling to maneuver a chair between the crowded restaurant tables. "Excuse me a moment. I really should help Billie with that chair." Joe turned his back on the men at the table and walked over to help. He took hold of the chair and looked closely at her fingers. *Good, no ring.*

"Thanks," Billie said. "These chairs are heavy."

Joe returned to the table and slid the bulky wooden chair into the open space the other men had created for him. "Sorry for the delay, gentlemen. I needed to help the lady." Joe's comment brought an unusual sparkle to Billie's eyes. This was a sparkle that the men had never seen in her eyes before, and it drew an uncomfortable moment of silence. Billie was special, and the truth be told, the men at the table looked after Billie, and Billie did her best to look after the men. One thing was certain: they were not at all sure how they felt about her taking an interest in a stranger … or about a stranger taking such an interest in her.

Art expected the talkative Sheriff Tom to break the prolonged silence, but in this case, it was the usually quiet Trapper who spoke first. "Are you the guy with the sports car and bloody windshield?"

Joe nodded his head. "I got hit by a pheasant out by the hunting lodge today."

"I saw the sheriff heading out that way this morning," the judge said to Joe while giving Tom a suspicious glance. "A person's got to be going pretty fast to shatter a windshield."

Tom squirmed. County coffers were low, and he didn't want the judge to know that he had given Joe a break on Art's behalf.

Trapper chuckled and helped Tom from his uncomfortable position. "The boys keep a pot of money out there. Every hunter throws in a buck, and when someone pulls off that feat, he wins the cash. The money piles up pretty fast and pretty deep. I'll bet somebody walked away with a big smile and more than a thousand dollars in his pocket."

"Forgive me if I don't celebrate his winnings," Joe said.

"The deal isn't as good as it sounds. The winner has to buy a round of drinks at the end of the day. I guess a pheasant in the windshield is as good a welcome to South Dakota as a man can get."

After a brief lull in conversation, Art inquired about Trapper's wife. "How's Millie doing, Trapper?"

"Not well."

"I'm sorry to hear that."

Trapper nodded. "Thanks."

Art didn't want to belabor Trapper's pain and quickly changed the subject. "Gentlemen, by the end of the week, I'm on full-time rest and relaxation: hunting, fishing, woodworking, and maybe a little community service from time to time." As a lifelong bachelor, Art's unspoken plan also included staying close to town and helping the twins and their mom, his widowed sister.

The judge looked at Art and smiled. "Are you sure that the commissioner has put his stamp of approval on that retirement deal this time?" He winked at Tom.

"Everything is signed and on file with Susan at the courthouse. Joe gets the benefit of one week of training, and then you'll find me down at the lake fishing."

"Joe, you have my sympathies. A week of training with Art is bound to be pretty tough duty," Tom said.

Father Riley, a kind and aging man himself, did not want to let the others spoil Art's moment in the sun. "You might consider spending more time in church, Art. You know, do some fishing for souls." As the word *souls* passed through Father Riley's lips, Pastor Dalton came wandering over from another table. "Excuse me. I have to go," Father Riley said as he got up to leave.

"Did I hear somebody say 'souls'?" Pastor Dalton asked as he barged over to the table.

Art whispered to Joe, "Look out. It's Pastor Dalton. He's here every morning, and *can* he be overbearing."

Dressed in black pants, a black shirt, white collar, and a black polyester suit coat, Pastor Dalton strutted up to the table. His right hand lunged forward to offer Joe a handshake. "Hello, I'm Pastor Dalton." Joe extended his hand in return, and the pastor administered the domineering and offensive handshake for which he was famous. Joe shook Dalton's hand and promptly forced his hand free from the pastor's intimidating, vise-tight grip.

Pastor Dalton had already picked up Dr. Joe's name from other customers. He went right to business. "I'm the pastor at Bethlehem Redeemer Church, Joe. I'm sure you'll need to call on me for spiritual guidance in your line of work."

"I'll have to see how things go, Pastor."

Dalton, having arrived late, saw that everyone was getting up to leave. "Sit down for a minute, Dr. Joe. Let's get acquainted. Where are you from?" he asked.

"I was working near Lake Superior before coming here," Joe said.

"Really? My brother is gathering a large flock in that area. Maybe you have heard of him, the Pastor Robert Dalton?"

"I can't say that I have, but the truth is I spent more time playing hockey than attending church."

"Joe, I want you to join us at Redeemer. We have a small and friendly congregation, so I know you'll be happy with us. Art will vouch for that."

"Thanks, but I'm going to spend Sunday mornings skating as soon as there's ice on the lake."

Pushing his recruitment effort harder, Dalton said, "What would you think about having a potluck at the church? You know, a special event to welcome you into the fold."

"That's nice of you, Pastor, but I'd like to get settled in before doing something like that."

"Joe, I bet you need a place to live. We've got a nice little house down by the church for rent."

"I do need a place. What's it like?"

"The last renter did some minor damage, but it's still a good deal for the money. There's one thing you might consider to be a problem though. We don't allow drinking on church property."

"I don't drink much."

As Art listened, he realized that his training plan had not included time for Joe to find a place to live. "Joe, why don't you take a look at that house? It's probably the nicest place you'll find in town." Art knew that Joe had stuffed what little he owned into his small car. "The place is furnished," he added. "I'll just get out of your hair. If you like it, take the rest of the day to get settled in." That said, Art seized the opportunity to escape.

"Just a minute, Art. I need to talk to you. Excuse us for a moment, Pastor," Joe said.

"I'll run ahead and get the keys while the two of you talk."

Joe waited for Dalton to walk away. "What's the place worth, Art?"

"I wouldn't pay a dime over three hundred and seventy-five dollars a month, and that should include utilities."

"What do people get for a deposit around here?"

"Don't give him one. The place has been empty for five months." Art saw a look of hesitation on Joe's face. "What's wrong?"

"I don't know for sure, but I can't say that I like the man."

"The pastor does have a way of getting on a man's nerves, but I'd grab the place. It's the best deal you'll find. Oh, one more thing. Be careful. The preacher has the power of persuasion, and he'll use those convincing blue eyes of his to fleece an extra fifty bucks a month out of you."

"Thanks for the warning," Joe said.

"I'll get your coffee, Joe. The first time is on me." Art stepped to the counter where Billie was minding the cash register. Looking at Joe, she handed her uncle a handful of change. "Don't be a stranger, Dr. Joe."

Revelations

While Joe and Art were talking, Dalton walked home to get the keys for the rental house. He stepped in, closed the front door, and looked for his wife, Debra. "Where's that worthless woman?" he grumbled.

Debra, who was snuggled on the coach with her head tucked under a thick, patchwork quilt, heard his crass remark. She slowly pulled the quilt below her chin and revealed her auburn hair and pale but pleasant face. Then, unlike ever before, challenging words slipped off of her tongue. "I'm tired of you saying things like that about me, Derrick."

"Watch your tongue," Dalton admonished.

When Debra was young, many had considered her to be a plain Jane. Accustomed to coping with overbearing parents during her childhood, she was pleasant yet submissive and easily coerced. It was the plain Jane and timid nature in Debra that had convinced Dalton she would be the perfect pastor's wife. In his eyes, the younger Debra was sensual but not so sensual as to create any kind of sexual distraction, and he liked her that way. But people change, and Debra was no exception. Now at thirty-four years of age, maturity had blessed Debra with a natural appeal—an appeal that came without makeup or fashionable attire. Strangely, Dalton had no appreciation for Debra's emerging beauty. It, along with other things, was causing him to bloat with insecurity.

Dalton loathed the bolstered sense of self-confidence and budding assertiveness that accompanied his wife's transformation. The challenging words she had uttered just moments ago told Dalton that he was at risk of losing control over what once was a submissive and moldable personality. Dominating and brow-beating, Dalton knew that it was once again time to school Debra on her proper place as a pastor's wife.

Debra had been living out Dalton's script for years in what she saw as a spiritual obligation to her husband. While she strove to be the perfect wife for Pastor Derrick Dalton, his thirst for dominance never seemed to be satisfied. Debra was caught in a trap. The more submissive she became, the more harshly Dalton exerted his control and intimidation. If she tried to step out of her assigned place in life, Dalton saw this as progress lost, and he got angry, very angry. By the time Joe came to town, Dalton's verbal brow-beating had mushroomed into physical abuse. Hands that Debra once thought to be guided by God and by love had struck her on more than one occasion. But Dalton saw to it that his wrath was well hidden behind closed doors. Finally, in the pastor's mind, there was one more issue, a bigger issue. Debra had not blessed him with children, and Dalton now sought to have this obligation fulfilled.

A barren home, a dwindling congregation, and his brother's success were cutting deep into Dalton's pride. "Mind your place, Debra. You have no cause to complain and certainly less cause to complain than me," Dalton said.

"What do you mean by that, Derrick?"

"You're to call me Pastor Derrick. How many times must I remind you? I'll repeat that since you seem too stupid to remember—Pastor Derrick."

The inadvertent words spoken earlier from underneath her quilt had awakened something deep within Debra. She was growing ever more tired of Dalton's insults and abuse. "I can repeat too," she said, venturing a deliberate challenge. "I asked a question. What did you mean by that?"

"I'll ask the questions. Your place is to listen and to serve, but where are you? Lying on the couch in the middle of the day. Get up and find me the keys to the rental. I don't have all day. There may be a renter for the old house."

Debra stood up from the couch and squared around. She faced her husband but stopped short of making direct eye contact. "I asked what you meant by that comment."

Dalton saw the spark of empowerment flickering within his wife. He could see her feelings about him and their marriage were changing, and her words stuck him like a dart. She had never been this testy with him before. He glared at Debra and took an intimidating step forward. "Show me my children, woman, and tell me how often you try."

"Maybe if you treated me—"

"A wife that produces no fruit and tries so little is worthless."

"You're right, Derrick. We have no children. But this isn't just about us, is it? Your brother has three children, and you're envious. 'Thou shall not covet,' Derrick."

"This is not about my brother," Dalton snarled. "This is about you and your lack of effort to bless this home. I have provided well for us, and it's time you do your part."

"You scare me, and you hurt me. Why should I try?"

Dalton's anger escalated at Debra's newfound persistence. "I told you, woman, mind your place." Dalton raised his hand in preparation to deliver a harsh backhanded slap across Debra's cheek. His hand started to swing forward, but he jerked and stopped it just before smacking her on the face.

"See, you want to hurt me."

Debra's courageous challenge drove Dalton into a mental rage. He put his face right next to hers and lifted his hand for a second time. "I should teach you your place right now."

"Go ahead, Derrick. Hit me again. I lived through it the other times. I'll live through it again."

Dalton stepped back and turned from his wife. Pacing frantically back and forth trying to think, he stepped on Buff, Debra's small housedog. Buff ran to cower at Debra's feet. Dalton turned and glared at Debra again. "If I have to enforce God's rule by my hand, I will. And you can explain your disobedience while standing before the congregation on Sunday."

"You wouldn't dare beat me like that, Derrick, not in this day and age. The congregation is already leaving you as it is." When Debra heard the raw defiance in her own voice, a flood of emotions rushed through her mind. *Where did that come from?* she wondered. The words that escaped so fluidly from her mouth were confusing, scaring, and liberating all at the same time. She felt strengthened. Her chin came up, and her posture straightened.

Dalton knew that Debra was right. Should the congregation become aware that he beat his wife, he would be finished. Seeing Debra's empowered posture angered him all the more. His submissive wife was suddenly out of control, and he needed to take action. Dalton's hostility exploded. His face turned red, and he pushed forward until his chest crushed against hers. He glared at her downcast face and jerked her chin up. A slight string of drool ran from the left corner of his mouth. In an emotional eruption, Dalton thrust back his leg and violently kicked Buff from under Debra's feet. Buff flew across the room, where she crashed into a floor lamp. Buff yipped and then bolted under the couch to hide. The violent explosion eased Dalton's rage, but while his jaw relaxed, a bulge formed in the front of his black, polyester pants. "Just get me the keys to the old parsonage, woman. I said there might be a renter."

Upon seeing her husband's arousal, Debra realized that Derrick was a dangerous man. At this same moment, Debra also sensed her own entrapment. Timid by nature and browbeaten, she could see no way out. She was a pastor's wife. How could she break her wedding vows? Who would suspect Derrick to be such a violent man? Even if she spoke out, who would believe her? Acutely aware of what happened to Buff, Debra went to the kitchen and got the keys from a drawer. She dropped them on the coffee table in front of Dalton. "Who's the renter?" she asked.

"The new psychologist Art brought to town."

Buff came out from hiding, and Debra went over to comfort her. She picked up her pet and held her tight against the chest. Tears fell from Debra's eyes while the whimpering pet nudged its nose against her cheeks. "I'm so sorry, Buff. That was my fault."

Dalton looked at the dog. "For once, she's got something right, Buff." He looked at Debra and pointed his finger at her. "And don't forget what you just saw."

Moments later, Dr. Joe rang Dalton's doorbell. Pastor Dalton came to the door and held it open. "Hello. I'll be out in a minute," he said. Meanwhile, Debra hovered on the far side of the living room with tears in her eyes. There, the voice from deep within her told her to stay visible. Debra cautiously eased her way into Dr. Joe's direct line of sight. Clutching Buff tight against her breast she prayed that this new psychologist would notice her tears.

Joe's eyes instinctively flashed toward Debra. *That's strange,* he thought. Such a plain dress and unpretentious appeal would not generally catch his eye. Yet, there was Debra, vivid, emerging from the shadows, somehow attractive, trembling, and in pain of some sort.

Suddenly, Joe felt that bitter cold block of ice in his gut again. There was something very wrong here. Joe could sense it. Debra's soft, brown eyes cried out, "Help me," but her voice said nothing. *None of this makes sense—not in a minister's home.* Disarmed by the pastor's professional calling, Joe minimized Debra's unspoken plea with a casual question. "Is everything okay?"

Dalton was quick with answers and even quicker with convincing lies. "Everything's just fine now. Our dog almost got run over a moment ago. Little Buff is like an only child to us, and the near miss scared my wife half to death."

Debra fumed at Dalton's innuendo about children. Joe looked at her as if asking for confirmation of her husband's assertion. However, Debra did nothing to visibly confirm or deny what the pastor said, at least not that Joe could see. She simply stood there comforting Buff. "Liar," she whispered softly into Buff's ear.

When the men stepped outdoors into the sunlight, Joe took a closer look at Dalton. *This guy's a misfit. I've seen his look somewhere before.* As they walked to the rental house, Joe searched through the memories he had acquired during intern rotations, but nothing seemed to fit. Dalton stood about five-foot eleven. He had dark-black hair and appeared to be somewhere around thirty-six years of age. His stature was stout, and he carried a thin layer of soft, sagging fat. The sunlight revealed numerous flakes of dandruff clinging on his black suit coat. *Sleaze ball,* Joe thought. But, oh, was Art right about the pastor's eyes. They were powerful tools. These Pacific blue eyes were hypnotizing and, as Art suggested, dangerous.

Dalton sensed that Joe was sizing him up. Uncomfortable with the scrutiny, he created a distraction by starting a conversation. "Let's take a look at the house. Did I mention it's partially furnished?"

"No, but Art did."

"It's really quite the setup. There's a stove, dining table, two kitchen chairs, sofa, easy chair, bed, and nightstand."

"Is there a refrigerator?"

"Yes, but I own that. You can rent it for an extra ten dollars a month."

"What are you asking for the place?"

"I can let it go for four hundred and fifty dollars a month, provided you have a month's deposit, and the ten dollars for the refrigerator."

"Let's look around first. We'll talk more about price later." Joe looked inside the white refrigerator. After closing the door, he ran his finger over the kitchen countertop. "The place is pretty dusty."

Dalton nodded his head in agreement. "We've been without a renter for some time. The church council gives me a percentage for watching over the place. I'll have Debra get over here to clean it up. She needs a project."

"It's not very big."

"I know it's a bit small, but there's a basement."

"Does it get water in it?"

"In the wet years, but it's good for storage if you keep things off of the floor."

"I see."

"You're responsible for mowing the lawn in the summer, raking leaves, and shoveling walks in the winter."

"I don't have a mower."

"The church owns a push mower. You're welcome to use it. The youth group rakes the leaves for contributions."

"That could work."

"Like I said before, though, no booze on church property. The council is fussy about that."

"Can I assume there's an exception during the playoffs?"

"Hockey playoffs, baseball playoffs, football playoffs—there are too many playoffs, Joe. Sorry. We don't allow booze."

While it was true that Joe did not drink very much, the thought of self-imposed prohibition seemed a bit much. "Let me think about that." He and Dalton continued on through the small living room to inspect the bedroom. Joe opened the top drawer on the night stand next to the bed. "What's this, Pastor?" Joe asked as he took out two pornographic magazines and a faded snapshot of a topless teenager.

The pastor stepped forward. "Oh my," Dalton said with mock surprise.

"Pastor, I saw some pretty bad stuff in the locker room, and I can tell you, this is not run-of-the-mill porn. This is garbage."

Dalton snatched the material from Joe's hand. "Debra really does need to do a better job of cleaning when we change tenants." He tucked the snapshot into his shirt pocket and folded the magazine in half before stuffing it into his back pants pocket.

"I'd burn that trash if I were you, Pastor. It's illegal." The front cover of one magazine read, "Revealing Features from Fourteens and Younger." Joe shook his head in utter disdain. "And whoever took the snapshot is a criminal."

"Well, do you want to rent the place, Joe?"

"All I can afford is three-fifty a month, including the refrigerator, and I don't have a deposit."

"Come on, Joe. You make good money."

"I've got a lot of bills from graduate school to pay off, too."

"You've been talking to Art. Three hundred and sixty dollars a month and the place, plus the refrigerator, is yours. On top of that, I'll get my wife over here to clean it up. You owe me a favor for the price, but I stand firm on the no booze rule."

Joe hesitated one more time before answering. A gut reaction told him that something with the Daltons just wasn't right. But he also knew from talking to Art that his options were extremely limited. "Well…okay, it's a deal." As Joe walked back to the courthouse to bring his car home, the distasteful snapshot flashed through his mind. For some reason, the young girl in the faded picture looked familiar.

Behind Closed Doors

Pastor Dalton watched Joe walk away with keys to the little house in hand. *Naïve fool,* Dalton thought as he pulled the pornography from his pocket with a sinister smile. He momentarily savored the images. Then, he went home, stashed the porn in the garage, and went into his house. It was time to deal with the matter of having children.

Dalton stepped into the kitchen where Debra was washing dishes. He squeezed her shoulder with his vise-like grip. "Get to the bedroom and prepare yourself; it is time you have a baby."

"Derrick, we need to talk, not have children."

After their earlier dispute, Dalton was in no frame of mind for resistance. He grabbed Debra with both hands, jerked her around, and shoved her hard in the direction of the bedroom. Debra hit her head on the doorway and fell to the floor. Trembling, she looked up at Dalton in fear.

"Do as you're told. Now!" Dalton yelled.

Debra was terrified. She went to the bedroom, took off her clothing, and threw herself on the bed. Dalton followed promptly behind her. Naked and uncovered, Debra said, "If this is how you want things between us, Derrick, do what you will."

Debra's sarcasm enraged Dalton even more. He tore off his shoes and pants. "I have coddled you too long."

Debra tossed her arms back toward the pillows and turned her head to the side so she would not be facing her husband. "Just get it over with, Derrick." Fighting back the flood of pent-up emotions, Debra closed her eyes and bit her bottom lip in preparation for what was to come.

Dalton pushed hard against Debra's body and made a dry, painful thrust followed by a second and then a third. In the complete absence of either erotic provocation or resistance, the insecure pastor fell limp. He pushed himself off of his wife and shook his head in anger and disgust. In complete denial of his own failing, he belittled Debra. "Cover your worthlessness." Dalton put his clothes back on and left the house. After he left, Debra breathed a long sigh of relief and lay on her bed staring at the cross that hung on their bedroom wall.

In Training

D r. Joe and Dr. Art devoted the rest of the week to training and to taking care of transitional issues. For the most part, this meant fulfilling the bargains Art made with Tom. He passed along the contrived coffee arrangement and delivered the flat screen TV to Tom's house. Having recommended that Joe buy a replacement to fill the office void, they stopped at D.C. Appliance. Joe bought a thirty-six-inch demonstration model to serve the purpose. Since new TVs are rather complex, they spent part of a day installing, programming, and field testing the new piece of office technology.

"When will you be seeing your patients?" Joe asked.

"My schedule is clear this week, so I can work with you."

On Thursday morning, Art sent Joe on patrol with Sheriff Tom for half a day. That afternoon, they changed the password on the office computer. Art concluded the day by giving Joe a set of keys for the office door and for the fireproof file cabinet. On Friday, Susan hosted a surprise "drop by anytime" open-house retirement tribute for Dr. Art. After that, Art did his best to bow out of mental health services in Dakota City. He didn't want to be in Joe's way.

Building a Practice

U nlike his predecessor, Joe was not one to be comfortable
sitting back and waiting for retirement. His little red sports
car made that perfectly clear. Joe's arrival brought a new
personality into the Dakota City mix, and it would prove to be
impetus for big change. This young psychologist came to town with
the sincere desire to make a difference. But even in Dakota City, Joe
would be haunted by his past and discover that being on probation
was akin to wearing handcuffs. He came to work bright and early
on Monday morning eager and ready to dig into his new job. The
first order of business was to brew coffee so it was ready and waiting
for Sheriff Tom. *A deal's a deal.* Tom came into Joe's office right on
schedule and filled his travel mug. "Good morning," Joe said.

"Good job, Joe. It smells like the coffee is ready."

Joe nodded.

Tom filled his cup and walked over to look out the window. He
looked across the lake and took a sip of coffee as his fishing boat
emerged through the morning haze. Art's distinguished head of
gray hair bobbed gently up and down on the water against the back-

drop of a orange sunrise. "It's sure going to be different without Art around here."

Realizing that Tom was lamenting his friend's absence, Joe nodded his head in agreement and sat down at his desk expecting a half-hour chat. But change was already afoot in Dakota City. The sheriff gulped down his coffee, turned from the window, and started out the office door. "Sorry, Joe, I've got to run."

"What's the rush?"

"The judge did a bunch of paperwork over the weekend, and I have three subpoenas to serve this morning. If I'm going to be at Kelsey's in time for coffee, I better get a move on."

"The judge must work some unusual hours."

"He goes in and out of that office like a gopher goes in and out of its hole. Tom waved a handful of the subpoenas in front of Joe's face. "When I stopped in last night, the judge handed me these. I think he was expecting me all along."

"At least you have something to do. I don't suppose there's anything in that pile of papers that involves me?"

"Not unless you care to settle a dispute over free-roaming cattle. The darn things cross fallen-down fences and then the farmers fight about who owns them."

Joe shook his head. "Are you serious?"

"Yes. I got called down to the City Bar a week ago to break up a push and shove match. With a deer rifle hanging in the back window of every truck in the county, the judge decided to settle the matter in court."

"That sounds a lot more exciting than looking through Art's records and trying to figure out who his patients were."

Tom smiled. He knew full well what a look at Art's records would reveal. "Oh, I suspect you might find that job more interesting than you imagine."

"What do you mean by—"

"Sorry, Joe. I have to run." With that said, the sheriff made a quick departure.

Dr. Joe rolled his office chair over to the three drawer file cabinet. First, he opened the bottom drawer labeled "Sporting Events and Pools." It was completely empty. The middle drawer was labeled "Fishing Reports and Hunting Information." This drawer was also empty. Expecting the top drawer to be packed with records, Joe saved it for last. Labeled "Records, Daily Logs and Calendars," this drawer contained files, spiral-bound notebooks, as well as pages torn from a desktop calendar. Joe grabbed the handful of files and quickly scanned through them. Having been trained to always look for patterns, he gathered his thoughts. *Number one, mostly assessment work. Number two, all referrals from Tom and the county court plus a few additional psychological assessments from the school. Number three, no ongoing therapy progress notes.* Placing the files back into the drawer, Joe grabbed the front-most notebook, rolled his chair back to his desk, and read the log from the back page forward.

> September–Week Four: No patients and no referrals. Consulted with the sheriff and did outreach at Kelsey's.

The report for weeks three, two, and one read exactly the same, except for a notation about doing a Drug and Alcohol Assessment in the first week of September. Joe turned his attention to the calendar pages. The little boxes contained daily pencil entries. "Monday and Tuesday–Total News Channel (TNC), Wednesday and Thursday–Complete News Channel (CNC), and Friday–Exclusive Sports Network (ESN)." *I'll bet Art's clinical records are on the computer.*

Before checking the desktop computer, Joe rolled his chair back to the file cabinet. Digging deeper into the top drawer, he finally found something of interest: a folder labeled "The snowman." Joe turned toward his window and took his first close look at the snowman. *There seems to be a community mystique about you, Mr. Snowman.*

Why do people rib old Art about you, and why does Art duck the hits? Let's see what I can learn. In hopes of lifting the shroud of silence that surrounded this fiberglass contraption, Joe ripped into the file. But to his disappointment, all he found were three pictures of the snowman, and all of them had been used in a game of darts.

A Second Look

After tearing through the file cabinet and finding nothing more of significance, Joe dug into Art's old desk. Excluding two dry pens, a short pencil without an eraser, and some fingernail clippings, it, too, was empty. After Joe dumped the drawers in the trash basket, he sat in utter frustration for a few moments. *I don't think Art had any active patients. No, that can't be true.* Joe sighed and looked at his wristwatch. *Maybe that's why Art thought I needed a TV.* Joe hit the remote switch and turned on the television to kill some time before going to Kelsey's. The table generally filled up at ten, but Joe's plan was to go to the restaurant a bit later. *Ten thirty-five should be about right.* Joe alternated between flipping channels and looking at his watch. Time moved in slow motion. *If I go to Kelsey's now, the regulars will expect me to join them. I want to talk to Billie.* A mental alarm clock went off in Joe's head when his watch read 10:35. He hit the power button on the remote, locked his office, and headed to Kelsey's, hoping to repair his image with the attractive and engaging hostess. When Joe stepped into the restaurant, Billie looked up from a pile of receipts. *Good. She noticed me.*

"You made it in without falling this time," Billie said with a big grin on her face.

"That was embarrassing."

"You're late. The table has already cleared out, but you can sit down with me if you like."

"Thanks. The fact is I wanted to talk to you."

"Do you want to order anything?"

Suddenly, Joe was struck with a feeling of empty discomfort that originated from his left, rear pants pocket. He didn't have his wallet. "Ah … ah … water will be fine."

Billie shook her head. "My, aren't you the big spender."

"I forgot my wallet."

"Hmm … let me think out loud. A new sports car, a broken windshield, a young psychologist who moves to Dakota City, and no wallet. Dr. Joe, did you forget your wallet, or are you broke?"

Joe felt the ice melting beneath his feet. "Okay, I admit it. I'm between paychecks right now, but I really did forget my wallet."

"What do you want, Dr. Joe? I'll buy. Call it payment for mopping up our floor."

"Water will be fine."

"Are you sure you don't want anything else?"

"I'd like a chance to talk with you. Do you have a moment?"

"Why on earth would a psychologist want to talk to me?"

"I want to apologize for my rude behavior the other day. I was looking where I shouldn't have, and I'm sorry."

Billie laughed. "I don't know what you saw, but I'm quite certain it wasn't anything more than people see when I'm on the beach."

The thought of seeing Billie in a swimsuit caused Joe to push the puck right down the ice. "What I saw was the most beautiful woman I've ever laid eyes on. I couldn't help myself, and as I said, I'm sorry."

Billie blushed. "My, you don't waste much time, do you?"

"Look, that didn't come out right. I didn't mean to sound forward."

Billie couldn't resist giving Joe a hard time. "What do you mean that didn't come out right? Either I am the most beautiful woman you have ever seen, or I'm not. Did you mean what you said, or did you come over here to feed me a line?"

By now, Billie had Joe stammering. "You know what I meant. I'm trying to apologize. Do you accept?"

Billie laughed. "Okay, thanks."

"Good, I appreciate your understanding."

"Joe, you can be such an idiot. The 'thank you' was for the compliment, *not* the apology." Billie laughed again and got up to wait on a group of ladies with gray and blue hair. "The second shift is here, Joe. I have to go."

Joe chugged his water and left thinking. *She's a testy little creature.*

The Competition Exposed

After mending fence with Billie, Joe went back to the courthouse hoping to check in with Susan, but she was doing business with the commissioner. Joe kept his distance until the commissioner handed Susan a stack of papers and started to walk away. Just as Joe stepped forward, the commissioner made a sudden turn back. "Did you check on that new piece of equipment we ordered for the park? I'd like to have it installed before the festival."

"It was still on back order as of last week," Susan said.

"Did you get a shipping date?"

"They wouldn't make any promises but said it should be here around Thanksgiving."

"That's a little late, I'm afraid." The commissioner stepped back from Susan's desk, greeted Joe, and left. Joe stepped forward. "Hi, Susan. Have there been any calls for me?"

"Only one. Sheriff Tom was wondering if you were going to coffee."

"Were there any drop-ins?"

"No, Joe. No drop-ins either."

For Joe's own piece of mind, he needed to confirm that Art's caseload was basically nonexistent. So, he fidgeted in front of Susan's desk.

"Did you want something else?" she asked.

"Susan, were things always this slow for Art?"

Susan rolled her eyes. "Things were usually slower for Art. He worked harder training you last week than he has worked in years."

"You're kidding me, right?"

"Why are psychologists always asking me that question? No, I am not kidding you. In fact, if you're trying to predict your workload, you may as well know the truth. Things will be especially slow this time of year. The snowman opens for business before too long, you know."

"Okay, Susan, I'll bite. I've been hearing comments about the snowman ever since I got to town. What do you mean, 'he opens for business'?"

Susan let out a long sigh, showing her frustration, and stalled by twisting her long red hair. "Ah ... let me guess. Art didn't tell you about the snowman, did he?"

"No. He left a couple of old pictures of him in his office. Other than that, all I know about the snowman is that Art gets teased about him."

Susan gave a short sigh. "It seems like I have to do everything around here."

"I don't mean to trouble you."

"Sit down for a minute, Joe." Susan paused to think. "Now, how should I say this ... Art would have you believe that he worked nearly to death the last twenty-eight years. But, the truth is, ever since the snowman showed up, there hasn't been much need for a psychologist in Dakota City."

Joe threw up his hands in disbelief. "Are you saying that the snowman has some kind of magical power and fixes people's problems?"

Susan shook her head. "No, Joe, the snowman is not magical. Let me try to explain it in another way. Every year on the first of November, someone, and no one knows who, crawls into the fiberglass snowman and turns on the lights. This is the snowman's way of telling all of us that he's ready to listen to our problems and help us. He likes to get his work done before Christmas. The holiday seems to go better that way."

"Do you mean to say that people stand outdoors in the cold and disclose personal information to that stupid-looking thing?"

"Yes, Joe, that's what I'm saying. I know that it sounds silly, but all year long, people around here stuff their psychological issues into a bag and wait until Snowman turns on his lights. Then, when the lights come on, folks go and talk things out with him."

"I refuse to believe that rational people seek help from someone hiding in a fiberglass snowman!"

"Believe what you want, but you'll see for yourself. All you have to do is watch out your office window. But, Joe, just so you know, the snowman is not stupid."

"Isn't that risky? I mean, talking to the snowman without know-ing who's inside listening?"

"It's either talk to Snowman, someone we've all been able to trust for years, or be seen going to the psychologist's office and have folks think you're crazy. Joe, you have a problem. Anybody and everybody can see who goes in and out of the mental health office. I don't know what it's like where you come from, but people around here worry about what others think."

"You're telling me that there is a stigma attached to talking with the psychologist?"

"Yes."

"But it's fine to stand in the public park and talk to the snowman?"

"That's right, Joe. Now you've got the picture."

"I see. So I'm skating second line behind the snowman?"

Susan hesitated before answering. "Joe, you may as well know the truth. Actually, you're skating third line. You're in competition with the ministers, too. Father Riley is highly regarded."

Joe scratched his head. "Susan, have you been brushing up on hockey?"

Susan smiled. "Yes. I can see where knowing the game will help me keep you on task."

"Why does the commissioner hire a psychologist if everyone talks to the snowman?"

"I'm not sure, Joe. I've heard him refer to your job as economic development, if that clarifies anything for you."

Joe found his visit with Susan productive—or at least sort of. He left her desk with a better understanding of his new job and where he fit into the scheme of things in Dakota City. *I am the only psychologist desperate enough to come here.* Joe went to his office and checked the computer files for patient records just in case he had missed something. However, all he found in the computer were three games. One game was called "Buck Hunt," another was called "Techno-Golf," and the third was called "Trophy Fishing." Joe tried the fishing game for five minutes and shut it off in frustration. *I don't like playing third line.* With that in mind, Joe called it a day. He stepped out of his office and into the hallway.

While Joe fumbled with his keys, the sound of Sheriff Tom's now familiar footsteps echoed through the courthouse hallway. "We missed you at coffee this morning," Tom said.

"I went down a little later. I needed to talk to Billie."

"Watch yourself, Joe. She's a spunky one, and, just so you know, people around here think the world of her. She's the icon of community kindness, and woe to the man that hurts her. I can't blame you for being interested though."

"Who said I'm interested?"

"Art."

"Is she seeing anyone?"

"Not to my knowledge. Listen, Joe, Art asked me to watch over the two of you when he's out fishing. He has kept a close eye on the twins ever since their dad passed away."

"I wish Art would have told me as much about my new job as he fabricates about Billie and me."

Tom heard frustration in the young psychologist's voice. "Is something wrong, Joe?"

"Sheriff, I want to know who the snowman is. And, Tom, if you want your coffee warm in the morning, you better be straight with me."

"That's a complicated question, Joe."

"Don't give me that 'it's complicated' line, Sheriff. I've been looking around, and the only way anyone can get into that giant fiberglass bulb is through the tunnels that come in and out of the courthouse."

"And the door to the pump house," Tom added.

"I stand corrected. You're in charge of security around here, and figuring out who the snowman is can't be that complicated. Now, I want a crisp, clear answer."

"I'll be as straight as I can, but you aren't going to like what I say."

"Try me."

The Sheriff encroached into Joe's personal space. "Okay, Joe, crisp and clear. I don't know who the snowman is, and I don't want to know. In fact, I go out of my way to help the snowman, whoever he is, keep his identity a secret. People haul their personal trash to the snowman, and he takes care of it for them. With the trash gone, crime stays low. And, Joe, when you're in the law enforcement business, a low crime rate is a good thing."

Joe held his ground. "A person needs a license to practice psychology in this state. What the snowman is doing is against the law. It may even be worse than parking in the cul-de-sac."

Sheriff Tom felt the barb in Joe's comment. "Now calm down, Joe, and look at it from my point of view. I'm an elected county official and serve at the will of the people. If I try to uncover the snowman or stop him from talking to folks, I'll be out of work and out of pay. Joe, I'll say this to you as a friend: leave the snowman alone. I have a wife and two kids to support."

"Tom, the silly looking thing is sticking its big carrot nose into my business. Plus, it's an eyesore. Look at it."

The sheriff was listening to Dr. Joe. In fact, he was listening very carefully. "I can't do anything based on accusations."

"What do you mean *accusations?*"

"Have you seen anybody even do so much as light up the snowman since you've been here?"

"No."

"Have you heard anyone say anything to the snowman that so much as remotely resembles a psychological therapy session?"

"Well, no."

"That's what I'm talking about when I say 'accusations.'" Tom paused. "Now, have you calmed down?"

"Okay, Sheriff, maybe I'm overreacting, but *I'll* tell *you* something as a friend. I don't like playing third line."

"I understand that. Maybe this snowman thing will work itself out. Let's go, Joe. I'll buy you lunch at Kelsey's."

After lunch, Joe shuffled home and took a nap. He startled awake at a quarter until two. His first waking reaction was to feel a twinge of guilt for having overslept his noon hour and being late for work. He rubbed the sleep from his eyes and listened to his conscience. *What difference does it make? I may as well stay home. I don't have any patients anyway.* But another internal voice countered with, *You're going to do things right this time, Joe.*

An Offer Rejected

With the end of Joe's second week of work fast approaching, he knew that things were not going well. Being on probation weighed heavily on his mind; it seemed to constrict his spontaneous and generally confident nature. He had been tricked into moving to a town with no ice. He had gotten off to a bad start with the county sheriff. He had yet to see a single patient, and he'd discovered that he had some rather unusual competition. Worst of all, he had embarrassed himself in front of the most beautiful and intriguing woman he had ever met. Dr. Joe needed to develop a game plan, and for him, doing so required spending some time on the ice—real ice. On the ice, Joe found that complex and confusing matters came into clarity.

Joe turned on his office computer. *Bingo! I have a hit, the Sioux Falls Hockey Association.* Sioux Falls was situated a mere ninety miles away and, unlike Dakota City, had an indoor arena. Even better, there was an "open league" comprised of former players who got together on a regular basis to knock the puck around. Their next game was scheduled for Saturday morning at 8:00 a.m. The website read, "Fresh legs welcome—bring a ten-dollar ice fee." *Perfect*, Joe thought. *Tomorrow is Friday and payday. I can drive down to Sioux Falls Friday night, spend the night in a hotel, and be on the ice by seven thirty getting my legs back.*

On Friday morning, Joe woke up full of anticipation for a change. He went to his office, needlessly hung around for a while in hopes of a drop-in patient, and wandered over to coffee. When he walked in the door, Billie was standing at the cash register. He found the very sight of her was inspiring. *Maybe she'll spend the weekend with me in Sioux Falls.*

"Good morning, Dr. Joe," Billie said.

"Billie, if I'm going to ask you to spend the weekend with me in Sioux Falls, I'd rather you call me Joe."

"My, I might be the one to fall on the floor next. Are you asking me out?"

"Yes."

Billie enjoyed making Joe squirm with her banter. She could tell that even though the teasing annoyed him, it didn't really intimidate him. In this case, Joe had simply ignored her. "What do you have in mind?" she asked.

"Have you ever seen a bunch of old men play hockey? There's a game in Sioux Falls on Saturday morning, and I'm driving down tonight. You could come with me and watch." Joe waved his paycheck at Billie. "After that, I'll buy you dinner. You can pick the restaurant."

"Is that all you had in mind?"

Joe was starting to see through some of Billie's games. She was playing with him, doing her best to keep him off balance. It was time to start playing back. "Actually, no, I thought I might put you to work. I need help picking out an automatic coffee pot because I'm tired of getting up early to make Tom's coffee."

"Joe, I'm flattered by the offer, but isn't it a bit fast to plan on spending the night together?"

"Spending the night together? I wish I had thought of that. Why was I planning on paying for your room?"

Billie knew she had just been beaten in their game of flirtatious banter. "Joe, under those conditions, I would've gladly accepted your offer, but I can't go. I have to work."

"Do you ever take a day off?"

"Not many. I couldn't leave Bobbi with three shifts in a row, not with this short notice. That would be asking too much."

"But you would go if you didn't have to work?" Joe asked, having heard a glimmer of hope.

"Yes, Joe, I'd love to go with you if I didn't have to work. It sounds like fun. What time is the game?"

"They drop the puck at eight," Joe said as he left Kelsey's. Since he was going to be on his own, he left for Sioux Falls early.

Getting Some Ice Time

A t seven thirty Saturday morning, Joe was the first person out of the locker room. He rushed directly to the rink, jumped over the boards, and onto the ice. Taking a deep breath, he filled his lungs with the cool moist air that hovered over the ice. Here, where the world was divided by blue lines, things seemed to make sense. In the practice of psychology, the lines were blurred. In hockey, the mental game was important, but so was being physical. In fact, being physical was encouraged and even applauded.

Joe dropped a puck and pushed it effortlessly around the rink while the other men made their way onto the ice one and two at a time. Once all of the players were present, teams were chosen, and Joe was back in the game. Eighteen minutes of play flew by. The buzzer blared out a two-minute warning. The first period was about to end. Joe's team was playing a man-to-man defense as an opposing wing-man eased the puck down the ice in front of Joe. Joe skated backward. Since everyone on the ice was tired, game etiquette mandated that the defense not pressure the opponents until they brought the puck into the neutral zone. The gap between the players closed at center ice.

Suddenly, Joe's assigned man jerked his chin upward and used it to point into the stands. "Is the babe in the seats with you?"

Joe looked into the stands, and there sat Billie in the eighth row smiling and waving at him. As usual, the very sight of her caused him to freeze. Joe's opponent seized his distraction and broke away, uncontested. The net popped backward, and the score changed to three to two. When the buzzer sounded, Joe was still standing on the blue line. *What's she doing here?*

Billie ran down to the boards to greet Joe, laughing all the way. Joe skated over to her. "Is that what you call defense?" Billie asked.

"What are you doing here?"

"I came to see you play, and as I recall, I was invited."

"I thought you couldn't come?"

"I said I couldn't come *with* you. I didn't say I couldn't come. Weren't you supposed to stop that guy from scoring?"

"I would have, but I was distracted by an unruly fan. How did you get out of work?"

"I traded a shift with Bobbi, but I need to be back by three, so don't get your hopes up about me spending the night." The buzzer sounded, calling the players back from their break. "Joe, can I give you some advice?" Billie asked.

"What if I say no?"

"I'll tell you anyway."

"For some reason, I believe that. You may as well go ahead."

"If you kept your eyes where they belong, things might go better for you."

Joe knew Billie was not just talking hockey. "Billie Kelsey, whether I'm on or off the ice, you have a way of taking me out of the game. Do you have time to stay for lunch?"

Noticing that Joe was surrounded by the smell of the game, Billie waved her hand in front of her nose. "Do you have time for a shower first?"

"Yes."

"Okay, it's a date." After the game, Billie took Joe to a quiet corner in an Italian restaurant, where they enjoyed a leisurely dinner. Later, they went to a discount center, where Billie picked out an automatic coffee pot. With that mission accomplished, she drove back to Dakota City, and Joe stayed overnight for a second game on Sunday morning.

The Game Plan

Joe came off the ice with a brighter outlook and a plan to take back to Dakota City. *Be visible. Be friendly, and never, ever gossip. Keep a regular routine. Work out in the park early in the mornings. Clean up. Check in with Susan, and go to coffee. After coffee, browse businesses, walk the streets, and visit.* Of course, the acute awareness that tomorrow might be a difficult day at work was stuck in the back of his mind. Tomorrow was November 1, the day that the snowman was said to open up his seasonal practice. If Joe was to have any chance of being successful in Dakota City, he had to earn the people's trust. On Monday morning, Joe stood by Susan's desk with sore legs and a renewed gleam in his eye. "Good morning," he said.

"Did you have a good weekend?" Susan asked.

"I had a great weekend. How about you?"

"I've had better. I spent a lot of time with my mom."

"How's she doing?"

Susan shook her head, and tears formed in her eyes. "Not well, Joe. I don't expect her to live through the week."

"I'm very sorry to hear that, Susan."

"Thanks for saying that."

Susan was visibly upset, so Joe stayed close by her desk in case she wanted to talk through some feelings. The fiercely independent receptionist fought back the tears and turned her attention to paper-work. "Look, Joe, it's nice of you to hang around, but I'm okay."

Joe excused himself and left to mingle on the sidewalks. When he returned in the afternoon, he stopped at Susan's desk again. "Were there any calls for me?"

"No, I'm sorry, Dr. Joe. No calls." Susan's phone rang, and Joe was hopeful that it might be a referral for him. Susan answered the phone with her customary and professional tone of voice. However, it was quickly apparent to Joe that this was a personal call. Susan's vibrant color turned pale, and her eyes grew wide. As Susan listened to the voice on the other end of the line, she winced in obvious distress.

Joe watched from across the desk in dismay and sympathy as Susan completely lost her office composure. By the time she hung up the phone, large tears fell from her eyes, and Susan was sitting in stunned silence. Her hands covered her mouth. Susan had clearly received very bad news. "Is that about your mom?" Joe asked.

Susan looked at Joe with a panic-stricken face. She repeatedly shook her head. "No."

"What is it?" Joe asked. He stepped around Susan's desk and put his arm around her shoulder. "Is there anything I can do?"

"This is terrible, Joe, terrible—and at the worst possible time too." Susan put her head down on her desk and wept.

"Would you like to come to my office where you can have some privacy? We can talk."

Susan shook her head again. "Dr. Joe, if this was about anything else, I'd be glad to do that, but I can't talk, not about this.

"Susan—"

"I'll be okay, Dr. Joe. Really." Susan sat up in one brisk motion as stubborn proof of her fortitude.

"Are you sure?"

"Yes, I'm sure. Just give me some space," Susan snapped at Joe.

Joe heard the bite of anger in Susan's voice. "Okay, I'll be in my office. Let me know if there's anything I can do."

Susan's tone softened. "Thank you. I'll keep that in mind. I may need your help later, but not now."

"Let me give you my cell phone number." Joe wrote down his phone number on a yellow notepad and placed it in her hand. "Now, don't be afraid to call me."

Susan nodded in appreciation. "On second thought, there are some things you can do for me."

"You name it."

"If I'm not in tomorrow morning, I'll be gone for several days. Tell the commissioner that I took vacation before I planned."

"Okay, consider it done. Is there anything else?"

"Find my dad and tell him I'm sorry—very sorry for leaving."

Joe was shocked. "Susan, how can you leave your mom now?"

"Joe, I want you to call on her for me, you know, in my stead. If her time comes before I'm back, you tell her that I love her. Say my good-byes for me, Joe. Please?"

"Susan—," Joe said, protesting the difficulty of his assignments in the face of his coworker's agony.

"Joe, don't pressure me. Please, just do what I've asked." Susan picked up the phone and called Vickie. After asking her to cover the phone from the Register of Deeds office, she cleared her desk and left the courthouse in a frantic hurry.

Joe went to his office and began digging through the box of college textbooks that he had brought with him from Minnesota. He searched and searched for an explanation to Susan's behavior. The look of panic on her face was unlike anything he had ever seen. Even more disturbing for Joe, her unusual requests left him feeling inadequate and ill prepared. *What could cause Susan to leave her dying mother? What will I tell Trapper? How does a stranger say a final farewell for someone else?* The inexperienced psychologist got lost in his studies. Time escaped, and bright daylight turned to dusk. While he had not found any answers, Joe was tired and ready to go home. He looked out the window. "At least that's encouraging. No snowman," Joe said to himself.

The Snowman Opens Shop

Joe had no more than spoken when the snowman suddenly lit up and a human silhouette became visible through the translucent fiberglass shell. *Who is that?* As tired as Joe was, he stood at his window and watched as the snowman's patients immediately began to emerge from the deepening shadows. One by one, and respecting each other's privacy, they walked up to the snowman and talked with him.

Of course, Joe couldn't hear the problems that the people were talking about. "Snowman, I lied to my husband." "Snowman, I cheated on my wife." "Help me, Snowman." Dim light turned to darkness, and the snowman's radiance sent a comforting yellow glow through Dr. Joe's window. Within an hour, Joe had seen as much as he cared to see. He pulled on his hooded sweatshirt and looked out at the snowman one more time. What he saw made him freeze in his tracks. He blinked with shock, and his jaw dropped in disbelief. There was Susan standing in front of the snowman pouring her heart out in anguish.

That really hurts, Joe thought. His pride boiled in disappointment as he watched Susan open her purse and take out a tissue to dry her eyes. Eventually, she pulled herself away from the snowman's support and walked away.

I'm not going to accept this without saying something to her. Joe hurried out of the courthouse and ran to catch up with Susan. She heard him coming and jogged toward her pickup in hopes of making an escape. Joe picked up the pace and burst into a full sprint. Susan could hear that he was closing in on her fast. She conceded defeat and made a sharp turn to face him. "I was afraid you were watching. That's why I waited until your office light went off."

"Why did you do it, Susan?"

"You're with my dad at coffee all the time, Joe. Sooner or later, whatever I tell you will slip out—no matter how hard you try to keep things quiet."

"You're wrong about that, Susan. I'm a professional, and I'm good at keeping confidences."

"I appreciate you telling me that, and I'll keep it in mind."

"What did the snowman say to you?"

"You really don't want to know, Joe."

"You're wrong again, Susan. I do want to know."

"Okay. The snowman told me I should get your phone number, and before this is over, I'll have to call you for help."

Joe was at his wit's end and started churning out more questions. "Before what's over? And another thing, Susan, how can I talk to your parents when I don't have the foggiest idea about what you're up to?"

"Listen, Joe. I'm sorry. I really am. But I can't talk about this—not now. Please just do what I've asked."

"How can I say your good-bye when I've never even met your mom?"

"Please do your best. I know what I'm asking is not easy."

A Very Long Trip

S usan jumped into her blue midsized pickup and hurried to her apartment. After throwing a few clothes and personal things into a suitcase, she hit the road. By ten o'clock that night, she was speeding toward Interstate 90 and had clicked off one of the twenty hours it would take to drive to Las Cruces, New Mexico. A hint of orange sunlight reflected in her rearview mirror as she crossed the Nebraska and Colorado state line. Tired and without sleep for over twenty-four hours, she pulled off of Interstate 76 in Sterling, Colorado, for rest. She found a cheap hotel, caught a few hours of uneasy sleep, and was on the road again by early afternoon. In another eight hours, Susan would be in Las Cruces. There, her six-year-old son, Tony, was on life support and dying as a result of a curbside hit and run accident.

As Susan's heart rushed to Las Cruces, her pickup seemed to crawl even at eighty miles per hour. Wide-open prairie, sand hills, dry desert, and sagebrush don't offer a heartsick mother anything in the way of emotional support. This was a long, lonely, and difficult trip. When Susan grew weary of praying, she listened to the hum of her pickup tires as they replayed conversations from the pre...ng thirty-six hours.

Hum…"He's been run over, Susan. They don't expect h...to live." *Hum*…"You need to hurry." *Hum*…"You can't leave your mom now." *Hum*…"Who should I be with, Snowman, my son or my mom?" *Hum*…"If there's anything I can do to help." *Hum*… "I'm good at keeping confidences."

These repetitive thoughts turning over and over in Susan's mind like the thumping of tires on hard pavement morphed into a throbbing headache. Susan rubbed her temples and turned on the radio again. Even though the pace of traffic was moving five miles per hour over the speed limit, these slower-moving vehicles held back her progress and annoyed her. When at last she came over the Organ Mountains and saw the lights of Las Cruces, she called her ex-boyfriend, Gary, on the cell phone. "What room are you in?"

"Room 312, and, Susan, you better hurry."

Susan pulled into the hospital parking lot and sprinted through the wide automatic doors. She jumped in the elevator and poked the third floor button. *Come on. Come on.* She stepped out of the elevator and saw Gary standing at the nurse's station.

Gary turned at the sound of the elevator's ring. He walked to meet Susan. "Susan, I'm sorry."

"What do you mean, 'you're sorry'?" The truth was that Susan knew what Gary meant, and she started to cry. She had not made it in time. Angry at her loss, she snapped. "Why weren't you watching him? Why do I send you all that money to take care of him?"

Gary not only felt terrible, but he had risked his life trying to save Tony. "I tried, Susan. I tried my best," Gary said, showing her a white cast on his broken arm. "The drunken jerk came speeding by at the same time Tony ran into the street after a ball. It all happened so fast. I dove and tried to shove him out of the way, but I was a split second too late."

Susan spent the night tossing and turning on a couch in Gary's apartment. At eight o'clock Wednesday morning, she and Gary were at the funeral home making arrangements. "Can I see him now?" Susan asked the mortician.

"Visitation begins this afternoon," the mortician said.

Susan stood with her feet planted firmly in front of the mortician. "I can't leave him here."

The mortician reassured Susan. "I promise you he's in good hands." He looked at Gary.

"Susan, let's go somewhere and wait until we can visit Tony this afternoon," Gary said.

Susan would not leave the funeral home until she clarified what she was trying to say. "I mean, I can't leave him here in New Mexico. This isn't where he belongs, not for eternity. What do I need to do so I can take him home with me?"

"You could fly him home from El Paso," the mortician said.

Susan shook her head. "That won't work."

"I could drive him for you."

"You don't understand. I don't have that kind of money, sir."

"I see," the mortician said.

"Susan, think about what you're saying. You're talking about a 1,250 mile drive," Gary said.

Susan was grief stricken and guilt ridden for not having made it in time to hold Tony's little hand. "I'm going to take him home with me," she insisted.

"I'll come with you," Gary said.

"No, I need some time alone with him."

Gary turned away from Susan to collect his thoughts. Then, he turned back to plead that she be more reasonable. "Susan—"

"Will you people please listen to me? I *need* to take him back by myself."

The mortician offered to defer expenses. Susan decline "A you absolutely sure you want to drive him back yourself, mad ?"

"Yes. All I need from you is to tell me what I need to do."

"Where do you live?"

"South Dakota."

"You'll need permits to carry your son's body across state line can get them for you."

"How long will that take?"

"I can have them by noon tomorrow."

"Thank you," Susan said.

Snaring Beaver

Meanwhile, back in Dakota City, Dr. Joe got up early and worked out in the park. When he was finished, he sat down to rest. Taking a seat on a park bench under a large cottonwood tree located near the lake's edge, he exhaled. His warm breath drifted away into the cool morning air. Joe looked through the prism of colors reflecting off the water just a few yards from his feet. Despite the beautiful array of purple, orange, and yellow hues glistening off the water, all Joe could see was the agony on Susan's face before she left him standing on the street. *What could have happened?*

As Joe stewed about Susan's perplexing behavior and unusual requests, a large golden leaf fell from the cottonwood. The dew-soaked foliage tumbled toward earth and gently touched his shoulder on the way down. Its tender tap stirred him from his contemplative trance. Joe sat up straight and took in a deep breath of the brisk air. The rich full aroma of fall filled his lungs, but there was more scent floating in the air than the smell of decomposing leaves. Joe took a second deep breath and looked at another cottonwood tree a few yards to his left. Part of the tree's trunk was freshly gnawed, and several finger-sized wood shavings lay at its base. He looked beyond the tree and across the water. Forty yards out into the lake, a beaver paddled on the surface leaving behind a long, V-shaped wake. Joe stood up to get a better look but moving gave his position away. The beaver slapped its tail and dove under the water.

"The darn things try to cut this tree down almost every year," Trapper said, startling Joe from behind.

"This particular one?"

"Yes."

"There are several other trees. Why this one?"

Trapper looked deep into Joe's eyes as if he was looking into the depths of Joe's soul. "There's something special about it. Maybe it gives off a certain smell or a special vibration. You know, like some people you meet." As the men talked, the beaver surfaced farther away from shore, and Joe squinted through the sun to get a better look at it. "You can see one up close tomorrow morning if you like," Trapper said with a lethal confidence in his voice.

Joe inched backward. *Don't be intimidated. You need to hold your ground with this guy.* "I'll be here," Joe said.

Trapper looked at the ground and pointed toward the beaver sign. In addition to the white wood chips, there were two trails made slick and shiny with water at lake's edge. "See where they've been sliding in and out of the water?"

Joe nodded.

Trapper clipped off a few small tree branches to use as bait, organized them into a pile, and stood back upright. "I'll be right back with a couple of snares and set them in those trails."

"And you'll have the beaver by morning?"

"Odds are that will be the case. Look, Joe, I don't have much time to talk, not if I'm going to do right by Millie. The doctor told me last evening she's not likely to make the day."

"I'm sorry to hear that, Trapper."

Trapper's head dropped. "I'm not inclined to talk about the two of us—not with what people say about her around here. But, Joe, I love her."

Joe realized that Trapper needed to say that to someone other than Millie. *Love means less if not confessed.* Joe also knew that since Trapper had taken a personal risk, this was the time to tell him about Susan. If he didn't tell Trapper about his daughter leaving town now, Trapper would never respect or trust him. Still, he hesitated and watched as the rugged outdoorsman walked away. *I've got to talk to him.* Joe cleared his throat and called out with a raised voice. "Trapper, we need to talk."

Trapper stopped along the trail and turned back to face Joe. "Can it wait?"

"I'd rather it not," Joe said with a tone certain to catch Trapper's attention.

Trapper walked back and faced Joe. Joe made a friendly step forward. "Did you talk with Susan last night?"

"No. Is something wrong?"

Joe could tell from Trapper's tone of voice that he did not know Susan had left town. "I was afraid of this."

"Afraid of what?"

"I don't know how to tell you this, but Susan left town last night."

"What? What happened? What were you doing with my daughter last night?"

"I don't know what happened. And as far as being with your daughter, it's not like you're suggesting. Susan and I work together, and that's all. Listen to me, Trapper. Something is wrong, seriously wrong. She got a phone call yesterday, and I've never seen anyone get as upset as Susan did."

"Did you talk to her?"

"I tried."

"What did she say?"

"Not much. She said something terrible had happened, and she had to leave town for a few days. That's all she'd tell me."

"Good heavens, Joe, her mother is dying as we speak. Why didn't you stop her?"

"I tried, Trapper, but your daughter has a mind of her own."

"Darn that girl. She's always doing stuff like this. I thought psychologists were supposed to help people. You know, guide them toward reason." Trapper turned and gazed out over the lake to sooth his irritation. "Where's she now?"

"I have no idea. The last time I saw her was last night just after dark."

"What was she doing?"

"She was in the park talking to the snowman. When she left him, I had to run after her. If I hadn't done that, I wouldn't know the precious little that I do."

"Did she say anything else?"

"Yes. I'm to tell you that she's sorry for leaving, very sorry."

Trapper gave a thoughtful look toward the ground and shook his head. "What kind of girl runs off and leaves a mother in her final hours?"

"Trapper, there's more. She asked me to make regular calls on her mom. If Millie's time approaches, I'm to extend all of Susan's love and explain that she's very sorry for not being here."

A Bedside Visit

Later that day, Joe made a bedside call on a complete stranger who lay drifting toward her eternal home. "Millie, my name is Dr. Joe."

Millie's voice was feeble and weak, her breath slow and labored. "Susan told me you're a nice man."

"I'm glad to hear that. Millie, I have something difficult to tell you. Susan had to leave town, and she asked me to stop in and see you."

Millie's frail, limp hand reached to take Joe's. "I know, Dr. Joe. Trapper told me."

"Susan wants me to tell you that she loves you very much and that she is very, very sorry that she can't be here."

Millie gazed out the window and looked beyond this world into the next. Then she gave Joe a faint smile. "Joe, could you tell Susan I understand everything? Tell her that I love her and that whatever she has to do is okay."

Joe squeezed her hand in support. "I'd be happy to do that for you."

"Joe, Susan is going to need someone to help her through this, someone she can count on. Trapper was so strict with her, and there's such a big wall between them. She'll need an understanding ear somewhere close by. Will you look after her?"

"I'll do my best." Trapper came into the room, and the men took turns holding Millie's hand until the staff dismissed Joe. It was time for Millie and Trapper to say their final good-bye.

Three hours later Trapper called Pastor Dalton. Blinded by the trust that he placed in the cleric's collar and completely unaware of the evil hiding from even his keen eyes, Trapper asked Dalton to conduct Millie's funeral service.

A Dirty House

Joe signed out of the assisted living center and picked up a small bag of groceries on the way home. Along the way, he made a rare sighting. Debra was outdoors and rushing to gather a basket of clothes off the clothesline before the evening dew settled in. Even though Joe and Debra had been next-door neighbors for several weeks, Joe had only seen her three times: once inside the new parsonage, once when Pastor Dalton brought her over to clean the house, and right now. Joe watched Debra's graceful but hurried movements. *Why isn't she out and about more?*

Joe went inside, sat down on his couch, and within an hour, the lonely boredom of the empty little house overtook him. If counting the pieces of snack-food confetti strewn across a living room carpet can be considered entertainment, Joe was having a great time. *This is crazy,* Joe thought once he had counted to twenty-five. *Maybe Debra has a vacuum cleaner.*

Joe started toward the parsonage but saw Debra walking into the side door of the church. By the time Joe caught up with her, Debra was in the church balcony struggling at the piano keyboard.

He walked softly up the choir-loft stairs and paused out of her line of sight. Joe wanted to hear Debra play without the pressure of an audience. *Good rhythm but timid and forced. She's afraid to play.* After a moment's listening, Joe stepped to where Debra could see him and cleared his throat. "Excuse me," he said.

Debra was startled and jumped up from the piano bench. "You scared me."

"I'm sorry."

"I hope you weren't listening. I'm terrible." Debra stood up and stepped away from the ivory keys.

Joe shrugged to let Debra know he had been doing a little eavesdropping. "Practice always helps."

"I've been embarrassing myself ever since Millie got too sick to play for the church service. Pastor Derrick insists that I play for her funeral, but she deserves better than me."

Joe motioned toward the piano. "May I?"

"Please, go ahead."

Joe sat down and pulled the piano bench forward. Debra listened as he played an improvised version of Pachelbel's "Canon in D." "Now I'm really embarrassed. You play so well."

"Thank my parents. Ten years of lessons helped."

"I can't get my fingers to do what I want them to," Debra said as Joe stood up and got out of the way so she could sit back down.

Standing at Debra's side, Joe showed her his hands palms up and fingers open. "May I touch you?"

"If you think you can help me."

Joe stepped in close behind the pastor's wife and pushed his palm firmly on the flat of her back to straighten her slumping and defeated posture. He gently pulled back on her shoulders with one hand and kept pressure against her lower back with the other. "Don't move." Joe released his hands and pushed his hard abdominal muscles against Debra's back to prevent her from slouching the minute he let go. Stomach hard against Debra's back, Joe reached his arms around his student from both sides and took a firm grasp of her hands. He adjusted their posturing and gently manipulated her delicate fingers into proper position. Then he held them there, and after a moment, he let go. "Now, play like you mean it."

Debra played and heard a subtle but immediate improvement. She also heard the same voice that emerged while she was fighting with her husband. The voice told her Joe's strong hands were different than her husband's, and Debra became acutely aware that she liked "different." Pleased with her immediate improvement, Debra tossed her head back into Joe's chest, flipped her auburn hair to the side, and giggled. "Thanks. That helps."

"You're welcome. Maybe you can return a favor. Do you have a vacuum cleaner I can borrow?"

"Sure. There's one in the janitor's closet. Let me show you."

Teacher and student walked out of the church together. Joe carried the vacuum cleaner. Debra talked music. Unbeknownst to either of them, Pastor Dalton had been watching them in silence through the little window in his office door. "This guy is trouble," Dalton snarled to himself. Annoyed by what he had witnessed, Dalton went to his desk and stabbed at the numbers on the phone. "Brother Robert, how are things going in Minnesota?"

"The flock continues to multiply in leaps and bounds," Robert said. "But I see by the regional report you're still struggling to fill the pews."

"Attendance could be better."

"It's not like you to call on a week day, Derrick. You must need something."

"Indeed I do, Brother. See what you can find out about a Dr. Joseph Doyle, would you? He practiced psychology in your neck of the woods until recently. I would like to know more about him."

"There's no need to do research on that matter. The man is embroiled in controversy. He had an affair with one of his patients, and, I might add, my parishioner. I've personally been trying to piece her marriage back together. Dr. Doyle earned himself an ethics violation, a probationary status, and was encouraged to leave the state."

"Ethics violation and probation ... You don't say?"

"Yes, and what burns in me is that the devil saved the adulterer from his own mess, too. The ethics committee clearly should have revoked his license. Don't tell me Doyle has landed in your fold?"

"Not in the fold, but the devil's angel dwells all too near, I'm afraid."

"I'd keep a watchful eye on him. Say, Brother Derrick, is that wife of yours with child yet?"

"No, but I'll soon be seeing to that matter. Peace, Brother. You've been very helpful."

An Unexpected Honor

While Joe vacuumed his floor, he was weighed down by worry for Trapper. He hurried through the work, returned the vacuum cleaner to the church, and walked to the assisted living center to check on his friend who was grieving at Millie's side. "Hi, Trapper. I'm sorry about Millie."

"Have you heard anything from my daughter?" Trapper asked with a hint of anger in his voice.

Joe understood the reasons for Trapper's angry tone. "No. Have you heard anything?"

"Not a word, and I have to plan Millie's service."

"You have my sympathy, Trapper. This has to hurt."

Trapper's eyes were dry and cold. "Joe, excuse me. I need some more time alone with Millie, and they're getting ready to take her from me."

"I understand. Call me if I can help." Joe turned and started out the door.

Trapper called him back. "Will you be a casket bearer?"

"I'd be honored." Having agreed to help place Millie at rest, Joe left the assisted living center and walked back home. Before going inside, he paused by his back door to contemplate and looked up at the stars. *What Millie and Trapper had was good.* As he grabbed the door handle to his empty, lifeless house, Joe remembered the many hours of late-night study during graduate school. *I'm sick and tired of being alone.* He opened his door and stepped in the entryway. "Hi, Billie, it's nice to see you," Joe said aloud. *Saying that felt good.* Of course, Billie wasn't there to hear him, so Joe tried to call her by phone. "The party you are trying to reach is not available. Please leave a message." *Come on, Billie, turn on your phone.* Since she didn't answer, Joe went to the courthouse and turned on his TV. At nine o'clock, he looked out his office window and watched in disbelief as Trapper shared his grief with the snowman. Joe shut off the TV and stared at the screen while its light slowly faded away. Feeling betrayed once again, Joe vented his frustration out loud. "What is it about this Snowman?"

Matters of Perspective

O n Wednesday morning, Joe worked out in the park and, as was now his custom, finished by the park bench. When he approached his usual resting place, he saw a beaver slide smoothly from the bank and into the water. The snared animal slapped its tail and splashed out of sight. Joe expected the captured beaver to rise back up and struggle violently against the Trapper's device. But the frightened beaver stayed under water and held its breath for as long as possible. Only after several minutes did Joe see a small nose and two beady eyes rise slowly to the surface.

Once again Trapper approached silently from behind. "Good morning, Joe." The beaver saw Trapper's movement and dove under the water again.

"How are you doing, Trapper?"

"I've been better, but thanks for asking. I wish Susan was here."

"I don't envy your situation."

Trapper nodded and pointed at the ensnared beaver. "I see I caught a beaver. Did you get a good look at it?"

"Not really. It slid into the water pretty fast considering how big it is, and it's of no mind to come back up."

"That's the female. You can have a better look at her in a moment." Trapper looked at the other snare that he had set. "The male is bigger, but I see I didn't catch him."

Joe nodded his head in agreement.

"Well, Joe, there's work to be done. I need you to step back a few yards. Sit down on the ground, and don't move." Trapper stepped toward the large cottonwood tree and hid in its shadow. He raised his rifle, stood motionless, and focused all of his attention on the beaver. After a few moments, the beaver's eyes and nose rose just above the surface of the water again. Trapper blocked everything else out of his mind and aimed the gun's sight just behind and below the beaver's eyes. Then he pulled the trigger. *Thud!* The crack from the rifle shattered the morning silence and spit out in all directions across the lake. An echo recoiled off the courthouse, making it sound as if Trapper had shot the animal twice. The beaver lunged outward and dove down, twisting against the thin cable snare. The thrashing slowly subsided, the water grew still, and the dead beaver floated to the surface in the bloodstained water. Trapper pulled the beaver from the water and cut the snare with his pliers.

Joe looked at the dead beaver. "Do you ever wonder if you are doing the right thing?"

"Do you mean when I kill a beaver?"

Joe nodded.

"I used to, but not anymore."

"How come?"

"Doing the right thing is often a matter of perspective, Joe. The beaver was going to kill the tree. I killed the beaver. One way or the other, something was going to die." Trapper pulled the heavy brown animal from the water and showed Joe its long orange teeth, sharp claws, and flat scaly tail. He carried it to his pickup, threw it into the box, and drove away. Joe filed what Trapper had said about right and wrong into his memory and lingered on the bench worrying about Susan until the red blood floating in the moss-green water turned brown and finally disappeared.

Billie had been watching through the restaurant window, and although too far away to see exactly what had happened, she had her suspicions. *Joe's sensitive, and that's going to bother him.* Since business was slow, she snuck away with a Styrofoam cup filled with hot coffee. "Did Trapper save the tree again?" Billie asked, handing Joe the cup of coffee.

Joe took the coffee and allowed the cup to warm his cold hands. "Yes, he did."

"You look rather distant sitting down here by yourself. What are you thinking about?"

"The water."

"Staring at it won't make it freeze any faster."

"No, but I wish it would. I could use some ice time again. How did you get away from work?"

"Art came in for breakfast, and I left him in charge of the till."

Joe chuckled. "You're a risk-taker, Billie Kelsey."

Billie knew that Joe's comment about needing ice time was his way of telling her that he was troubled by something. She also knew that when he called her a risk-taker, Joe was indirectly asking if there was any hope for their relationship to grow into something more. "You don't like it here, do you?"

"Why do you ask?"

"I have my reasons. For one thing, new customers are hard to come by around here."

Joe wanted to push the discussion beyond playful banter. "I like you," he said.

"That's not what I asked, Dr. Doyle, and you know it." Billie stepped behind Joe and put her hands on his shoulders. "You're bored here, aren't you?"

Joe slumped forward on the bench and looked at the ground. "It's not the place, Billie. Sure, I miss real ice, but I like the small-town feel."

"What's on your mind then?"

Joe needed to vent, and Billie was offering a listening ear. "I'm not in the game, and I don't like sitting on the bench. Do you understand what I am saying? I'm not making any contributions—no goals, no assists, and not a single therapy session in over two weeks. To make matters worse, the first referral I'm bound to get will be from that ridiculous Snowman everybody talks to. So why am I here? Don't bother answering that. Susan already told me. I'm economic development."

"I was teasing about needing new costumers."

Joe sat up straight. "You were?"

"Of course. Look, Joe, I know that going to the snowman for help seems bizarre. But listen to me for a minute. The people around here are proud, and they are private, at least with their personal problems. It takes time to win their trust."

"They protect him, Billie, and he's not qualified."

"You can't say that, not for sure. No one knows who it is. There aren't a lot of resources in a small town like this, and it's important for people to have a choice." Billie began massaging Joe's shoulders with her delicate fingers.

The sensual movement of her hands made Joe hungry for a glimpse of Billie's pretty face, but turning around would pull his shoulders from the supportive touch that he so craved. He pushed back further into her soothing hands. "That feels good."

"Referrals will pick up. Word in the restaurant is that people like you."

"Things better pick up. I can't sit on the bench and wait for retirement like Art was doing. I want to help people."

Joe Makes a Contribution

B y early Thursday morning, a thin sheet of ice clung to the shore and to Trapper's snares. Joe kept watch for Trapper from his favorite bench, and as he expected, even in grief, Trapper would not leave the trees in danger. Nor would he be so cruel as to allow a captured animal to suffer longer than necessary in a snare. The outdoorsman approached, and, having put aside his camouflage ball hat for the season, he now wore a beaver pelt hat with large fluffy earflaps folded up.

"I didn't get him, did I, Joe?"

"No, you didn't."

"We don't always get what we want."

"No kidding," Joe said, letting his tone of disillusionment escape.

"I know what I'm looking for down here by the water. But tell me, Joe, with all the time you spend on this bench, what are you hoping to find?"

"Ice, Trapper. I love hockey."

Trapper knew that Joe was being evasive and took a guess. "There are a lot of gray areas in life, and you won't learn right from wrong sitting on a park bench. Don't ever tell anyone this, but I have let some pesky critters go in my day—if they weren't hurt."

"Why?"

"Because I thought it was the right thing to do. The point is, a man's got to face what life throws at him and make one decision at a time."

Joe scuffed his running shoe in the dirt and thought about what Trapper said.

"As far as the ice is concerned, don't get your hopes up. It's going to warm up today and melt what little ice there is."

Joe shrugged. "I figured as much. What happened to the other beaver?"

"I may have scared him off like I've done with Susan. Joe, if she calls you—"

"I know, Trapper. I'll tell her what has happened and that she should get back here as soon as possible."

"I'd appreciate that. By the way, Joe, services are at the Redeemer Church tomorrow. I decided to put Millie to rest with or without Susan."

"What time?"

Trapper pulled up the empty snares. "Two o'clock, but you need to be there at twelve thirty to help with the casket."

"Okay. I'll see you then, Trapper."

"Joe, I have another favor to ask you."

"What's that?"

"Millie loved piano music. She played so grand out at the Big Dog. I wish you could have heard her. Everyone danced and had such fun when she played."

"Debra told me Millie played very well."

"I understand that you play very well too."

"You've been talking to Debra, haven't you?"

"Actually, I caught that piece of information from the pastor. Would you play something at the funeral for us?"

"Debra was planning to play."

"Debra plays, but the truth is, she's not very good. We've talked, and both of us want better for Millie."

"I don't normally play in public—"

"But you would play for Millie's sake. Thanks. I knew I could count on you to do the right thing." Trapper bent over and reached down by Dr. Joe's feet. He picked up a flint arrowhead and gave it to him. "It's amazing what one can find if he keeps his eyes open, Joe."

Joe looked at the arrowhead and smiled. "Did I just swim into a snare?"

"Like I said before, a man's got to face what life throws at him and make one decision at a time."

"People here are strange, Trapper. Everybody worries about confidentiality, but nobody can keep a secret." *Except the snowman,* Joe thought.

Susan Comes to the Surface

*J*ust as I am—a fitting message for Millie, Joe thought as he finished playing the recessional. After a long line of cars with lights on made their way to the little country cemetery, Pastor Dalton said a few words and sprinkled dust over Millie's casket. Trapper stayed long after the other people walked away so he could talk with Millie and see her securely to rest. "Where's our daughter? What have I done?" he asked Millie. There was nothing more to say. Trapper dropped a single rose on Millie's burial vault as a symbol of his love. He left the graveside and returned to the church where the women's group served a light lunch.

Joe joined Billie, Bobbi, and Art for a bite to eat and then went home to change out of his suit. *I hate these things,* he thought as he tore off his dark-blue tie.

Joe found himself between taking off suit pants and putting on sweat pants when his cell phone rang. "Hello," Dr. Joe said.

"Hello, Dr. Joe. This is Susan."

"Susan! Where in the devil are you?"

"Let's not talk about that now. How's my mom?"

"She's gone, Susan. We buried her today."

"I was afraid of that. How's Dad?"

Joe wouldn't buffer the frustration he felt with Susan's behavior, nor would he minimize Trapper's anguish. He raised his voice and answered. "Understandably upset, Susan."

Susan ignored the scolding. "Did you call on Mom for me?"

"Yes, Susan, I sat with your dad, and we took turns holding her hand. I told her everything you asked me to say."

"Thank you. What's the weather like?"

"Susan, your mom was buried today, and you want to talk about the weather?"

"Joe, I'm serious. What's the weather like? Has it been cold?"

"No. I can't believe—"

"So the ground isn't frozen?"

"No, but ice has started to form around the edges of the lake."

"Good. Is it cloudy there?"

"Yes."

"That's even better. Listen, Joe, I need your help."

"I think I deserve some answers first," Joe insisted.

"Weren't you the guy who said 'anything I can do to help'?" Susan snapped back.

"Calm down. I haven't said no. Now, where are you?"

"Before I tell you, you've got to promise to keep everything confidential, and I mean *everything*. You told me you were good at that, remember?"

"Yes, Susan, I remember. Now, it's your turn to talk. How could you run off and leave your parents at a time like this?"

Susan was stressed, exhausted, and irritable. "I had my reasons, Dr. Joe, and I'm in no mood to be judged by you or anyone else."

"Look, Susan, I wasn't much into religion before I came to town, but I've been praying for you. I've also been praying that you wouldn't call me. Your dad expects to hear from me the minute you show up. And you ... you want me to keep secrets. Susan, your dad asked me to be a casket bearer."

"I was afraid of this. You'll run right to Kelsey's and tell my dad everything."

"Susan—"

"I should've never opened my big mouth and asked you for help."

"All right, I'll keep things confidential, but you're making this very difficult for me. Where are you?"

"I'm on my way back to town, and I have my son with me. Joe, I need your help with him."

"You have a son?" Joe thought for a moment. "Your dad doesn't know that, does he?"

"No, and I plan to keep it that way."

"He might be more understanding than you think."

"Don't play dumb with me, Joe. You know what my dad is like. I'll bet that my parents and I are the only people that Art told you about during your training. Everybody talks about the Trapper and his prostitute wife. Did Art tell you that Dad used to walk around town checking on my moral integrity?"

Dr. Joe cleared his throat.

"See, it's just as I expected. Are you going to help me with my son or not?"

"Okay, I'll help."

"Good. I need you to go to Vickie's office and get some papers. She'll give them to you in an envelope. Bring the envelope to me. We'll meet behind the gravel pile north of town."

"When?"

"At one o'clock tonight. Dress warm, and don't let anyone see you. Good-bye." Susan hung up on Joe before he could ask any more questions and immediately dialed Vickie. "Vickie, I need a favor."

With help and papers arranged, Susan pulled into a hardware store in North Plate, Nebraska, where she bought a big tarp and some tools. She loaded them in the truck and was back on the road.

What Twins Won't Say

illie and Bobbi left the church and walked back to the restaurant. As usual, business was slow after a funeral, and Billie hung around to help her sister pass the time. She sat down at a table and found herself dwelling on Joe's situation—a situation that had set her mind and heart in conflict. It was not going to be easy for Joe to compete with the snowman, and Billie knew it. This meant that the odds of Joe hanging around Dakota City were not good. Even if he did stay, he certainly wasn't the type to fall in love with. But on the other hand, Joe was sensitive, attractive, exciting, and full of potential. Billie decided that she needed to spend more time with Joe so she could sort out her feelings about him.

"Bobbi, I need a favor."

Just like that, Bobbi unleashed the F-bomb. "Not another one. I traded shifts with you last weekend."

"Just hear me out, Bobbi. This one is different."

"Let me guess; it involves Dr. Joe. You're falling in love with him, aren't you, Billie?"

"Maybe, maybe not, but the way things are going, I'll never find out."

"How come?"

"He's not happy with his work."

Bobbi giggled. "What work?"

"Be serious. I'm afraid he's going to leave town before I have a chance to figure out how I feel about him."

"So what am I supposed to do about that?"

"You know how Mom is always on our case about swearing—"

"I see where this is going, and the answer is *no way*. I am *not* signing up to be Dr. Joe's patient so *you* can find out if you're in love."

"Come on, Bobbi. He doesn't have a single patient. The snowman is open for business, and he's kicking Joe's butt. Joe wants to help people. You know, make a contribution. With a patient or two he might hang around."

"Like I said before, no way."

"Please, Bobbi, just tell Joe your goal is to quit swearing and go in for a couple sessions a week."

"You swear as much as I do. You should go."

"He can't see me in therapy and go out with me at the same time. That would be unethical. Besides, I don't want him to think that I'm crazy."

"I see. You would rather that he think I'm the one who is nuts. If I have to quit swearing, so do you."

"Damn, you make a hard argument. Okay, here's the plan. You sign up for two sessions a week. That will give him something to do. He'll ask you some questions and start a treatment plan of some kind. You don't have to tell him anything really personal. After the first session, you can report to me on what you talked about. Then we'll switch places. I'll go to the next session and pick up where you left off. Even though we'll be taking turns with the sessions, Joe will think he's only treating you."

"That cuts the inconvenience in half, but I'm still stuck with the stigma of being Dr. Joe's patient."

"True. I'll make a deal with you. If you go to therapy, I'll cover your shift on the weekends here at the restaurant."

"For how long?"

"From the first of December through New Year's Day. That's the entire holidays, Bobbi."

Bobbi thought the offer over. "Okay, it's a deal. You never know. This might be fun."

Starting Cuss-Word Therapy

S usan had called late in the afternoon, so Joe got to Vickie's office right at closing time. "Hi, Vickie," Joe said.

Vickie quickly stuffed a couple of forms into an envelope, sealed it, and handed it to Joe. "Susan said I should give these to you."

"Thanks. I'll walk you out," Joe suggested, knowing that it was closing time.

"It's nice of you to offer, but I have a couple of things to do yet."

Joe looked anxiously at his wrist watch. He had a lot of time to kill before meeting Susan at the gravel pile at one o'clock. After taking the envelope from Vickie, he went home for supper. Within a few minutes, the dead silence in his empty home was adding to the anxiety he felt about Susan. There was only one escape: the TV in his office. Hoofing his way to the courthouse, Joe passed by Kelsey's along the way. Bobbi saw him stroll by and stuck her head out the door. "Are you going to your office?" she yelled.

Joe stopped on the sidewalk and turned back. Yes," he said, mistaking Bobbi for Billie.

"Could I come over for a few minutes and talk to you?"

"Sure, use the back door. I'll leave it open." *Finally, there's something to look forward to.* Joe hurried to his office in anticipation of having a moment of privacy with Billie. In a matter of minutes, there was a gentle knock on his partially closed office door.

"Hello," Bobbi said.

Joe walked over and pulled the door wide open. "Hi, Billie. Come in."

"Actually, I would be Bobbi."

"Please excuse the mistake. The two of you look so much alike."

So far so good; their plan appeared to be working. "We hear that all the time."

Joe offered Bobbi a chair and sat down at his desk. "What can I do for you?"

Bobbi got right to the point. "Actually, this is rather embarrassing. I want to quit swearing, and I thought you might be able to help me."

At the realization that he was talking with a potential patient, Joe jumped out of his chair and shut off the TV. He pulled the window shade closed so no one could look in. When he did, he looked out the window and cocked his head. "Hmm..."

Bobbi heard this utterance. "Is something wrong?" she asked.

Joe took a second look. "That's strange. The snowman is late. Bobbi, I need you to fill out some papers," he said handing her a stack of intake forms that he had created in his down time. While she was busy with the forms, he started half a pot of coffee. *I've got one on you, Snowman.*

Bobbi finished the forms and handed them to Dr. Joe. "Actually, I was hoping that there wouldn't be any record of this."

Dr. Joe did not want to lose his first and only patient over paperwork. He tore up the pile of papers and threw them in the waste basket. "You know, Bobbi, for what we're going to do, I don't see a need to start a clinical record."

"Thanks."

"So, tell me about your swearing. When did you start?"

"In high school, and it has only gotten worse since. Working with the late afternoon coffee crowd seems to keep me in practice, too. They're a tougher bunch than the group you hang around with in the morning."

"Do you swear a lot?"

"That's the strange thing. I really don't. In some ways, that makes the problem worse."

"Can you explain what you mean by that?"

"Well, out of the blue and just like that I'll let a really bad word fly, and it shocks the—oops, I almost did right now."

Joe smiled. "I see what you mean. How come you want to quit?"

"I do it in front of my mom from time to time, and she hates it." Bobbi was getting uneasy with Dr. Joe's gentle probing, so she subtly changed the conversation. "Billie swears too, you know."

"I've noticed that. But may I assume quitting is your goal, not Billie's?"

In this statement, Bobbi heard that Joe expected her to be committed to their work, and this made her even more nervous. She got defensive and threw herself back into the chair. "So what the hell do people talk about in therapy, Dr. Joe?"

Joe chuckled. "All sorts of things, but actually, we're not going to talk that much, at least not today."

"Are you serious? After watching Uncle Art all these years, I was convinced that all psychologists do is talk—and drink coffee."

Joe laughed. "Bobbi, I'm going to do things differently than Art. The way I see it, the more we talk, the more you're going to swear at me. That would be counterproductive."

Bobbi realized that Joe was trying to help her relax through the use of humor, so she gave him a warm smile in appreciation of the gesture. Now more at ease, Bobbi remembered that she came with plans of doing some probing of her own. If this guy was going to date her twin sister, she wanted to see if he could be trusted. Bobbi gave her hair a flirtatious flip, raised her eyebrow, and showed just a little more leg. "So if we aren't going to talk, what *are* we going do?"

Joe shook his head and cleared his throat in a way that told Bobbi he wasn't going to play along. Digging into his middle desk drawer, he brought out a small journal. "To start things off, I'm going to give you this green pocket journal. You're going to write a notation in it every time you swear. Write down what you said and what you were doing when you said it. When we meet, we'll talk about what happened and what you were feeling at the time that you cussed."

Bobbi was pleasantly surprised. Joe had stuck to business and did better with her little test than she expected. He was even making this therapy stuff seem easy. However, since she was not truly committed to the sessions, she withheld her full cooperation. Bobbi picked up the journal and examined it. "I don't like green."

Women. Joe reopened his drawer. Taking out a pink pocket journal, he offered it in trade.

"That's better. You surprise me, Dr. Joe. Do I have to do anything else?"

"No, I want this to be as painless as possible. That's all until the next time."

"How often do we meet?"

"I suggest three times a week."

Bobbi and Billie had agreed to two sessions a week. "I don't have time for three sessions a week."

"Let me explain. We really won't be having sessions. I want to keep our talks brief."

"How brief?"

"Very brief. Five to ten minutes at the most."

"That's all?" Bobbi took a moment to think. "Okay then. I'll see you Monday."

Having been uncomfortable in the role of a patient, Bobbi wanted to escape Joe's office as quickly as possible. She stood up and pulled the door open. Bolting out before looking, she ran smack-dab into Pastor Dalton, who happened to be inviting himself into Joe's office. Bobbi made an abrupt turn backward and tried to push the door shut. Bobbi unleashed the F-bomb again. "What's he doing here?"

Joe pointed at Bobbi's journal. "That can be your first entry."

Pastor Dalton pushed the door wide open and bull-dozed his way in. "I happened to see that your light was on, Dr. Joe. I hope I'm not interrupting anything important." Bobbi brushed at her hostess skirt in an effort to look casual. The motion of her hands immediately drew Dalton's eyes toward her slender legs. He gawked until he saw the small scar on her calf. Bobbi saw Dalton's stare and walked closer to Joe as if for protection. Dalton looked at Joe. *I'll be watching you, adulterer*, Dalton thought.

Joe held up the green pocket journal and tried to use it in an effort to cover for Bobbi's confidentiality. "Thanks for bringing this over for me, Bobbi. I need to be more careful about what I leave in the restaurant."

Bobbi recognized that Joe was setting up a smoke screen for her. "No problem, Dr. Joe. I made sure no one looked at it." Bobbi darted out the door and left Dr. Joe alone with Dalton.

Comparing Notes

B illie, anxious for Bobbi's return, was keeping a keen eye out the restaurant window. Bobbi and Joe had met only on two brief occasions, and since this was their first truly personal encounter, Billie was eager to know how things went. She pounced on Bobbi the moment she came through the door. "What did you think of him up close and personal?"

Bobbi was expecting this interrogation and played with her sister's emotions. "He ticked me off."

Billie's eyes fell to the floor in disappointment. "What happened?"

"He insisted on having three sessions a week. You and I agreed to two. I couldn't get him to change his mind. Then if that wasn't bad enough, he gave me a pea-green journal that I'm supposed carry with me so I can take notes about my cussing. It looked so ridiculous, I threw the ugly thing right back at him."

"You didn't."

"I most certainly did. Plus, I made him dig into Art's desk and get us a pretty pink one."

"I wish you would've been nice to him."

Bobbi laughed to let Billie know that things had gone better than she made them sound. "Other than poor taste in notebooks, I have to say he was a pleasant surprise." The girls sat down to talk. Bobbi told Billie all about the journal and the planned course of treatment. "All we have to do is write down every time we swear." Bobbi slid the notebook across the table to Billie. "I've already made one entry, and the next session is yours. You can write down your own cussing."

While the twins compared notes on Joe, Joe was stuck with Pastor Dalton. "Pastor, this is a professional office. I need to ask that you knock before entering. What are you doing here this time of night anyway?"

The fact was Dalton had watched Bobbi enter the back door of the courthouse and assumed she'd be talking with Joe. The thought of the two of them being together bothered Dalton, so he followed her and intentionally interrupted. "I was just going to ask if everything is okay in the rental house."

"You could've stopped by the house."

"I knocked on your door, but obviously you weren't home. When I walked through the park, I saw the light in the office and figured you were watching that TV. I had no idea you were with a patient."

"Bobbi's not a patient." *For a minister, this man is hard to stomach.* "Look, Pastor, everything is fine at the house. Thanks for checking. All I'm asking is that you knock before entering." Joe inched closer to Dalton in hopes of getting him to turn and leave the office.

Knowing Joe's history, Dalton was of no mind to move. "You know, Joe, I take it upon myself to stop in from time to time to offer you and the sheriff a spiritual uplift. I know the work that the two of you do can be stressful."

Joe heard Dalton's indirect implication. He planned on doing what he wanted when he wanted. *He's beyond hard to stomach. This guy is pushy.* Joe countered Dalton's assertion. "Father Riley does rounds here at the courthouse. The sheriff and I can get pretty busy, so I'm not sure we would have the time to visit with both of you."

"You're right about that. But you probably don't know, Father Riley is having knee surgery soon, and he'll be in a wheelchair for quite some time. I wouldn't want the two of you to be without spiritual guidance while he's recovering."

Clearly, Dalton wasn't going to be easily deterred. *Maybe he can be pawned off on the sheriff.* "I'm in and out of the office a lot. You might be able to catch up with Tom from time to time though."

Joe's mention of the sheriff did nothing but invite more conversation with the abrasive pastor. "The sheriff is president of my church council. Did you know that, Joe?"

"No, Pastor, you've got me there. That's something I didn't know." Joe concluded that there was only one way to get rid of Dalton, and that was to go home. He put on his sweatshirt and started to walk out of his office. "I've got to go have some dinner, Pastor." Joe held out his arm to let Dalton know that it was undoubtedly time to leave the office. Dalton strutted into the hallway, and Joe was stuck with him for the short walk home.

Killing Time

After ditching the pastor by the church, Joe stepped into his house and looked at his wrist watch. *Nine o'clock.* There were still four hours to kill before meeting Susan behind the gravel pile. He took a sneak peek out his bedroom window to make sure that Dalton had left. *I certainly don't want him following me down to the Farmhand for supper.* Joe put on a warmer coat and walked down to the steakhouse. This was the perfect opportunity to have a leisurely dinner and try his luck at video lottery. Fifty dollars and two hours later, Joe walked home empty-handed. *This waiting is killing me.* Joe grabbed his favorite music, jumped in his car, and went for a drive. *I have no idea what Susan is up to, but I suspect she doesn't want her dad to know she's back.* He drove thirty-five miles north of Dakota City, turned around, and drove back toward the gravel pile. *I bet she wants me to help hide her son from Trapper.* Joe looked in his rearview mirrors to make sure that no one was following him. *Good, nothing but darkness.* Confident that he had the road to himself, Joe turned off the highway and drove behind the gravel pile at five minutes to one. Susan was there waiting. Joe pulled alongside her pickup. Susan opened the pickup's driver-side window, and Joe opened the window on his car. "Thanks for coming, Joe," Susan said.

"Where in blazes have you been, Susan?"

"I'll explain later."

"Have you called your dad? He's pretty upset with you."

"No, I haven't called. I have to go to the cemetery first, and I want you to come with me."

"You want to go to the cemetery right now?"

"Yes."

"Susan, it is one o'clock in the morning, and I feel like I'm sneaking around under cover of darkness."

Susan gave a frustrated sigh and started her pickup. "This isn't going to be easy for me, Dr. Joe. Are you coming with me or not?"

"Don't I get to meet your son first?"

"He's—"

"Asleep. I'm sorry. It's late. What am I thinking?"

Relieved that Joe had answered his own question, Susan continued to pressure Joe. "Can you show me Mom's grave or not?"

"Yes, I was just there this afternoon." Joe started his car and led the way to the cemetery.

The Bethlehem Cemetery was one of those remote little cemeteries that you might see driving down a back road and think, *Oh, how peaceful*. It was located one mile north and one mile east of the gravel pile, a location that placed it in uninhabited countryside and away from the lights of town. Joe turned his car onto the cemetery driveway. As the car's headlights swung over the narrow gravel approach, Joe noticed the woven wire fence that surrounded the five-acre piece of sacred ground. A wrought-iron gate hung between two stout brick gateposts; each post was capped with a gray concrete cross. The gate had been closed after Millie's funeral, and now it blocked Joe's passage onto the narrow vehicle trail that ran down the middle of the cemetery. Joe got out of his car to open the gate. Susan stopped behind

Joe and shut off her lights. She stuck her head out the pickup window. "Shut your lights off, Joe. I don't want to be seen."

In addition to the trail that dissected the cemetery east and west, two other narrow trails crisscrossed the burial ground north and south. Millie's grave was located thirty yards to the south of the second road. Joe squinted through the dark looking for an occasional white tombstone or any faint glimmer of polished granite that might help him guide the car over the narrow pathway. As he got close to Millie's grave, he stepped softly on his brakes to give Susan advanced warning that he was about to stop. Joe shut off his car and got out. "Your mom is buried about one hundred feet to the right."

"Thanks. Will you walk over there with me?" Susan took out a small flashlight.

"Of course, Susan." Joe put his arm around Susan's waist in support, and they walked together to her mother's grave. At first, Susan stood over the grave, trembling in silence. Her hands slowly came to her face and covered her mouth. Tears started to pour from her eyes and drip onto her fingers.

Joe felt Susan's grief and remembered Millie's message. "Your mom said to tell you that she understands everything. She said that she loves you and that whatever you have to do is okay. It might help to tell your mom what's on your mind," Joe said.

Susan wiped her tears into brown jersey gloves, sniffled, and nodded her head. "Yes, I think that would help." Susan looked down toward the earth. "Mom, I'm so sorry for everything … everything I've done and everything that I need to do. I love you. I should have told you some things, but I couldn't do it. It would have broken Daddy's heart. He tried so hard to bring me up right."

Joe listened and tried to piece together what was happening with Susan. After standing in silence a bit longer, Susan led Joe back to her pickup, where she opened the cab and took a large tarp off the driver's seat. She handed it to Dr. Joe. "Hold this for me." Next, she pushed the passenger seat forward and took out a sand shovel.

"Just what are we doing here, Susan?"

"*You* don't have to do anything if you don't want, Joe, but I am hoping for your support. I didn't know who else to turn to."

"Susan, where's your son? There was no one in the cab when you opened the door."

"He's in the pickup box, under the topper."

Now Joe was beyond suspicious. "Susan, what are you thinking? He has to be cold. People get charged with child abuse for doing things like that."

"Yes, Joe, he is cold, very cold."

When Joe heard Susan's remark, he finally realized what Susan was doing. *I can't be a part of this, not in my situation!* "Dear God, he's dead, isn't he, and you're going to bury him with your mother! Susan, what happened?"

Susan nodded, tears dripping to the ground like rain. She told Joe the story of her son's death. She told him about the choice she had to make, and why she'd talked to the snowman. Half dazed, she described the long drive home from New Mexico. "I needed some time with my little boy. Was that wrong?"

Joe put the tarp down on the pickup hood. He took Susan and held her in a warm embrace. "No, Susan, that wasn't wrong."

"I couldn't leave him there, and I don't have any money for a plot. I want him to sleep here with his grandma." Joe was taken aback. Not knowing what to say, he picked up the tarp again and walked with Susan back to Millie's grave. "Let's spread out the tarp," Susan said.

A sick feeling grew in Joe's stomach while they spread the large blue tarp over the earth next to the grave. *Maybe if I just watch, I won't get into trouble,* he thought as Susan began digging with vehemence toward her mother. Torn between fear over his own situation and pity for Susan, Joe sat at graveside watching as Susan threw one shovel full of cold, loose dirt after another into a pile on the tarp. *I have to do more.* "Susan, you don't have to do this. I'll buy a plot for you right here in this cemetery. I wouldn't expect anything back."

Joe realized that his offer might offend Susan's independent pride. "I mean, if you think it's necessary, you can pay me back."

"Thanks, Joe, but it's not that simple. I can't let Dad know about any of this. It would break his heart to find out that I had a baby outside of marriage."

I'm on probation. "Susan, is doing this even legal?"

Susan looked up from her digging and toward the flashlight that Joe was holding for her. "You know, Joe, for once in my life, I'm not exactly sure."

"Susan—"

"What do you think, that I called Sheriff Tom to ask if it was okay to bury my son on top of my mother in the middle of the night?"

While Joe held the small flashlight, his best friend's daughter alternated between crying and shoveling. Even in dim light it was easy to see that the commissioner's commanding secretary, the rough and tough Trapper's daughter, was emotionally and physically exhausted. *She's in such agony. This isn't right. How can I not help her?* Joe could not stand the sight any longer. He stood up and stretched his arm out toward Susan. He motioned to her slowly with his fingers. "Here, give me that shovel." Susan let the shovel's handle fall into Joe's hand. He gave her his coat. *I'm going to do things right,* Joe thought, and he started to dig.

"Thank you," Susan said. Her body went limp in relief. Joe gave Susan his other hand and helped her from the shallow grave. She took the flashlight and, trading jobs with Joe, sat on the ground holding the light. There, in complete fatigue, Susan's head grew heavy, and the weight of grief pulled her head low toward her mother's grave.

Joe paused from his digging and looked through the dim light. "Susan, how old is your son?"

"He was six." Susan thought for a moment and realized the full intent of Joe's question. "A small six," she clarified.

Susan watched, and Joe dug deeper. Soon she heard the hollow echo of the shovel scraping against the top of Millie's burial vault. "I want to place him as if he is asleep in his grandma's loving arms."

"I understand." Joe finished cleaning off the burial vault as best he could. "That's as deep as we can go, Susan. The grave is ready." Susan nodded, stood up, and, holding out her hand, helped Joe from the depth. Through her stiff grasp, Joe felt the traumatic shock and intense pain that had overtaken Susan. She pulled hard on Joe's cold hand, and, struggling to pull himself from the grave, Joe stumbled forward, and his chest bumped into hers. As they stood face-to-face in near embrace, all Susan could say was, "Oh, Joe." Joe took Susan in his arms and held her tight.

Joe knew what came next would be very difficult for both of them, but it would be especially traumatic for Susan. He spoke softly in her ear. "I helped carry your mom. Do you want me to carry your son?"

"No, I need to do that myself."

Joe eased his embrace. *Does she really have enough strength left to do this? How is she holding herself together?* "Are you sure you don't want me to carry him?"

"Yes, I'm sure, but it's time to put him to rest. Thanks for being here, Joe."

Joe walked with Susan to the pickup, and together they carried the heavy cardboard box with Tony's body to graveside. Susan opened the box and lifted the black bag that held Tony's body. After cradling her son for a long and final moment, Susan looked deep into the dark grave; then she looked at Joe. "I can't just drop him in from up here. Will you please hold him for me?" Joe took Tony and held him while Susan crawled down into the grave and onto the burial vault. Feeling bad for disturbing her mother's eternal rest, she said "Forgive me, Mom." Joe handed Tony to Susan, and she gently laid her little boy down. She unzipped the body bag and looked at her son. She kissed her index finger and softly touched Tony's lips. "Good night. Sleep tight, honey." Susan zipped the bag again and turned Tony's body facedown, where it would rest over his grandma's breast forever.

"We should say a prayer," Joe said.

"A prayer? Where have you been, Joe? I've been praying all night. No, Joe, I've been praying all week. Let's finish this and go home. I don't have a prayer left in me."

Joe and Susan took turns shoveling the dirt back into the grave. They lifted the tarp and shook the remaining loose soil onto the fresh mound of dirt. After carefully reshaping the soil, they gathered the tools and walked to their vehicles in pensive silence. Soft blue and gray colors began to emerge in the eastern sky while the two coworkers drove back to town under what little cover the diminishing night offered them.

Strange Disappearances

Susan followed Joe home, drove into his driveway, and jumped out of her pickup. She ran over to her now-trusted confidant, threw her arms around him, and gave him a warm kiss of appreciation on the cheek. Dalton, an early riser, was sitting at his kitchen table looking out the window and saw the kiss. Unfortunately, the intent of this kiss was different than it appeared. The preacher smiled and made a mental note of what he had witnessed. *This adulterer should be easy to keep in his place.*

Even more unfortunate for Joe, there was another witness to this parting at sunrise, at least a portion of it, and in Dakota City, things never seem to go well when one attractive woman sees another attractive woman leaving a man's home at that time of day. Billie, having taken note of Joe's late-night absence, had driven by his house to check on him on her way to work. After seeing Susan back her pickup from Joe's driveway and speed away, Billie went to work steaming mad.

Joe went inside and crawled into bed. Every time he closed his eyes, images of Tony's body floated through the black void between his face and the ceiling. When he did manage to drift to sleep, he dreamt. Time and time and again, he was awakened by a gentle voice that Joe attributed to little Tony. "See to my blessing," the voice said. By midafternoon, Joe dragged himself out of bed with a throbbing tension headache. He took a shower, ate a cold cheese sandwich, and shuffled toward his office.

When Dakota City is at peace, there's a certain feel—a feel that Joe had already come to recognize. On the other hand, when all is not well, it feels as if a cold, heavy fog lifts from the lake and settles over the town, confining it under a dome of pure tension. Joe knew the minute he saw Sheriff Tom and Art coming from the courthouse and heading for coffee on Saturday afternoon that life in Dakota City was out of order. He just didn't know what was wrong. *Did the sheriff see me at the cemetery with Susan last night?* The three men met on the sidewalk. "Is there something wrong?" Joe asked, looking at Art.

"You should maybe join us for coffee, Joe," Art said.

Joe's suspicions soared. There was definitely something in the air. "You're going to coffee on Saturday afternoon?"

"Joe, you better come with us," Sheriff Tom said as if giving an order.

Once inside Kelsey's, it didn't take long for Joe's suspicions to be confirmed. He passed by the cash register smiling at Billie, but she refused to give him as much as a single glance. No doubt, there was a bitter chill blowing his way. Joe followed Tom and Art to the table where the judge, Father Riley, and the commissioner had already settled in over steaming cups of coffee.

Something big must be going on, Joe thought as he pulled up his chair. An uncomfortable silence surrounded the table. "It's a bit tense around town this afternoon."

"You noticed," Art answered.

Tom began the inquisition. "Where were you last night, Joe?"

"Last night? Ah... I had a stressful week and went for a late-night drive."

"And this morning?" Tom asked.

Joe squirmed in his seat. "This morning... I was catching up on some sleep. Why?"

"Some of us were afraid you had driven off the road," Tom said.

"And that we'd find you wrapped in barbed wire and dead in a ditch somewhere," Art added.

"At least that's what we thought until Pastor Dalton put most of us at ease over breakfast this morning," the judge said.

"And how did the pastor do that?" Joe asked.

"He told us that you were just fine. After all, he saw Susan kissing you good-bye at sunrise," the judge said with a slight frown.

Joe ignored the frown. "The pastor is a pain. He should mind his own business."

Father Riley nodded his head in agreement.

"I suppose Billie heard him say that too?"

"Actually, no. Billie had pretty much figured things out on her own by that time," the commissioner said.

"Billie was all worked up last night. She thought something bad had happened to you," Art said.

"What on earth made her think that?"

"From what I understand, she sent Bobbi over to your place late last night with some leftover chocolate chip cookies from here in the restaurant. You didn't answer the door, and Bobbi noticed your car was gone. Bobbi told Billie that you weren't in, and Billie got uncomfortable. She called and asked if I would patrol the highway to look for you," Tom said.

"You've got to be kidding me?"

The judge looked at Art. "Art, do you want to tell Joe how this story ends?"

"There's more to this insanity?" Joe asked.

"Sure, Judge," Art continued. "Billie was still worried this morning, so she drove by your place on her way to work. Of course, when she saw that your car was back, it put her mind at ease for a moment. When she saw Susan leave your driveway at sunrise … well, that lit her fuse. The truth is, that little tidbit didn't go over very well with any of us either," Art said, revealing his irritation. He would not have Joe treating his niece in such a way.

Seeing Art's anger, Tom took over the explanation of events. "Billie's pretty embarrassed about sending me out to look for you."

"Oh man—"

"When Billie brought coffee over to the table this morning, she apologized for bothering me so late at night. About that time, Pastor Dalton butted into the conversation."

"And what did that jerk have to say?" Joe asked.

"Well, let me put it this way. He made sure Billie knew you were kissing Susan at sunrise."

"He didn't?" Joe got sick to his stomach. *No wonder Billie's wrath is kindled. No wonder I'm ducking questions about my whereabouts. Dalton is stirring the pot.* Joe was so upset he jumped out of his chair.

"It's never wise to kiss the help, Joe, even if you don't supervise them," the commissioner added. Art gave Joe a cold stare, reminding him of the commitment he made the day he came to town.

Joe returned the stare long enough to read Art's thoughts, *You said you were going to do things right this time.* Joe turned away from his predecessor, knowing that it would be necessary to patch things up with him later. Scanning everyone at the table, Joe unleashed a verbal attack. "That preacher, I'd like to kick his butt. The more I see of that man, the less I like him."

"Now calm down," Tom said.

"Was Trapper here when the preacher was saying all that stuff?" Joe asked.

The judge answered this question indirectly. "I don't think Trapper is having the kind of day he was hoping for, not after putting Millie to rest yesterday."

Joe sighed in disgust. "Dang it. Where's he now?"

"He's taking Susan out to visit Millie's grave," Art said.

"Great." *Of all the places for them to go,* Joe thought as he started to make an escape.

Not having heard an explanation for Joe's antics, Art was boiling with anger. "Look, Joe, Billie is special, and she deserves to be treated that way. If you can't do that, then leave her alone."

Art's comments cut deep, and for the first time, Joe was really angry with Dr. Art Bowen. He of all people should know better than to make assumptions. He looked at Art and shook his head in disgust. "You don't think I know that, Art?"

Art heard the sincerity in Joe's voice and took a deep breath, trying to calm down. "And, Joe, before you leave, there's one more thing you might want to know."

"What's that?" Joe snipped at Art.

"The snowman failed to show up for work last night. That's something that hasn't happened since he started his practice fifteen years ago."

"I already know that, Art." Joe looked sternly at everyone at the table. "You folks aren't the only ones to see what goes on in Dakota City after dark." The mild challenge stunned all of them into a silence, and Joe felt a morsel of appreciation for the snowman. With a bit of luck, the snowman's disappearance would distract from his own. "If you gentlemen are done poking into my private affairs, I'll be leaving now." Joe stomped away from the table and left Kelsey's, knowing that there was absolutely no way to explain things to Billie. He had to protect Susan's confidence.

$\mathcal{A}$ $\mathcal{P}urple$ $\mathcal{D}ress$

$\mathbf{A}$s Joe hurried out the door, he tripped over a folding sign on the sidewalk and accidently kicked it over. *Dang this place. I'm always tripping.* Joe put the sign back upright.

Community-wide Rummage Sale Today
High School Auditorium
9:00 am to 7:00 pm.

Saturday's rummage sale was an annual Dakota City highlight. Every fall, the women organized the event to accommodate the exchange of winter coats for the children. Of course, anything and everything, including secondhand ladies' apparel went on sale as well. This year, more than other years, the sale had captured Debra's interest.

Dalton had historically forbidden Debra's attendance at the sale. In his view, fashions were always changing, and whatever the new look was, it was inappropriate for a pastor's wife. Instead of letting his wife shop for clothing, Pastor Dalton made Debra's wardrobe his personal responsibility. Once or twice a year, he put out a call to the congregation and asked for hand-me-downs. Dalton collected whatever clothes were donated and sorted them to his taste. Whenever Debra needed new clothes, he would dole out a portion of the collection and proclaim, "The Lord hath provided for you, Debra. Remember to give thanks."

The pastor's proclamation and the lack of any fashion in her wardrobe added to the list of things troubling Debra. This year, the sale was drawing her breakaway spirit like a magnet draws iron. Debra just knew she'd enjoy this community event. Plus, there was an idea floating around in the back of her mind. As far as Debra was concerned, the decision was made. This evening, she would sneak off to the rummage sale while Dalton was in a scheduled meeting with a confirmation student. Debra stepped nervously into the school gymnasium, and at first the large number of tables spread across the entire basketball court overwhelmed her. Eventually, she made her way to a table and hanging rack that Billie and Bobbi had arranged.

"Hi, Debra. It's nice to see you out. Are you enjoying the sale?" Billie asked.

"Oh, yes." Debra took a closer look at Billie. "You're Billie, right?"

"You're good, Debra," Billie said, giving the pastor's wife credit for a lucky guess.

Debra browsed through the clothes on the table. "I've never been here before."

"It's always fun. You should come more often."

"How come I don't see you in church anymore, Billie?"

"I have to work on Sunday mornings. It seems like everybody in town wants breakfast after church."

Debra already knew that her husband was falling from the good graces of his congregation. She wondered what others in town might be thinking, so she used the opportunity to probe. "Is that the real reason you don't come?"

The truth was that Bobbi talked Billie out of going to church years ago, and Billie wanted to avoid Debra's question. "Are you finding anything nice?" Billie asked.

By now, Debra had turned her attention to the rack of hanging clothes and was running her fingers down a deep-purple evening dress that Bobbi wanted to sell. "Not until now, but this is beautiful."

"It's Bobbi's. Do you want to buy it?"

"I'm afraid it would be a smidgen too small."

"As I recall, Bobbi had it taken in a bit." The ladies examined the inside seams, and Billie pointed at the stitching. "See, you could let it out."

"I could, couldn't I? How much does she want for it?"

Billie knew from watching the Daltons in the restaurant that Debra would not have much money. She quickly pulled off the $25.00 price tag before Debra saw it. "Gee, it's not marked. I remember now. Bobbi said I should ask for an offer. Would you like to throw out a number?"

"I don't know. I'm not sure the pastor would approve of this dress. On the other hand, I'd love to come to the holiday festival looking nice once. I have a dollar. Would that do?"

"Sold! Debra, you're going to catch eyes in that. I promise."

"Do you really think so?"

Billie nodded with a smile and put the dress into a plastic sack. "There you are," Billie said, handing the bag to Debra.

Nervous about being in a forbidden place, Debra held out her shaky hand and gave Billie four quarters. She carefully stuffed the dress deep into her large purse. "Thanks, but I'm afraid there's a lot of work to be done before I catch any eyes." Debra hurried from the gym and smuggled her purchase home before her husband left the church.

All Things Hidden

Having made it home without her absence being discovered, Debra's nervous tension subsided. In fact, the little excursion gave Debra's recent sense of empowerment a small boost. She folded the dress and tucked it into her sewing machine case, where it should be safely hidden and at the same time readily accessible. Her plan was to let it out while Pastor Dalton studied in his office and worked with his confirmation students.

When Pastor Dalton walked in the back door, Debra was the first to speak. "How was your session?"

"Not very good; the girl struggles so."

"Which girl?"

"Laura Walter."

"What does she struggle with?"

"With accepting God's will; she knows that it's her place to grow up and bear children. Yet the devil tempts her with talk of careers and fashion."

"I see."

"The poor girl. I try to teach her God's way, but she resists it so. I hold her, shelter her … I let her feel the love to be found in a man's arms."

Dalton's words kindled Debra's worst fears. She had recently started to worry about what her husband did with his students, and his remarks gave her an upset stomach. "Watch yourself, Pastor. Hearts are tender, and passion runs high at that age."

That Debra should be so bold as to give him advice immediately sent Dalton into one of his ugly moods. "You know nothing of passion or of a man's work for that matter, so mind your tongue, wife. Now is exactly the time for Laura's passions to be aroused."

"Why now?"

"So she can confront them in the shelter of her pastor's protective embrace."

Growing Discomforts

W hen Joe read the word *community* on the rummage sale sign, it gave him a growing sense of apprehension about his future in Dakota City. *I don't fit in here.* He went for an early afternoon walk in City Park hoping to find some peace of mind. Unfortunately, the confrontation at Kelsey's had quickly become a mental obsession. *People don't trust me. Need I wonder why?* Leaving the park, Joe sought the shelter of his own home, but even there, he could not find tranquility. In the quiet emptiness of the old parsonage, a little boy's voice cried out in his mind. *Bring a clergyman.* Joe fought the voice until early evening but eventually jumped in his car and drove to the cemetery, thinking that calling on the grave would help. "Listen, Tony, I don't want to answer more questions about my late-night activities."

After the graveside visit, Joe drove back to town and went down to his office. He needed to know what was happening with the snowman tonight. Joe peeked from behind the drawn shade on his window. Even before complete darkness, people hovered around the snowman in hopes that their old friend and counselor would light up. As Joe watched them, Sheriff Tom came by and started to snoop around the snowman. *Unbelievable. I'll say this much, Snowman. You have a faithful following.*

By early Sunday morning, Dr. Joe was in no frame of mind to mill about Dakota City, at least not in the daylight. It was best to avoid Billie. She was angry with him, and he had yet to devise a suitable explanation for his behavior. After his clandestine activities with Susan and being confronted by his friends, he didn't feel comfortable at the table. If these things were not bad enough, Joe was being upstaged by the snowman that, even when failing to show up for work, had more patients than he did. Frustrated, afraid, and embarrassed, Joe got up early and drove to Sioux Falls for the hockey game where one look at the black puck had him thinking about a black body bag. *How do I get his body blessed without breaking Susan's confidence?* When the Zamboni dropped a load of ice shavings, it reminded him of the snowman. *Why did he suddenly disappear? Will he be back tonight?* Since there seemed to be no escape from Dakota City, Dr. Joe put in his ice time and rushed back to the office wondering if his competitor would be open for business.

Just as the night before, people gathered around the snowman. And, once again, the snowman did not light up. This evening, Joe talked to the snowman through his office window. "So what's up, Snowman? Did you get injured? Did you retire? I certainly didn't run you out of business. Yeah, well, you aren't the only one with problems around here."

This was the third evening in a row that the snowman had missed work. Still, his patients continued to come, and Joe was getting a belly full. "I've seen enough of this, Snowman. I'm going home." He stepped out of his office and turned to lock his door. As he fiddled with his keys, he thought about one of his first conversations with Dr. Art. "*Things don't always go as planned in a business as complex as ours."* He looked down the hallway at the stairwell leading to the tunnel. He walked over to the chain barrier that hung across the stairs. He read the "Do Not Enter" sign. He looked up and down the hallway. There was no one around.

During the recent weeks, Joe had walked by the prohibited stairwell numerous times, but tonight something was different. Tonight, Joe saw an opportunity. The low drooping chain seemed less an obstacle. The "Do Not Enter" sign read as a provocative invitation to run down those eight measly steps. *Should I?* He looked up and down the hallway again. *There's no one here.* The door at the bottom of the stairwell beckoned him. This had to be one of the doors leading to the snowman. *Why not do this?* Joe hopped the chain and ran down the stairs. He held the brass door handle and wrestled with temptation. *I'm not helping anybody in my office.* Joe gave the handle a sharp snap down and backward. Nothing happened. *I've got to do something.* He snapped the door handle harder. This time, he jerked up and backward. Just like that, the old door popped open, and Joe was stunned. *I have access to the snowman.* Joe stood by the door and looked down a dim-lit tunnel. Cobwebs hung from the ceiling. *Is breaking into the snowman's office the right thing to do? Not tonight.* Joe closed the tunnel door, scuffed his tracks from the dust on the floor, and went home. He would take the night to think about making a break-in of his own.

Reading the Sign

As life in Dakota City grew ever more complicated, Joe got less and less sleep. Thoughts of Tony's unblessed body continued to weigh heavily on his mind. He tossed and turned trying to come up with a way to repair things with Billie. After failing to call Trapper about Susan's return and disturbing Millie's grave, he was very worried about coming face-to-face with Trapper. Plus, he now had a decision to make about the snowman. Monday morning followed a miserable sleepless night, and Joe woke up with another throbbing tension headache. *Who poured motor oil in my head? Maybe if I worked out I could relieve some stress. But if I do that, I'm likely to run into Trapper.* If Trapper had accurately read the sign out at the cemetery, he was bound to be livid.

I can't avoid him forever. Joe pulled on his sweat clothes and went for a jog in the park. When he finished, he sat at the edge of the lake praying for ice and looking for Trapper.

As usual, Trapper approached Joe from behind. "Have you seen any sign of that beaver?"

"No, I haven't, Trapper."

"He must have moved on. Let me tell you something, Joe. Critters always leave behind signs when they go about their business. Beavers cut trees, and badgers dig holes."

"Have you seen any badgers?" Joe asked with growing apprehension.

Trapper didn't answer this question—at least not with words. He handed Joe a wilted flower petal.

"What's this?"

"It's a petal from the rose I placed low in Millie's grave on Friday." Joe's head dropped. "I see."

"Joe, I was ready to shoot you the other day when I heard the rumors about you and my daughter."

Joe looked at Trapper's rifle. "I figured you might be. Is that why you're here, to shoot me?"

"No, the thought crossed my mind though. I'm here because you and I need to talk about right and wrong some more."

"That's a subject I'm still struggling with."

"I figured you might be. You know, Joe, I've learned something new about judging right from wrong the past couple of days."

"What's that, Trapper?"

"Sometimes it's necessary to measure what a man does against the intentions of his heart."

Joe pondered what Trapper was saying. He realized that even though Trapper had read the sign, he and his friend were at peace. Joe smiled at Trapper in relief. "You're a good friend, and you make a good point."

"You have a good heart, Joe."

"Thanks, Trapper. That helps me a lot." Trapper started to walk away, but Joe called out to him.

Trapper turned back. "Yes, Joe?"

"Does Susan know you've pieced things together?"

"No, Joe, she doesn't, and please don't tell her. I've driven her to this over the years, and she's been through a lot. The two of us need some time and space to work things out."

Susan Sees a Problem

Susan reported back to work on Monday morning, and when Dr. Joe made his rounds, she was sitting at her desk looking as if last week's events had not transpired. "Good morning, Susan," Joe said.

"Good morning, Dr. Joe. I understand you and my father have been talking down by the lake from time to time."

"Yes. In fact, we talked this morning. Our paths seem to cross quite often since the beaver have gotten active."

"The truth is I knew the two of you talked. Dad told me. Did you tell him about Tony?"

"No, Susan. I haven't said a word."

"Thanks, Joe. Thanks for everything." Susan looked around the rotunda. There was no one there. "I feel like giving you a hug."

"I'm sorry, Susan. It might be better if we don't do that."

Susan had heard the rumors about Billie being angry with Joe, but she didn't know Joe was in hot water at the table too. "I understand that my kiss is costing you with Billie."

"Yes, Susan, it is. The two of us are rather distant right now."

"I'm sorry about that. What did you tell her?"

"Nothing. We haven't talked since Saturday. That ice is too thin to venture on."

"So you're not speaking at all?"

"No, not at all."

"I'm sorry about you and Billie. The two of you look good together. You're the first man I've seen her with that I can say that about."

"Has she been in a lot of relationships?"

"Enough to know what kind of men to avoid, but none that brings out that delightful glow in her eyes like you do."

"All I see in Billie's eyes is anger."

Susan gave Joe one of her disgusted sighs and smiled. "Men can be so blind. Say, talking about Billie reminds me . . . Bobbi called earlier this morning and said she wanted to review a journal with you at nine o'clock. You better hustle down to your office, or you'll miss her."

Cuss Word Therapy

Of course, Dr. Joe had no idea that it was Billie's turn at cuss word therapy when the charming imposter knocked on his office door. "Come in," he said. But the invitation wasn't necessary. Joe looked up from his desk as a beautiful bundle of raw attitude came charging his way. Billie was prepared for this therapeutic encounter. She sat down in front of Joe's desk and slapped open the little pink journal.

"I brought my notes," Billie said.

"Good, Bobbi. Are you ready to review them?"

"Sure," Billie said.

"Great, let's get started. This is simple, Bobbi. All you need to do is read me your entries."

"Okay," Billie said. She opened the pink journal and read as if she were Bobbi. "I said, 'Where in the hell is he?' when I knocked on your door late Friday night. I said, 'damn him' when Billie told me you spent the night with Susan. I really cut loose with a long list of words when I heard about the two of you kissing at sunrise. I can read them all if you like."

"I get the point; we can skip the rest of the list." Joe cleared his throat. "Is that all?" he asked.

Billie thumbed through the journal and saw Bobbi's lone entry. "Oh, and then I cussed when I was leaving your office after our first session. You heard that one, so I won't read it. How am I doing with my journal, Dr. Joe?"

"Ah … you're doing great, Bobbi."

Billie got tears in her eyes. "How could you do that to my sister, you jerk?"

Dr. Joe did not want to lose his only patient after two brief sessions. "Bobbi, our work together is about *your* swearing, not about Billie and me. I want to repeat what I said before. Bobbi, you're doing a great job."

"I swore more this week than I did the week before I started therapy. What's so great about that?"

"The good part is that I can see response patterns in your cussing."

"Are you going to explain that mouthful of mashed potatoes?"

"Yes. The way I see it, you love your sister a great deal. You don't want anyone to hurt her, and that's why you swore at me. You think I'm hurting her. The second—"

"How would you feel if—"

"Please, allow me to finish before you ask your next question. The second pattern that I see is this: you are quick to react. If you're going to quit swearing, you'll have to practice biting your lip before you speak. In this case, you may have reacted in defense of your sister without knowing all of the facts."

Billie found Joe's firm, gentle voice and sense of composure to be calming. "Why don't you tell me the facts then, Dr. Joe?"

"Bobbi, confidentiality is very important in what I do, and there are some things I can't talk about."

Billie took a deep breath and sat for a long moment in silence. "Is that all you have to say?"

"That's all I can say. Would *you* like to say more?"

Billie silently debated Dr. Joe's question for a moment. On one hand, she was angry and wanted to give him an even bigger piece of her mind than she had. It would serve him right if she chewed his butt and stomped off. On the other hand, Joe didn't cower when she let him have it a moment ago. *Why?* In fact, Joe went so far as to suggest that there was more to the story than she knew. *Could this possibly be true?*

Joe's question had Billie lost in thought. "Bobbi, would you like to say more?"

"Maybe. Being in therapy is different than I expected."

"How's that?"

"I thought we would need to spend more time together. Our sessions seem to be so … in and out." *I really didn't just say that, did I? You must be going insane, Billie Kelsey. You actually like this guy.*

"I thought we agreed to short sessions."

Billie was torn between her anger and her desire to spend more time with Dr. Joe. Today, anger won. "Well, you seem to work day and night with some women around here."

"Bobbi, I understand that you're angry with me, but I asked a question. Would you like to say more about your swearing?"

Billie thought for a moment. "Okay … how do I learn to 'bite my lip' as you like to say?"

"The first thing you need to do is think before you speak. You could also try relabeling the swear word; change it to something less offensive."

"Do you mean like saying darn instead of damn?"

"That's a perfect example. Or, simply use 'F' for the big bomb."

"I'll try that."

"Is there anything else you would like to ask?"

"No, Dr. Joe, that's all." Billie got up from her chair and left Dr. Joe's office with some things to contemplate.

Holiday Preparations

J oe waited for a moment's time to pass before leaving his office. He didn't want Bobbi to feel like he was following her. After a short delay, he got up and walked past Susan's desk.

"Where are you going, Dr. Joe—in case anyone calls?" Susan asked.

"Out to be visible; you can call me on my cell phone." Joe continued on his way and stepped out of the courthouse. As he reached the cul-de-sac, Sheriff Tom pulled up in front of him. "Jump in, Joe. I want to talk to you." After Joe jumped into the sheriff's SUV, Tom drove around the cul-de-sac and away from the courthouse. At the far end of Main Street, he swung across both lanes, parked, and turned on the emergency lights.

"What's up?" Joe asked.

"This is about what's not up. And what's not up are the city's Christmas lights. They need to be hung before the festival."

"I see what's going on here. You want me to help kill time while you sit and block traffic for the work crew."

"You're no dummy, Joe. I'll give you that."

Once again, Joe let his annoyance with the sheriff be known. "They didn't give me a PhD for being stupid, Tom."

"That new coffee pot you bought was sure a smart move. For all these years, Art and I were taking turns getting up early every other day to make coffee. You're here less than a month, and we have a new coffee pot with an automatic start. Just like that, there's no need for anyone to come in at the crack of dawn."

"Did I hear that right? You and Art traded every other day?"

"Oops, I'm busted, aren't I?" Tom was now forced to weasel out of the embarrassing spot he had put himself in. "Actually, that's what I wanted to discuss. I've been feeling a little guilty about that coffee pot. How about I pay for half of it?"

"That would be great. Your half is thirty-two dollars and fifty cents."

"Ouch, they don't give those things away, do they?"

"No, and I picked it up on sale in Sioux Falls. I'll give you a break and cover the cost of gas myself. That's a better deal than you giving me a break for parking in front of the courthouse for five minutes."

"Okay, I get your point."

"Since we're talking shop, what do you think happened to the snowman?" Joe asked.

"Is this just between you and me?"

"Sure, no problem. Between you and me."

"Exactly what happened, I don't know. But I got a note saying that he'd be gone for the rest of the season."

"That's interesting." Joe's face turned from stern to forlorn.

The expression on Joe's face surprised Tom. "I figured you'd be happy about the snowman's disappearance."

"Like him or not, the people keep coming to the park in hopes that he'll return. They need somebody to talk to. Are you going to make a public announcement?"

"I don't think that would be wise. They'll figure it out on their own soon enough anyway."

Joe nodded in agreement. "Let's change subjects. Pastor Dalton tells me you're president of his church council."

"Yes, I'm three years into a four-year term. Why do you ask?"

"Something's not right with the Daltons. I was in the parsonage the other day, and Debra looked scared."

"Debra's different. She's always been on the timid side, and she's gotten more so over the years. I have a hunch your being a stranger could have scared her."

"I don't know. My gut reaction tells me it was something more than shyness. What's their history?"

"They moved here eight or nine years ago. Pastor Derrick wasn't too long out of the seminary and had been serving a church in a small town northwest of here. He delivers a passionate message, and from the sounds of things, it might have been too passionate for the congregation's liking. He rubbed people the wrong way, and the flock split into three factions. Only a third of them stayed with Dalton. The church ran out of money, and the regional administration reassigned him to us. He's been here ever since."

"Don't they transfer pastors around from time to time?"

"They do, if they can arrange an agreeable match. Unlike his brother, who has climbed the church ladder, Pastor Derrick has been left to serve in a more remote assignment, and we're it."

"So his brother is climbing the ladder, and Pastor Dalton is stuck in Dakota City. That sounds like a perfect formula for envy and anger."

"That could be. You're the psychologist, Joe. I'll say this: he hasn't improved his standing around here any over the years. Attendance is down, and there are those among us calling for his release, Art included. He and the entire Kelsey family were faithful members years ago, but the girls fell by the wayside right after confirmation. Their mom and Art still attend but not as often as we'd like."

Hmm…dwindling numbers and an unhappy congregation, Joe thought. "Do you go on a regular basis?"

"You'll find my family in the third row back every Sunday."

"The Daltons don't have any children, do they?"

"No, no kids."

"How come?"

"I try to mind my own business, so I really can't say. Like I said, Debra is rather timid; maybe that has something to do with it."

"Interesting."

"I wish my term as president was over. That movement to remove Dalton could cost me votes and my job."

Confession

Monday night brought Joe more bad dreams and restless sleep. Whether his eyes were open or closed, all he could see was Tony's body lying on top of Millie's burial vault. At four fifteen, Joe flopped over in his bed and sat up. *Tony, this obsession is killing me.* Joe tossed and turned until six and got up to workout. After seeing the words *bless me* drift through the warm fog in his shower on Tuesday morning, Joe decided it was time to take action. *I'm tired of this, Tony. You aren't letting me sleep, and I'm running out of energy. We've got to do something, don't we?* By eight o'clock, Joe was in St. Peter's Church sitting in the front pew. Father Riley showed himself in due time and came limping down the aisle with a wooden cane. He put his free hand on Dr. Joe's shoulder. "What brings you here, Joe?"

"Nightmares—nightmares and a search, Father."

"What are you searching for?"

"Some peace of mind and some sleep."

"You surprise me, Joe. I had the impression that Trapper was your counsel."

"Trapper is a good man with good advice, but he can't be my go-to guy with this problem."

"I see," said Father Riley. "Do you want to tell me about this problem of yours?"

"Maybe."

"Maybe? Oh, I understand; this calls for confidentiality. Joe, I have the tightest lips in the state. If I didn't, I wouldn't be in Dakota City. Your confidence is safe with me so long as you do things right."

The phrase "do things right" made Joe's ears perk up. "What do you mean?"

"Have you ever gone to confession?"

"No, but I've heard of it. So you want me to go into a little booth and tell you about my sins?"

"And about your problem. Once I'm in the confessional, I'm bound by a sacred oath of silence."

"I get it. How do I get started?"

"Go in the confessional booth, pull the curtain closed, and say, 'Forgive me, Father, for I have sinned.'"

"What if I haven't sinned?"

"Joe, we both know that's not true. If you get stuck, just follow my lead."

Joe stepped into the confessional booth and sat down. Father Riley stepped into the opposite side, and they pulled their curtains closed at the same time.

"Are you there, Father?"

"Yes, Joe, I'm here."

"Forgive me, Father, for I have sinned."

"What are your sins?"

"I looked at Billie's legs when I fell down."

Given the distraught look that Father Riley had seen on Joe's face before entering the confessional booth, he was expecting a more meaningful disclosure. "Joe, you can do better than that. Even I look at Billie's legs. Why don't you kick it up a notch?"

Joe took a deep breath in preparation for his confession. "Okay, Father. Here goes. Susan had a son. Trapper doesn't know about him. The boy was killed in an accident in New Mexico. She brought him back here, and Susan and I buried him on top of Millie under the cover of darkness. His body hasn't been blessed, and the boy's spirit is haunting me. Oh, and Father, no one can know. I promised Susan my confidence."

While Father Riley had encouraged Joe to get to the point, he wasn't expecting *this* level of admission. He fell silent for an extended moment to contemplate what he had just heard.

"Father, are you still there?"

"When you kick it up a notch, Joe, you really kick it up."

"Can you bless the boy in confidence, Father?"

Father Riley was back on task. "Yes, my son. Now, Joe, listen to me. This is the hard part, but for you, it's also the important part."

"Yes, Father, I'm listening."

"Joe, go and sin no more."

"That's it?"

"That's it, Joe."

Go and sin no more ... I wonder if he says that to everybody? Dr. Joe left St. Peter's feeling better. He went home and slept for the better part of the day. With some rest, maybe he could focus his attention on reconciling with Billie.

Making Adjustments

Joe woke up shortly after three o'clock and went to his office around four. In the absence of other things to do, he searched the Internet for a new job. An hour later, he concluded that everybody was looking for five years of experience, clean records, and that sort of thing. *Nothing that seems to match my background.*

Darkness comes early in the late fall, and before long Joe was looking at the snowman through his office window. There was no light from within, and the snowman seemed to disappear into the shadows of night. *You look rather pitiful, Snowman.* As indistinguishable silhouettes came by to call on the empty shell that was once their therapist, Joe felt his compassionate heart beating. *Look at them—hopeful shadows each and every one, all in pain and all waiting for the snowman to light up again.* The compassionate force that carried Dr. Joe through the torture of graduate school was awakened. He saw beyond his envy of the snowman and empathized with the people. *Like the snowman or not, these people need his listening ear.*

A confusing flood of thoughts rushed through Joe's mind. *Measure the intentions of your heart. I'm in this business to help people.*

I'm going to do things right. Suddenly, clarity struck like a slap shot hitting the glass, and Joe made a decision. *I'm in a mess, and I need to do something.* What was once unthinkable now seemed to be the right thing to do. Joe locked up his office, sneaked down the stairwell, popped open the tunnel door, and entered the dim-lit tunnel.

The damp tunnel offered Joe only enough height to walk so long as he bent way over. One careful quiet footstep at a time, Joe moved closer to the ladder that would take him up to ground level and into the bowels of the snowman. Joe cringed at the sound of the crumbling pieces of loose concrete under his feet. Cobwebs pulled on his hair, and he brushed the sticky threads from his face using his fingers. He spit them from his mouth. *I must be taller than the snowman, or maybe he comes in another way.* Joe took hold of the rusty ladder and gave the top rung a hard pull. *It should hold me.* Then without further hesitation, he climbed up into the fiberglass shell, flipped the light switches, and turned on the speaker. Dr. Joseph Doyle, PhD, took over the snowman's practice.

Working at Home

Debra worked on the purple cocktail dress every chance she got. So far, she had taken out the seams, flattened folds, sewed the dress to fit, and ironed the creases. She hid the dress in her portable sewing machine case after every session. By now, Debra had lost count of how many times it had been stashed away. Extra sessions with Laura, Dalton's confirmation student, were keeping her husband from home at night, and Debra's work was nearly complete. Still, as Debra sewed, she worried. *If only I was more attractive. I really don't think he should be alone with Laura.* Were it not for her work, Debra would have been unable to escape her terrible fears.

Tonight, Debra was trying to adjust the hem, but the task was not going well. Another set of hands would be helpful. Fortunately, Billie's curiosity had gotten the better of her, and she was just dying to see how Debra looked in Bobbi's old dress. Billie rang the Daltons' doorbell, and Debra answered. "Hi, Debra," Billie said.

"Hello. Are you Billie or Bobbi?"

"I'm Billie." Billie extended her arm and held out a plate. "I have a pie for you guys."

"Thank you. I'll be sure to tell the pastor you brought t by."
Debra looked at the wall clock. *Good, there's still some time. N e I
can get her to help me.* "Billie, I—"

Billie assumed she was about to be hastily dismissed and cu in.
"Debra, my curiosity is killing me. How's that dress coming? I nt
to make sure you get your money out of it."

"That's what I was trying to say. I'm so glad you came by. he
hem is giving me all kinds of trouble. I don't know where it sho ld
fall, and I can't get it straight. Can you give me a hand?" Debra h ld
the door open and stepped to the side so Billie could come in.

"Sure, I'd be glad to." Billie stepped in the house.

Debra looked out the door at the pastor's office light. "Come on.
We have to hurry. The pastor will be home in a half an hour, and I
don't want him to see it. It's going to be a big surprise." Debra put
on the snug dress.

Billie took one look at Debra and was taken aback by the transformation standing before her. "Wow, you are gorgeous. If that
doesn't surprise the pastor, nothing will."

"I hope so."

Billie turned the hem up. "How do you like this length?"

Debra looked in the mirror. "Is that where it belongs? I've never
worn anything like this."

"It belongs where you like it, but I like it right here."

"Me too." Billie pinned the hem, and Debra slipped off the dress.
She hid it and promptly put away the sewing machine. "Thank you."
With the dress stowed safely away, Debra took a quick peek out of
the living room window and checked her husband's office light once
again. It was still on. "Billie, can you give me some ideas for my
hair?" The women tossed Debra's hair this way and that until she
saw the pastor's office light go out. "You've got to go, Billie."

Billie heard the panic in Debra's voice and let Debra's hair fall.
She was making her way out the door when the pastor came home.
"Hi, Pastor."

Dalton looked down at Billie's legs. *What's she doing here?* "You won't reach the kingdom without coming to fellowship, Billie," he warned.

"I'll keep that in mind, Pastor. Good night. I have to run," Billie said as she continued out the door.

"What was she doing here?" Dalton asked Debra.

Debra heard Dalton's suspiciousness. "She brought a donation—a pie."

The edgy pastor probed some more. "She was here snooping for a reason. You're either too dumb to know why or you aren't saying."

Debra didn't want to run the risk of escalating Dalton's anger, not with her dress so close to being finished. "I thought it was nice of her to stop. Would you like a piece of that pie?" The Daltons ate pie and went to bed. Debra crawled under the covers and fell asleep envisioning herself in the purple dress. Maybe she would steal a few glances at the festival.

Minding the Snowman's Business

Time started to fly the moment Joe turned on the snowman's lights. The snowman worked difficult hours, and, most nights, clients came one after the other to talk things out with him. *At least I'm in the game.* At first, the people's problems seemed routine. "Snowman, I don't have enough money for Christmas. What can I do?" "My boss is a jerk. Should I quit my job?" "My boyfriend is going to propose. Should I accept?" Although the work wasn't complex, it was clinical work, and Tuesday night was soon lost to Friday morning. Joe woke up, mind spinning and already at work. *Friday night... the bar crowd will be out. Listening to problems distorted by alcohol is tough duty.* But before he was out of bed, Joe made a promise to himself. Today he would go to Kelsey's and do his best to work things out with Billie. *I can't stand another long, lonely weekend.* Joe walked to the restaurant storefront, where he came face-to-face with Billie. She was standing inside the door, and their eyes met through the glass.

Since Joe was too close for Billie to ignore, she forced an insincere smile and finished taping a sign on the glass door.

That was one cold smile. Give her a chance to escape. Recognizing that the time was not right for talking with Billie, Joe stalled outside, reading the sign.

Holiday Festival
November 27th
Volunteers Needed–Sign up with Billie or Bobbi

When Billie stepped away from the door, Joe entered the restaurant. Not knowing where else to go, he set off in the direction of the table. Today, only two people were there, Pastor Dalton and Father Riley. To Joe's surprise, Billie cut him off before he got to his destination. She'd repay him for accommodating her easy escape moments earlier. "I wouldn't go back there if I were you; they're arguing," Billie said flatly as Joe walked by.

"Thanks for the warning." Joe turned around and followed Billie away from the table. He took a stool by himself at the counter where he assumed that someone other than Billie would provide customer service. However, unbeknown to Joe, Billie ran the till and waited on the customers at the counter.

"What would you like, Dr. Joe?" Billie asked.

"Coffee, please."

"Did you bring money?"

"Yes."

"Regular or decaf?"

"Regular."

"To go?"

"To stay. And could I get that without ice, please?"

"Damn, that's strange, Dr. Joe. I thought you liked ice." Billie poured Joe's coffee and intentionally spilled just enough in the saucer to annoy him.

Joe wanted to calm the mounting hostility. "I was reading the sign you put on the door. Tell me about the festival."

Billie hesitated. Since it seemed a safe subject, she answered, "It's a community-wide gathering we have every year to ring in the holidays."

"What's involved?"

"The festivities begin early in the evening about an hour before dark. Things kick off with a special event, something the little kids can enjoy."

"Like what?"

"Last year we had a parade of lights. The year before, Santa and his reindeer were here. The year before that, a holiday train stopped in town."

"What are you doing this year?"

"A re-enactment of the nativity scene."

"Who's organizing that?"

"The preachers. That's what they're fighting about at the table."

"What's to fight about?"

"From the little I heard, they're arguing about who gets to play which character."

"You're serious, aren't you?"

"Yes, I suggested that they draw names from the hat. Father Riley was game, but Pastor Dalton just keeps on arguing."

"Dalton gets on my nerves. What's his problem anyway?"

"He keeps insisting that Laura Walter play the part of the Virgin Mary."

"Who's Laura Walter?"

"A local high school girl and one of Dalton's confirmation students."

"What sets her apart from the other girls in town?"

"That's a good question."

"Who gets to play the other parts?"

"That's hard to say. Pastor Dalton asked me who might be a good donkey, and I nominated you."

"You're kidding, right?" Joe said. Billie raised her eyebrows to intentionally create doubt in Joe's mind. "What happens after the nativity scene?" he asked.

"I have to work."

"I suppose you get a big crowd after an event like that."

"Actually, we close down the kitchen and keep the place open for a community potluck. The Farmhand Lounge hosted the dinner last year. This year, it's our turn."

"That sounds like a lot of work."

"We don't have to prepare any food, but putting up decorations and moving tables is a big hassle."

"Your regular setup doesn't work?"

"Not really. We have to squeeze in more tables and open up a backroom to accommodate the large crowd. Then we have to move the tables again to make room for the dance."

"A dance?"

"Adults only; the parents take the kids home and come back later, if they can find a sitter. We used to hire a band, but we switched to a DJ three years back. The music is cheaper and better."

"Did I mention I can dance?"

"Better than you play defense, I hope."

"I was distracted by a beautiful woman when that happened. Am I invited?"

"Everyone is invited, but I'm not sure you'd be comfortable there. It's not a hockey-jersey-and-sweatpants sort of affair. The women get dressed up, and the men try to do the same. For one night a year, fashion makes a statement in Dakota City. I'm sure Susan would love an escort. Maybe you should ask her to go."

She just has to push it, doesn't she? "Okay, I know how things looked, Billie, but things aren't always what they appear."

"Well then, Dr. Joe, this would be a good time for you to tell me how things really are." Billie took a cookie from a plate and slid it hard in Joe's direction. "You got the puck, Joe. What are you going to do with it?"

Joe fell silent.

"Just as I expected. No explanation."

"Maybe I should ask Susan. I'd rather go with you, but you'll be working."

"Go with me! Have you lost your mind, Dr. Doyle?"

Joe spun his index finger around his ear. "Are you saying a man would be crazy to go out with you?"

"Joe, I'll be honest. You hurt me, and I expected better from you. Do I need to say more?"

"What did I do that hurt you?"

"What did you do? Tell me that Pastor Dalton did not see Susan kissing you at sunrise."

"Billie, that was—"

"Tell me I didn't see Susan driving away from your house the very same morning."

Joe shrugged.

"See, just as I expected. *No explanation.*"

"I'm sorry you're hurt, Billie. I had no intention of that happening, and neither did Susan."

"That's all you have to say for yourself?"

"Billie, that's all I can say." Joe felt the conversation coming to an abrupt and very much undesired halt. It was nice talking to Billie again, even if she was mad at him. Joe grasped for anything to change the subject and keep their conversation going. "Does the snowman come to the dance?"

Billie laughed. "That is the stupidest question I have ever heard! No, Dr. Joe, the snowman doesn't come to the dance. It's bolted to the concrete."

"You know who I mean, the real Snowman. Does he come?"

"Don't be ridiculous. First of all, no one knows who the snowman is. For another thing, the festival is the busiest night of his work year. Why do you ask?"

"I was just thinking even the snowman deserves to have some fun."

"He's already taken time off this year, and that's a strange thing too. He's never done that before. Judging from what I've seen, he has a backlog now. Speaking about work, are you going to volunteer to help with the festival?"

"What needs to be done?"

"Art and Trapper are going to build a big manger using broken telephone poles and old boards in the park. There are a million other things to be done, too. I'm sure no one would turn down your help."

"I doubt that's true."

"You're wrong about that, Joe. No one turns down help during the festival."

"Well then, sign me up for the manger crew. Oh, and Billie, one more thing. Put me down to help you with tables in the afternoon."

"Dang it, Joe. That was a trap." *Why am I like this around him?* Even though Billie was shaking her head and glaring at Joe in disgust, she signed him up for both projects. As Joe stood up and dug into his pocket for money, Billie said, "The cookie's on me."

A Complex Case

As soon as dusk fell, Joe was eager to climb into the snowman and turn on the lights. "Snowman, I cheated on my husband. Should I tell him?" "Snowman, I spent the kids' lunch money on booze. Now what do I do?" "Snowman, I can't control my eating. How do I stop?" Snowman this and Snowman that. The snowman's business was brisk. Joe sat inside the chilly fiberglass shell listening as one voice after another passed through the muffled old speaker system. People talked, and Joe listened to their problems late into the night. Just when he thought the flood of patients was about to slow down, a silhouette stepped in front of the snowman and fidgeted in silence.

"May I help you?" the snowman asked.

"Do you still like Christmas songs, Snowman?" a timid voice said.

"Of course I do."

"Will you listen to me sing?"

"Gladly."

After a short pause, the delicate voice started to sing.

Jolly old St. Nicholas, Lean your ear this way!
Don't you tell a single soul, what I'm going to say.

The singing stopped, and the voice fell silent.

"You sing very well," said the snowman.

"Thank you," the timid voice answered. "Is that all you have to say, Snowman?"

She wants me to say more, but what? "You can trust me. Did you want to say something else?" But there was no answer. The girl left, and Dr. Joe sat encapsulated in the fiberglass shell wishing he could talk with her some more. *That was strange.* Joe shut off the lights and went home where, in his loneliness, he was now troubled by another young person's voice.

More Cuss Word Therapy

Monday rolled around, and Bobbi came charging into his office for cuss word therapy right on time. She too wanted to give Joe a piece of her mind. "Hello," she said coldly.

"Come right on in, Bobbi. Don't bother to knock."

Bobbi ignored Joe's lecture in manners. "Let's get this over, shall we?"

"You sound as if you are still angry with me."

"What the F do you think?" Bobbi said, trying her best to relabel bad language. "Of course I'm mad at you."

"Do you want to tell me why?"

"It's all in the journal."

Joe tensed and pushed himself back into his chair. "I guess I'll brace myself and listen to what you wrote."

"I said the F-bomb when Billie told me she talked to you in the restaurant. I said it again when Billie said you wanted to take her to the dance, and I said, 'Get the F out of here' when Billie told me that you offered to help her set up tables."

Dr. Joe rubbed his forehead. "Bobbi, I appreciate your effort to relabel, but you've just had what we call a relapse."

"Joe, you're what I call a complete idiot."

"Bobbi, do you remember when we talked about response patterns in the last session?"

"Sort of."

"Do you see any patterns in your swearing?"

"Yes, Dr. Joe, I do. I swear every time you mess with my sister."

"Billie means a lot to you, doesn't she?"

"We're twin sisters. We run a restaurant together. What do you think, Dr. Joe? Of course she means a lot to me."

"And you'd do anything to protect her, right?"

This question made Bobbi fidget in her chair. "Of course." Bobbi turned her face away from Joe's. She looked defensively out the window, and her bottom lip quivered ever so slightly. "Are we done talking?"

Joe caught the fidget and the broken eye contact, but he could not see the quivering lip. There was more going on with Bobbi than swearing, but whatever it was would have to wait until she was ready to talk with him. "We can call it quits for the day if you like."

"Good. I want to get out of here before somebody sees me again."

"I'm sorry about Pastor Dalton barging in like he did. Look, Bobbi, you're doing a great job with your journal. Keep it up. Remember, practice biting your lip, and keep looking for patterns."

Community Involvement

Joe rolled over in bed Saturday morning and slapped his hand on the small nightstand trying to find his cell phone in the dark. *Dang, who'd be calling me at this time of day?* In this case, it was Art, who, along with Trapper, was in route to pick him up. Art was in charge of manger construction and had declared today groundbreaking day. The men went to Kelsey's for breakfast and a quick cup of coffee. Then, they scurried off to beg enough broken telephone poles and rough lumber to build a structure fitting Pastor Dalton's specifications—specifications that, in Art's opinion, were far more expansive than necessary. Dalton demanded that the three-sided structure be almost equal in size to a single stall garage. The scope of such construction would have the three men busting their behinds from now until the day of the festival.

The men made an effective team. Art planned, did measurements, and supervised. Trapper's job was to keep Joe's mind on work. He did this by convincing Joe that the sheet of ice covering the lake wasn't safe enough for skating. Joe did the manual labor. After gathering the lumber, Art measured and marked places on the ground for ten post holes. Then he had Joe chisel through two inches of frosty ground and dig holes with an auger so that ten sawed-off telephone posts about twelve feet long could be set in place as uprights for the manger walls. Once the poles were set, the trio tacked wall boards into place, and Art declared that to be enough work for the first day. They could put up roof boards on Sunday afternoon. After that was done, the remaining work could be taken care of on weekdays during the warm period of the day, meaning the four hours following morning coffee break and late afternoon.

"Fellas, we make a great team. I think we can call it quits for the day and sneak in a road hunt," Art said.

Joe lifted the bill of his cap and wiped the perspiration from his forehead. "What do you mean, *we*?" Joe said, knowing that he had done almost all of the strenuous physical labor.

"Everybody made a contribution, Joe," Trapper said. Trapper knew that Art would have him driving up and down dusty backroads hoping to shoot a pheasant in the ditch until sundown. "I think I'll pass on that road hunt. I'm tired."

Even though the men had accomplished a lot, the roof boards still needed to go up, and the manger needed outdoor lighting. Also, they had to build a podium and direct bright flood lights at it. Dalton insisted on these features to draw everyone's attention toward him when he started the program. With a little luck and Joe's hard work, they should get done before festival.

Secrets Revealed

Another weekend had come and gone, and on Monday it was back to work for most people in Dakota City, including Dr. Joe and Susan. When Billie walked through the front doors and into the courthouse, she stomped past the reception desk. "Is Dr. Joe in?" she asked Susan with a scowl on her face. "I have a session with him." It was her turn for cuss word therapy.

"Ms. Kelsey, may I talk to you?" Susan asked.

Billie froze in her tracks, and after thawing a bit, she turned back toward the attractive receptionist. "Susan, we have known each other our entire lives, and you've never called me Ms. Kelsey."

Susan had intentionally addressed Billie in this manner. She looked around to be certain no one could overhear them. "You're quite right about that, Ms. Kelsey. I want to talk to you about Dr. Joe."

"What's to talk about?" Billie said, failing to hide her jealousy.

"Billie, please. Hear me out."

"Okay, Susan, what do you want to say?" Billie sat down in the wooden office chair beside Susan's desk.

Susan pointed at Billie's unblemished calf. "Ms. Kelsey, I believe that we both have secrets—secrets that could cause problems for someone we both care for."

Susan's confrontation captured Billie's attention in a heartbeat. "What are you talking about?"

Susan jumped right to the point. "You're in love with Dr. Joe, aren't you?"

"In love with him! I hardly know him."

"Billie, if you don't know that you're in love with Dr. Joe, you're the only person in town who hasn't figured it out. You fell in love with him the moment he dropped at your feet. From what I have heard, everybody there saw it happen. "

Billie was annoyed by Susan's bold assessment. "Even if I was in love with him, he can't be cut in half and divided—although, I'll admit I am tempted to try."

"Billie, please just listen for a minute. I think that Dr. Joe is a very nice man, and he means the world to me—"

"Pastor Dalton noticed that at sunrise a while back."

"Billie, you and I both know that things aren't always as they seem. Would you please just listen for a moment?"

"All right. Go ahead, Susan."

"Billie, my bet is that Dr. Joe thinks he's counseling Bobbi Kelsey, not Bobbi *and* Billie Kelsey. Am I right?"

"You could be." Billie knew that Susan was on to their ploy. "Okay, you know my secret. What's yours?" Billie asked with a jealous bite in her voice.

"Can I ask for your complete confidence? The things I need to say are very delicate and very personal."

Now Susan had Billie's full attention. "Go ahead."

"Understand when I say *confidential*, I'm excluding Dr. Joe. You can talk to him. In fact, the only reason I'm telling you any of this is because I want you to talk to Joe."

Billie's interest in this conversation continued to grow. "Why would you want me to talk to Joe?"

"Because he's my friend and because he's in love with you. And the way things are going around here, he will leave town before either of you admit it."

"Go on," Billie said.

Seeing that Billie had calmed down, Susan was ready to share her risk. "Billie, I'm going to tell you something—something Joe won't ever tell you because he is a gentleman and a professional."

"What on earth are you talking about?"

"Billie, I needed Joe's help the other night, and I made him promise not to talk about certain things."

"Continue."

"Billie, I have a son. I mean, I did until he was run over and killed in New Mexico last week. His name was Tony."

Billie's jaw dropped. "Are you serious?"

"I couldn't be more serious. Last week when I was gone, I drove down there and brought his body back in my pickup. I wanted to bury him in his grandma's arms. Billie, you know what my dad is like. He'd be devastated if he knew I had a baby outside of marriage." Susan started to cry. "Billie, I'm just going to tell you how it is. I didn't have enough money to bury him anywhere but with my mom."

"What does this have to do with Joe?"

"I asked Joe to help me bury Tony. I had no one else to turn to. Joe shoveled all night. He cradled my boy in his arms while I crawled into the grave with my own mother. Then, he promised to keep everything a secret from my dad, who's the only friend he has in town—except for you and me."

Astonished, Billie leaned closer to Susan. "Susan, I am—"

Susan interrupted. "You're making Joe pay a huge price for helping me. He's a good man, Billie."

Billie stood back up and put her hands over her mouth. She didn't know what to say.

Susan continued to speak. "Did I spend the night with Dr. Joe? Yes, digging up my mother's grave and burying my little boy under the cover of darkness. Did I kiss him in his driveway? Yes, in appreciation for what he had done, not because we're in love. Billie, I suspect Joe can get himself into all kinds of trouble, but he *did not* cheat on you." Susan took a deep breath and let it out slowly. "There. That's all I wanted to say."

Billie took her hands from her mouth. "Susan, I am so sorry about your son."

Susan gave Billie a faint smile and touched a finger to her own lips. "Please don't tell anyone. It will get back to Dad before I'm ready." Susan pointed her chin sharply in the direction of Joe's office. "Ms. Kelsey, I believe Dr. Joe is waiting for you."

Billie stepped forward to give Susan a hug. "Your secret is safe with—"

"Go. We've got to quit talking. Here comes Pastor Dalton," Susan said.

Another Break-In

W hile Billie ran for Joe's office, Susan gave Dalton a cold greeting as he approached her. "Pastor," she said.

"Is Dr. Joe in?" Dalton asked.

"Yes, but he's in a session."

The pompous pastor ignored Susan's implied directive and promptly followed Billie to Joe's office. Susan attempted to caution Dalton again. "Pastor, I said he's in a session."

"I heard you," Dalton said, ignoring Susan and strutting on only a hall length behind Billie.

Billie rushed to Joe's door, pushed it open, and tossed the pink journal in the air. Joe stood up and stepped out from behind his desk. "Is everything okay, Bobbi?"

Billie, so relieved by Susan's disclosure, stood before Joe, shaking her head and crying.

"Bobbi, what's wrong"

Billie could not contain herself. She ran to Joe, hopped up, and wrapped her arms around his neck. Joe had no choice but to catch her and hold her in his arms. With her feet dangling from the floor,

Billie kissed him and kissed him. Her tender lips chased Joe's as rising passions escaped … until Pastor Dalton barged into the office unannounced.

"Susan said you were in session, but I wanted to—"

Joe and Billie sprang apart. "Get out of here, Pastor. You have no business walking into my office like this," Dr. Joe barked.

Undeterred by Dr. Joe's order to leave, Dalton held his ground and stared at Billie's leg to identify her. Dalton gave Joe a sly grin. "Excuse me. I didn't mean to interrupt a personal moment. I can see you do some interesting things in therapy sessions, Dr. Joe."

Joe was fed up with Dalton but fought his physical instincts. *Don't lose your cool, Joe.* "Dalton, get out of my office before I boot you out."

In Dalton's mind, it was time to let Dr. Joe know who was in charge. "Kissing a patient? You could get into trouble doing that sort of thing, couldn't you?"

Joe felt Dalton's trap snap closed, and he lost self-control. He rushed Dalton and grabbed him by the lapels. "Dalton, I'm going to kick your—"

"I'd be careful if I were you, Dr. Joe."

All professional composure lost, Joe raised Dalton from the floor and shoved him in the direction of the doorway. "Get out of here, Dalton."

Filled with arrogance, Dalton recovered from a stumble and gave Joe a casual two-finger salute. "Have a good day, Joe."

Joe paced wildly back and forth across his office floor. "I'm sorry about Dalton, Bobbi. I simply need to lock my door when you're here."

Billie shrugged. "I think he got the point this time."

"I'm not so sure about that," Joe said in a surprisingly dismissive way. His mind was no longer on Dalton. Half stunned and legs wobbly from the passionate encounter, he stepped back and looked closely at Billie. *What a kiss!* "Bobbi, I don't know what that was all about, but I need to tell you I can't be kissing the people I counsel."

Billie blushed. "I'm sorry, Dr. Joe. I got carried away. If you don't mind, I'm going to run along. I'm not in the mood for therapy today." While Joe thought, *I'm done for*, Billie thought, *I need to talk to Bobbi.* Billie bounced toward the office door with a happy smile. "Good-bye," she said.

Joe sat down and frowned. "Bobbi, hang on a minute. I'd really appreciate it if you don't tell anyone you kissed me, especially Billie."

"But, Dr. Joe, we're twin sisters."

"Yes, I understand that, but you don't have to tell her everything, do you?"

"Not everything, but this was all pretty exciting by Dakota City standards."

"Bobbi, please—"

"I'll have to think about it."

"Think about it . . . why?"

"Billie and I made a deal in the eighth grade."

"What kind of deal?"

"We each get to keep one secret from each other. If we tell the old secret, then we get to keep a new one. I just promised someone else my confidence, so I'm out of slots. Sorry," Billie said as she closed the door.

Joe slumped further into his chair. As he lamented in the jaws of the preacher's trap, his eyes took on a distant look, and he scribbled "the situation is hopeless" on his desktop calendar.

Billie rushed straight to Bobbi and told her about kissing Joe but said nothing of Susan and Tony.

Bobbi was so stunned that she forgot about relabeling. "F, why on earth did you do that?"

"It's my secret," Billie said.

A Cold Wind Blows

Rumors of the big thaw between Billie and Joe spread through town like a prairie wild fire. Even though Art wasn't excited about the reconciliation, he couldn't wait to get to coffee on Tuesday morning. He was dying to know what had taken place between his niece and Dr. Joe. Art walked through the door expecting his favorite hangout to be filled with warm breezes, not the arctic chill that slapped him in the face. Sure, Billie was bubbly, but there seemed to be an arctic cold front hovering over the table. Art eased up to his friends and took a mental roll call: Trapper, Judge, Father Riley, Dr. Joe, and the source of the bitter chill, Pastor Dalton. "Hello, gentlemen," Art said.

"You're just in time, Art. We need another psychologist for this discussion," Father Riley said.

"Pastor Dalton's preaching a sermon on professional ethics in psychotherapy," Judge added.

"Now there's a topic with absolutely no relevance around here. With no disrespect, Joe, the snowman is the only one who does any therapy in Dakota City," Art said.

Pastor Dalton stared at Dr. Joe and gave him a disturbing grin. "I don't know about that. From what I've seen, Joe has a thriving practice."

Joe stared back at the pastor, but his gentle, compassionate eyes were no match against the evil that lurked in Dalton's deep blue eyes. Dakota City's young psychologist buckled under the pastor's dominating presence, and he slowly moved his chair back from the table. Dalton saw Joe's subtle retreat, raised his eyebrow, and smiled. Instantly, Joe realized Dalton was more than a simple annoyance; he was an intimidating force, a monster that fed on controlling others. *He's got me pinned against the boards.* Eager to escape, Joe said, "Excuse me. I forgot to do something." He got up and walked quickly away from the table. *It's time to adjust my game plan.* While Joe wasn't the type to hide out, in this case, he didn't know what else to do. *Maybe if I lie low and avoid Dalton, this mess will blow over.*

It took less than a day for Billie to notice Joe's vanishing act, and his scarcity caused her to keep keen ears open in the restaurant. By the time Friday rolled around, she overheard Trapper declare Dr. Joe to be "extinct," and this caused her worries to mushroom. It was time for her to talk with Bobbi and adjust their plan. "We need to quit having sessions with Dr. Joe," Billie said.

"I agree, but how come you want to quit?"

"Because I don't want to get him in trouble."

"So it has finally happened. My sister has fallen in love and fallen fast too!"

"Maybe... that's why we have to bow out gracefully. Otherwise, we might hurt his feelings."

"Be careful, Billie. That man's a gamble—a charming one, but a gamble just the same."

"You think I should get out now, don't you?"

"As if you could. Just admit it. You are *so* in love. Don't worry about dropping out of therapy. That'll be easy. I'll stop at Joe's office, visit for a bit without swearing, and tell him that I'm cured. You can back up my story at coffee, and we're out of those sessions with no harm done."

"That won't work. Joe would never buy it. Plus, he's desperate for patients. He'd convince you to come back. He talked you into three sessions a week, remember?"

"Good point. He does have an engaging way about him."

"See, Joe could talk you into staying in therapy just like that." Billie snapped her fingers. "I better handle the exit strategy."

"Okay, if you're sure. Don't do anything on my behalf that hurts his feelings. I like him, in a brotherly sort of way."

$\mathcal{L}$oose $\mathcal{E}$nds and $\mathcal{O}$pportunities

On Friday afternoon, Art and Trapper flushed Joe from his house to help build the podium by the manger. The men went directly to the park and got to work. "What's up with Dalton?" Art asked.

Joe didn't know how to answer this question without telling Art about kissing his niece in a therapy session. "Nothing I can't handle," he said.

Before Art asked a follow-up question, Billie, who had seen the men working through the restaurant window, came running over and interrupted. "Joe, I'm getting up early and going to Sioux Falls tomorrow. If you want to ride along, I'll drop you at the hockey arena."

"That sounds great. I could use some ice time again."

Trapper cleared his throat and held his hammer high. "Joe, aren't you forgetting something?"

Joe immediately dropped his head in disappointment. "I'm sorry, Billie. I promised to help finish here." *We'd be done if that jerk, Dalton, didn't want this thing built so big.* Joe turned his eyes toward Art as if asking permission to be excused.

Art shrugged his shoulders at Joe and held strong in support of Trapper's position. "A deal is a deal, Joe."

Hearing Art's unwavering position, Billie turned her pleading brown eyes on Uncle Art. He melted under the charming puppy-dog look. "Trapper, I think we can have this thing built by evening if we skip hunting with Tom this afternoon."

Trapper stopped nailing boards long enough to reconsider. He did owe Joe a favor or two for helping his daughter through a crisis. Plus, were it not for Joe, he and Susan wouldn't be talking out the lifetime of tension that had built up as a result of his overprotective parenting. "I can work late."

"Me too," said Joe.

"If that's the case, you kids should be able to go," Art said.

Joe looked at Billie. "What time are we leaving?"

"I'll pick you up at five forty-five."

Joe calculated the driving time against game time in his head. "That'll be perfect." Billie went back to the restaurant, and Joe immersed himself in the work. He nailed down the last roof board just in time to go to his office, sneak into the tunnel, and pull himself into the snowman. Thankfully, it was a slow night, and the snowman had a nap.

That Awesome Kiss

Billie drove into Joe's driveway in her fire-engine red SUV at precisely five forty-five. Joe was sitting outside on the back steps waiting with his hockey equipment. He waved good morning to Billie and opened the rear door on the SUV. Then he threw in his large black hockey bag and two sticks. Billie turned toward the rear seat. "Good morning," she said.

Until now, Joe had no comprehension of how Billie's voice could warm and brighten a morning. "Say that again," Joe said.

Not fully understanding the power she had to sway Joe's heart, Billie ignored the request. "Would you drive?" she asked.

"Sure."

Billie jumped over the console and bounced into the passenger seat. Joe climbed in and inhaled the wonderful aroma that surrounded her. He closed the door and pushed the electric button to adjust the seat. Billie immediately began to fan her nose. "Phew! Joe, that bag stinks." Billie let her window down in hopes that some of the thick stench oozing from the hockey gear would escape.

"Does it? I guess I don't notice it anymore. You'll get used to it in a few miles."

Billie choked back a gag. "I'll be dead in a few miles." She tipped her seat back, slipped off her clogs, and threw her feet on the dashboard. "You can't believe how good that feels. I'm on my feet all day." While Billie relaxed, Joe's wandering eyes slowly followed Billie's snug blue jeans from her waist, down to her knees, then to her ankles, and came to rest on her tiny toes. "You're gawking again," Billie said.

"You're showing off those sexy legs again. So what takes you to Sioux Falls?"

"Shopping. I need a dress and some new shoes for the festival next Saturday night."

Joe couldn't keep his eyes on the road. They were glued to the tips of Billie's cherry-red toenails. *Even her feet are sexy.* Joe pointed at her feet. "Let me guess, size seven?"

"Watch the road. There are a lot of deer out this time of year."

Joe pressed for an answer and embellished. "Size eight?"

"Six and a half, and that's usually a bit large."

Joe smiled. "I stand corrected."

"Joe, I wanted to talk to you before we get to Sioux Falls."

"Uh-oh, this sounds serious. What about?"

"About what happened between you and Bobbi the other day. She asked me to tell you that she won't be coming to therapy anymore."

Joe took one hand off the steering wheel and hit himself on the forehead. "I should've seen this coming. Bobbi told you about the kiss in my office, didn't she?"

"I know all about the kiss, Joe."

"You've trapped me in here to chew my butt, haven't you?"

"Joe—"

"Before you do, tell me something. Is Bobbi always so impulsive and, shall I say, passionate?"

"She can get carried away at times. Now, you tell me something. When Bobbi and I were in college, we argued about who kissed the best. How did you like her kiss?"

"What kind of question is that?"

"It's a simple question. I think I'm a better kisser than she is. She thinks otherwise. What do you think?"

This was a loaded question, and Joe knew it, but Billie was pressuring him. "Billie—"

"I answered your question. You have to answer mine."

"I've never kissed you, so it would be impossible for me to compare."

"Stop avoiding the question. Is she or is she not a good kisser?"

"You really want the truth?"

Billie smiled and nodded her head. "Yes, the truth. Give it to me point blank."

"Are you sure about that?

Billie was frustrated by Joe's avoidance. "Answer the question, Joe."

"Well, there was something special about Bobbi's kiss."

"Describe it for me."

"I think it was her lips. They're tender, soft, but firm at the same time. They're wildly passionate and enticed me to want more. Do you really want me to talk about this?"

"If there's more, I want to hear about it."

"I hardly know her, but that kiss had a special way of saying, 'I love you,' and, I have to admit, I liked the feeling."

Billie had Joe squirming in his seat, and she was enjoying every minute of it. "So she's pretty good?"

"Billie, Bobbi is your sister. Talking about this is making me very uncomfortable."

"I bet I'm just as good, if not better."

"Billie, if you kiss better than Bobbi, it would be like taking a full speed hit at mid-ice."

"Her kiss was that good?"

"The truth is, it was awesome, *really* awesome." Joe braced himself against the steering wheel and waited for an explosion that didn't come. To his surprise, Billie relaxed deeper into her seat and gave a contented sigh.

The Snowman Makes More Trouble

While Joe skated, Billie tore through four shops looking for the perfect dress, a dress that would knock Joe off his feet—again. And she found it. A red cocktail dress with a lace skirt cut low in back and high in front. The flowing dress would have a sensual sway when she was dancing, and it would feature her sleek legs from the front. Dress in the bag, Billie went back to pick up Joe. "How was the game?" she asked.

"Okay."

"Only okay?"

"My skates are wearing out. There's supposed to be a good sport's shop downtown. Do we have time to stop?"

"Sure. I need to look for shoes yet anyway." While Billie shopped for shoes, Joe looked for skates. An hour later, they walked up to Billie's SUV at exactly the same time.

Joe pointed at the plastic bag dangling in Billie's hand. "I see you found shoes."

"They aren't exactly what I wanted, but they'll do." Billie looked at Joe's empty hands. "I don't see any skates."

"They're already in the back seat."

Casual conversation consumed the trip home until they drove by the Big Dog Hunting Lodge. "Billie, would you grab those new skates from the back seat for me?" Joe asked.

"Sure." Billie turned to get the large bag and wrestled the box of skates forward between the bucket seats.

"Open the box. They're for you. Size six and a half as I recall."

"Are you kidding me? I can't skate."

"I'll teach you. Trapper says the ice will be safe by Sunday if the nights stay cold."

"I work until three. After that, I'd love to go."

"You'll need time to change into warmer clothes. Let's meet at three thirty."

"Great. I'll meet you at your bench." While Billie was excited about her gift and about spending more time with Joe, her cheery mood started to fade. As of yet, Joe had not asked her to the dance, and Billie fell silent. By the time they pulled into the driveway and stopped in front of the house, the silence in the SUV overpowered the smell of Joe's hockey equipment. He pushed his hair back and let out a deep breath. "Okay, what's wrong? Is this silent treatment about that kiss?"

Billie couldn't believe her ears. "No. This has nothing to do with the kiss."

"Well, then what's wrong?"

"Aren't you forgetting something?"

There was a razor-sharp bite in Billie's voice that Joe couldn't help but hear. "Let me think for a minute. We had a wonderful day together. Thanks for inviting me by the way. I bought you lunch and a gift. I asked you to go skating with me on Sunday, and you said you would love to go. What am I overlooking?"

"Joe, you are such an idiot. Why do you think I just dropped an entire paycheck on a new dress and shoes?"

"I assume you want to wear them to the dance next Saturday."

"How in the he … ck did you get a PhD?"

"Ah … Oh, I see. You want me to ask you to go to the dance."

"Boy, don't you catch on fast. Yes, Joe, I was hoping to go to the dance with you."

Joe sat in the SUV with Billie and with a dilemma. He had already hurt Billie's feelings once, and he didn't want to do it again. Of course, he also had a secret commitment with Snowman. The fact of the matter was Joe had to work on Saturday evening. "Billie, there's nothing on earth that I would rather do than take you to the dance, but I have to work."

"Work! You don't need to work. The snowman will cover things in the remote event that there's a cris—" Billie stopped abruptly. Remembering that the snowman had mysteriously skipped work for several nights and then suddenly reopened for business, Billie gave Joe a quizzical look. His head went back, his chin came up, and he looked away. Billie wasn't a psychologist, but she knew defensiveness when she saw it. She covered her mouth in shock. "Oh my—" Joe turned his face farther toward the driver-side window so Billie couldn't see it. Billie squirmed in her astonishment. "You're filling in for the snowman, aren't you?"

"Billie, I know you're out of secrets with Bobbi, so I'm not saying another word."

"Wow, I don't believe this. I'm dating the snowman."

"You don't have to tell Bobbi about suspicions, do you?"

"That's asking me to stretch the rules a long way, Joe."

"You're the one who said that the snowman needs to work on Saturday night."

"I did, didn't I? Joe, you have a way of shocking the s … ocks off me. Do you always live on the edge?"

Impending Doom

J oe's mind was racing when he woke on Sunday morning. Problems were piling upon problems, and his affairs in Dakota City had gone from bad to worse—except with Billie. His only patient had dropped out of therapy. His undercover status as the snowman had been exposed, and the words to "Jolly Old St. Nicholas" were still keeping him awake at night. He had to work during the festival, and everyone else, including Billie, would be having fun. Worst of all, Dalton had him in a trap. Joe threw off his bed covers and dressed for church. *It can't hurt to pray.* He slipped across the street to attend service at St. Peter's and took in Father Riley's message about "taking care of business." The Father was an inspiration, and Joe left church thinking that it was time to wrap up some loose ends of his own. So when Monday morning rolled around, Joe drove his car to work. *I better get that windshield fixed before I have to leave town.* On the way into the courthouse, he passed by Susan's desk. "Good morning," he said.

"You drove this morning," Susan said in recognition of Joe's deviation.

"I want to see about getting my broken windshield fixed."

"That's a good idea. Dad says you'd be smart to trade that little car off before winter gets here."

"I'll give that some thought. Say, how are you and your dad getting along?"

"Very well. In many ways, he's like a new man."

"Have you told your dad—"

"No, Joe, I haven't. I've been tempted, but I can't seem to get the words out of my mouth."

Even though Joe knew that Trapper had accurately read all the signs, he would not be the first to reveal confidential information. "Your dad might be more understanding than you think."

"Things like this can be very hard to explain, and I don't want to hurt him any more than I already have."

"I could sit down and talk with the two of you if it would help."

"Thanks, Joe. I'll think about that."

"Say, are there any messages for me?"

"Sorry. Not today, Dr. Joe."

Just in Case

With Susan's assurance that his schedule was clear, Joe drove his car to the dealership at the north end of town. He stepped inside and approached the service counter. The service manager, a short skinny man wearing a three-day-old shadow of whiskers and a blue shirt with red lettering, stood up from behind a desk. His shirt pocket, which was embroidered with the name Bob, came just above the countertop. Joe looked down. "Hi, Bob. I need an estimate for a windshield replacement."

"No problem, Dr. Joe. I heard you had a broken window," Bob said in an elfin pitch.

Bob bent down and grabbed a step stool. He carried it outside, and Joe followed. He took one look at Joe's car and shook the stool in frustration. "Darn, I forgot you've got a sports car. I didn't need this." Bob leaned over the hood and wrote down a long line of numbers on a clipboard. "That should do it. Let's get back inside where it's warm."

"It is cold out here."

"It always turns cold before the festival." Bob put his stool down behind the counter again and stepped up to reference his computer.

Once again, he wrote a bunch of numbers and started to add them on a pocket calculator. He carefully reviewed his work and looked up in frustration. "This isn't right. I have to go in back and look at a catalog. Excuse me for a minute."

"I'm in no hurry." Joe backed away from the service counter to browse in the small showroom. When he turned from the counter, Dalton strutted in the door. Their eyes met, and the pastor gave Joe a menacing look. "Spending some money, Joe? I bet it feels good to get a paycheck after a long dry spell," Dalton taunted.

"Mind your own business, Preacher."

"Oh, but I am, Joe. The way I see it, a man's wife is his own business."

"You're crazy, Dalton. What are you talking about?"

"Debra's piano playing sure has improved since you gave her that cozy little lesson in the church."

Joe mentally replayed the close physical contact between Debra and him. He felt Debra playfully tossing her head into his chest. He heard her gentle laughter at the satisfaction of immediate improvement. *Now I get it. The preacher's jealous.* "The piano lesson—that's what this craziness is all about? Dalton, you're overreacting."

"Dr. Doyle, you are an adulterer."

"Dalton, get a grip. Nothing happened."

"You're hardly in the position to be handing out advice, Dr. Doyle. You mind your business, and I might mind mine. Oh, and one more thing, stay away from my wife, or I'll be talking to that ethics committee in Minnesota. I'm sure they'd be interested to learn that you've been kissing your patients … *again.*" Dalton saw Bob returning. "I'll come back later, Bob, when you're not so busy." Bob shook his head, and Dalton walked out the door.

"That Pastor Dalton is a strange man," Bob said.

Joe nodded his head in agreement. "Strange is an understatement. I feel like the man is stalking me." Bob laid his paperwork on the countertop. "What's the bottom line?" Joe asked.

"The total would be four hundred fifty-eight dollars and sixty-two cents including installation and tax."

"When can you do it?"

"I'll have to order the parts, but if they get here, we could start Saturday morning. I should tell you, though, we close at noon, so it won't be done until late Monday."

"That works for me. I walk to work anyway. In fact, I can leave the car here today if you don't mind."

"Actually, that would be better for us. Things can warm up before we work on it. If the parts get here early, I'll try to slide it in sooner. But remember, no promises until Monday."

"Thanks."

Bob cleared his throat as Joe made a small step back from the service counter. "Can you leave a two hundred and fifty dollar deposit for parts?"

"Sure." Joe dug out his wallet and paid in cash.

Seeing the bundle of cash, Bob realized an opportunity. "You don't plan on driving that car over the winter, do you?"

"Why?"

"We all kind of look after the Kelsey twins around here since their dad died. That little red car of yours won't be the safest thing to drive this winter."

"How do you know about Billie and—" Joe cut himself off and shook his head. "Never mind. I know." *Small towns,* Joe thought. "Actually, I was thinking about trading. Do you have anything good on the lot?"

"We've got a nice midsize pickup coming in late on Monday; one owner, low mileage, four-wheel drive, well equipped, and clean. You could trade for less than five grand so long as your windshield is fixed. Did I mention that the pickup would be under warranty?"

"That sounds interesting, but I need to get some things worked out first."

"We'll check the pickup over and have it cleaned up so   ı can drive it home Monday after work."

"Do you have dealer financing?"

"Do you have equity?"

"Some, I've caught up on my payments if that helps."

"Art made big bucks, and I'd be surprised if they paid you any less. Here's how our credit plan works. Our business office will call Susan for a reference. If she says you're good for it, financing shouldn't be an issue."

A Shocking Patient

As daylight gave way to darkness, Joe went to his office. Even though the bad weather persisted, he eagerly waited for the first chance he could get to sneak into the tunnel. He climbed the ladder, turned on the snowman's lights, and sat shivering through the season's first arctic blast. A vicious north wind was shaking the snowman and caused an annoying echo to bounce around in the hollow fiberglass shell. The pounding reverberation gave Dr. Joe a headache. To make Joe's suffering worse, the cold and wind were keeping most people indoors. By nine o'clock, the snowman had not had so much as a single office call. Despite the cold, the snowman endured, and even though it was late, he would still see two patients, both of whom would shake him far more than the winter wind.

"What the F are you doing, Snowman?" a voice said. The voice carried a cold angry tone that stunned Joe for a moment. The intonation combined with the cold air to send a shiver down his spine. In his brief experience, no one had addressed the snowman in such crass terms. Joe was also quite certain that, in this case, he recognized the voice passing through the muffled speaker system. This voice belonged to Bobbi. Joe took a deep breath. "I was getting ready to close down for the evening," the snowman said.

"Pretty early to call it a night, isn't it?"

"You're right about that. How can I help you?"

Bobbi hesitated before answering. "Never mind. This is a mistake. I shouldn't have come."

"What makes this a mistake?"

"I can't talk to you."

"How come?"

"It's those blue eyes of yours, Snowman. They make me sick to my stomach. I hate them. Don't you ever shut them off?"

"No one has ever asked me to do that before, but I can shut them off." Joe turned off the snowman's eyes.

Bobbi's voice softened. "That's better, Snowman. I might come back and talk to you again sometime. But I won't talk unless you shut your eyes off."

"How will I know it's you?"

"You'll know my voice when you hear it. Good night."

"Wait—" The snowman had hopes of getting Bobbi to talk more, but she had already jogged off. *Why was her tone so cold, so angry... so detached? She sounds so very different than when in my office.* Joe was suddenly scared for her and for Billie. He turned the lights for the snowman's eyes back on. He looked at his wristwatch and began counting down minutes. *Another half an hour is about all I can take in this cold.*

Two minutes to go, and there's no one in sight. I'm going home. For the second time that evening, Joe was ready to call it a night. Then, at the last moment, someone emerged from the dark and stood in the yellow glow of Snowman's soft light. "Hi, Snowman. Listen to me," a soft voice said.

Joe recognized this tender voice from a prior session. Even if he was freezing, he could not turn a deaf ear on this patient. Joe sat back down on the little white stool inside the fiberglass snowman. "How are you this evening?"

"I'm scared, Snowman," the voice trembled.

"What are you scared of."

There was a long silence, and once again, the soft voice began to sing.

Jolly old St, Nicholas, Lean your ear this way!
Don't you tell a single soul, what I'm going to say;
Christmas Eve is coming soon; Now, you dear old man,
Whisper what you'll bring to me: Tell me if you can.

The song continued to puzzle Dr. Joe. He sat in silence, thinking.

Whoever was outside the snowman grew impatient waiting for an answer. "Are you there, Snowman? Can you tell me?"

"I'm sorry. I don't know what St. Nicholas will bring you."

"You think about it, and I'll come back. Maybe you can figure it out."

"I'll try."

"Thanks, Snowman. Good night."

Avoiding Dalton

The encounter with Dalton at the car dealership pushed Joe deeper into hiding. *I have no idea how to deal with that lunatic.* More and more, Joe found himself avoiding daylight activities. Going to Kelsey's was not an option because the pastor had taken up a menacing and controlling presence there of late. This he had done for the purposes of keeping Joe away from Billie and from any support he might muster at the table. Joe was also avoiding both Billie and Bobbi. Billie would take one look into his eyes and see that he was getting ready to leave town. She would also see that he was hiding something from her—hiding his worry for Bobbi. Stumbling into Bobbi would create a different problem. If he were to see her, he could never resist the temptation to try coaxing her back into therapy. Doing this would risk revealing the snowman's identity to yet another person. Monday passed, and the only reason Joe left his house was to go to work in the snowman.

On Tuesday, Joe called Susan and told her he wasn't coming into work. Late in the afternoon, he looked out his bedroom window and saw, to his relief, a heavy fog rolling off the lake. Fog was always accompanied by early darkness, and Joe was able to sneak through the damp, heavy air without bumping into anyone on his way to the snowman. He no more than sat down when Billie came by to talk with him. "Hi, this is Billie. You're avoiding me, and I want to know why."

"Billie, have you ever seen one of those he-should-have-told-her romance movies?"

"Only about a hundred of them. Why?"

"Because I don't want you and me to be in one of those movies. I need to be honest about some things."

"Things like you're planning to leave town?"

"What do you know about that?"

"Since your car is gone, I assume you're getting it ready for a road trip. Plus, I overheard Pastor Dalton talking about you at coffee this morning. His prediction is that you won't be here much longer."

"Dalton's a jerk. He's trying to force me out of town."

"How come?"

"He thinks I'm involved with his wife."

"Are you?"

"Of course not. All I did was help Debra with her posture at the piano. The preacher saw me touch her, and he's taking it out of context."

"I don't see how he can run you out of town with that. There's more to this story, isn't there, Joe?"

"Like I said, there are some things I need to tell you. Billie, the fact is, my license to practice psychology is on a probationary status, and Dalton knows it."

"How come you're on probation?"

"Because I was cited for an ethics violation."

"What kind of violation?"

"I kissed a married patient. Well, to be completely honest, I had an affair with her, and Dalton found out about it."

Billie thought matters through. "He's blackmailing you with my kiss, isn't he?"

Joe was stunned. "Did I hear that right? Your kiss?"

"Yes, Joe, my kiss. Bobbi and I were taking turns coming to ther-apy and didn't tell you."

"Oh man, I am such an idiot."

"What have I done, Joe? I'm so sorry." Billie started to cry.

"It's not your fault, Billie. I have a responsibility to know who I'm working with. I knew there were twins involved in the case when I started my work with Bobbi." Overcome with guilt, Billie ran off. Joe listened to her cry fade in the distance, and the sound burned into his heart like acid.

One crisis after another was pushing Joe deeper into despair. He tipped forward on the stool and leaned his forehead down against the snowman's cold hard stomach. "I can't go on like this."

"How come, Snowman?" a voice asked from the outside.

At first, Joe thought the fiberglass Snowman was actually talking to him, but then he realized that the two-way speaker was still on. He looked up, but the thick fog prevented him from seeing so much as even a silhouette. "Because I can't do anything right; that's why." Joe closed his eyes to think and hung his head in defeat.

"So you've had enough of my business, and you're ready to quit?"

"It's quit or be forced out."

"There's always another option. Can I give you some advice?"

Joe's gut reaction told him this was the original Snowman and he was talking to a comrade, not a competitor. "Why not?"

"Listen to the people. They always had the answers. They always will. If you listen to them, you'll know what to do."

Joe looked back up. "Who are you?" Joe asked. But whoever it was had left under cover of the dense fog.

Spiritual Guidance

B illie ran away from the snowman as Bobbi's voice darted in and out of her mind. *"You are so in love." "He's a gamble."* Suddenly, Billie was having a whole lot of second thoughts about Dr. Joe. *He kissed a married patient. He's always in trouble, and trouble always involves other women.* She wiped the crystalline flakes of frost off Joe's favorite bench and sat down to search her soul. *Okay, maybe I am in love with Joe, but I'm looking for a man I can marry.* Billie's head started to throb. *I need someplace to think, but where? St. Peter's complex... Father Riley is a good man. He can help.* Billie left the park and slipped into St. Peter's Church, where she took a seat in the back pew.

After fifteen minutes of utter silence in the dim candlelight, Billie saw Father Riley come limping down the aisle. "Billie Kelsey, you surprise me. The last time I checked, you were a member at Redeemer."

Billie smiled. "We don't cross the street very often around here, do we, Father?"

"Not when religion is involved."

"How's your leg doing?"

"The truth is that it hurts. The doctor wants to replace my knee after Christmas."

"I'm sorry to hear that, Father."

"So what brings you here at this hour, Billie? Love's passion?"

Billie sat forward in the pew and hung her head between her legs. "Or love's torment. I'm not sure which."

Father Riley gave Billie a gentle smile. "Granted, there are different ways of looking at things. Let's walk up front and sit where the light is better." Billie took hold of the old man's arm and helped him walk. "I never expected to walk down the aisle with you, Billie."

Billie laughed. "I'm sure you didn't, Father."

"Are you thinking about taking this walk with Dr. Joe?"

"Is it that obvious?"

Father Riley smiled and sat down in the front pew beside Billie. "That look on your face tells me we're going to be talking for a while. Let me guess; your heart says one thing, and your head says another."

"You just hit the nail on the head." Billie sat next to Father Riley and told him everything. She told him about Susan, about Joe's probation, about her kiss, about the piano lesson, about Dalton, and about the snowman.

Father Riley patiently listened late into the night until Billie was done venting. "I see your dilemma. Joe does push the limits."

"He's just too big of a risk, isn't he, Father?"

The kind old man's voice rose and became firm. "You'll have to make your own decision about that, Billie. But as I was saying earlier, there's more than one way to see things."

Billie laughed again. "You've been coming to coffee all these years, and I never realized how funny you are. There's more than one way to see Joe? This I want to hear."

"Dr. Joe is a talented young psychologist."

"He's talented all right—at finding trouble."

"Joe has been blessed with a special ear. He hears the voice of pain. It calls him, and he answers. It can be difficult learning to live with such blessings."

Billie heard a reverent seriousness in Father Riley's tone. She sat up straight and gave him her full attention. "The same kind of ear that brought you here at this time of night? The two of you are alike, aren't you, Father?"

Father Riley gently shook his cane and tapped it against his bad leg. "Yes, in some respects. But I'm getting old. We're blessed to have such young and sensitive ears living among us."

"You can say blessed. I can say cursed. Joe hears pain, but like I said, trouble finds him, and trouble brings women along with it. I don't know if I can live with that."

"Have you read Genesis?"

"Genesis? Yes, why?"

"Maybe you're Joe's helper. Lord knows a man like that needs somebody to keep him grounded."

Billie shunned the Father's point with a counterpoint. "Father, you're like Joe, and you're not married. Who keeps you grounded?"

"I'm married to the church. I don't think Joe's cut from that cloth. He spends too much time looking at your legs."

"And anything else he can get a peek at." Billie continued to fight emotion with reason. "My life would be a lot easier if he was married to the church like you."

"I'm not convinced of that. You fell in love with Joe the moment the good Lord dropped him at your feet, didn't you?"

Billie sat in silence fighting the truth.

"Am I right, Billie?"

"Yes," Billie admitted reluctantly.

"Imagine meeting Joe in my collar. Would you have loved him any less?"

Billie looked into the soft candlelight and contemplated the question in silence. She knew the answer to this question. It was no.

"Billie, you look exhausted. Why don't you spend the night with the Daughters of Rome? They'll look after you."

"Thanks, Father. I appreciate that."

Someone Takes a Risk

Billie came from spiritual retreat early Wednesday morning refreshed and empowered. The talk with Father Riley had helped her find a sense of clarity. She knew what she wanted, and she went to work wearing a smile. Meanwhile, Joe was still trying to sneak around Dalton's intimidating shadow. Without a clue about how to fight his way from the preacher's snare, he was inching nearer and nearer to complete resignation. Plus, the snowman's work had him mentally exhausted. *Is this what depression feels like? Oh, for a massage from Billie's supportive hands.*

By Wednesday night, it was all Joe could do to shuffle through the tunnel and climb the ladder, but his desire to help two particular patients pulled him into the snowman one more time. In Joe's mind, this would be his last night in disguise. He shivered as a mix of wind-driven snow and sleet pelted against the fiberglass shell. A shadow emerged, and Bobbi's intense anger cracked through the blustery night. It sped through the speakers and ricocheted inside the snowman. "F, Snowman, shut off those eyes."

Joe jumped at the command and shut off the deep blue lights in the snowman's eyes. This was anger steaming and ready to escape from its vessel if only he could find the words to help set it free. Joe carefully considered the advice he had been given. *Listen to the people.* He remembered his session with Bobbi. *Look for the patterns.*

Bobbi was annoyed by the snowman's silence. "F, Snowman. Are you going to talk to me or not?"

"Yes, I am. That word is important to you, isn't it?"

"What word."

"The 'f' word; you use it all the time."

"That is none of your business." Bobbi sat down on the park bench in front of the snowman.

The snowman would turn this talk into a battle of wills. Bobbi's legs stretched out in front of her. Her head fell forward and hung low to the ground. Her long hair brushed the snow-tinted grass, and the snowman heard a sniffle.

"F you, Snowman! Just F you!" Bobbi screamed out.

"There's that word again." The snowman heard Bobbi's sniffle turn to a sob, but she would not answer his probing question. The snowman pushed harder. "Why do you use the 'f'" word all the time?"

The snowman's aggressive questioning drove Bobbi to the point of explosion. She jerked her head up, looked at the snowman's face, and yelled. "Because, Snowman, that's what he did to me—not once but twice. There, Snowman, I told you. I hope you're happy." With her trauma revealed, Bobbi sat on the bench in front of the snowman, hanging her head low to the ground. Both angry and relieved, she sat in the cold night air where she cried and cried. Tears flowed until they melted circles in the new fallen snow.

The snowman waited for Bobbi to finish weeping. "Thank you for answering my question. That took courage. Who hurt you?"

Bobbi was afraid to say the name of her perpetrator. "You aren't stupid, Snowman. I've told you everything you need to know. Figure it out."

Dr. Joe's arms instinctively reached out to comfort Bobbi, but they could not break through the fiberglass barrier. Bobbi had taken a huge risk, and without supportive human touch, Joe was afraid that she might repress this pain forever. His clinical training told him that he needed to be more directive. "Make me a promise," Joe said.

"What kind of promise?"

"Promise me that you will share your secret."

Bobbi hesitated before answering and wondered what the snowman knew about secrets? "I need to think about that, Snowman. Good-bye."

The snow and sleet had stopped, and Joe listened as Bobbi's steps crunched down the sidewalk. He wiped a tear from his eye as he sat trapped inside the snowman contemplating Bobbi's victimization and her intense pain. His anger festered into rage. *But who am I angry at? Who violated her? When did it happen?* Joe's thoughts turned to Billie. *If Bobbi tells Billie about being raped, she'll go into shock. Both of them will need a lot of support.* Joe stayed in the snowman long enough to calm down, and then he closed for the night. He walked home and went to bed with a long list of questions on his mind. *What will St. Nick bring? Is it right to leave Bobbi alone in her pain? Will Bobbi tell Billie her secret? Should I tell Billie I'm leaving town?*

In Trouble Again

fter another sleepless night, Joe got out of bed at noon on Thursday with one more question on his mind. *Why did I leave my car in the shop?* He pulled himself out of bed and checked for messages on his cell phone. Billie had called twice just to say hi. She called a third time to say, "Give me a call." The messages gave Joe an idea. Not a good idea but an idea just the same. He called Billie at the restaurant. *She'll be glad to hear from me.* "Hi, Billie, could you sneak away and bring me some lunch? It would be great to see you."

"No, Dr. Doyle, I will not bring you lunch," Billie said with a sharp bite in her voice. "Where have you been the last two days?"

"The snowman keeps me busy."

"That's bull, and we both know it. The snowman only works at night."

"Okay, I should have called. I'm sorry."

Joe thought the apology would smooth things over, but Billie was just getting started. She knew what Joe was doing, and she expected better from *her* man. "Joe, you're hiding from the preacher, and I don't like it."

The sharp tongue-lashing surprised Joe. "Billie—"

"Look, Joe, I'm willing to help you with almost anything, but I'm not going help you hide out like a coward. Sitting on the bench is not like you, and I'm not going to be a part of it."

"Billie—"

"If you want lunch, if you want to see me, put on your skates, and slide the back half of your stinky breezers down here."

"Is the preacher there?"

"Come down here and find out for yourself."

Joe slumped around home for an hour or two, but with Billie having placed his pride at stake, he had to go to Kelsey's and see her. He paused outside the restaurant before entering. There was a new sign posted on the door, and he stalled by stopping to read it. "Thanksgiving Special - Senior Citizens - Half Price." Joe opened the door and looked toward the cash register. Billie was standing there ready to pounce on him the moment he stepped in the entryway. She raised her chin in stern greeting. "Hi. You look even worse than you sounded on the telephone. Sit down over there." Billie pointed to the table closest to the cash register.

Joe squirmed into a chair. "I'm tired."

"When was the last time you ate or came out in the light of day for that matter?"

"I don't remember. Things have been pretty crazy."

"I bet you didn't even know it was Thanksgiving, did you?"

"It is? What's to be thankful for?"

"Listen to me, Joe. What happened between us—that kiss—it wasn't your doing. I'll vouch for that."

"Thanks, Billie. I appreciate the gesture, but the matter goes beyond a kiss. It's about professional responsibility and competence.

I'm supposed to know who I'm working with, and I didn't even bother to ask."

"We—no, I took advantage of the situation. I didn't trust you when I asked Bobbi to play along with my therapy scheme."

"I figured as much. No one trusts me around here." Joe turned his eyes away from Billie.

"I'm sure that hurts, but look at me, Joe. Look in my eyes." Joe turned back toward Billie. "I'm sorry for doing that, but I trust you now. Did you hear me? I said *I trust you.*"

"Thanks."

"Let me tell you another thing. You trusted *us.* That's a good thing, not a bad one, and that's why *we* are in this mess. You have big heart, Dr. Doyle, and don't forget it."

"*I'm* in this mess because I get into relationships with my patients and because I'm playing behind that ridiculous Snowman."

"What are you talking about? You *are* the snowman."

"Come on, Billie. You and I both know that the real Dr. Joseph Doyle is not in the game. I'm a bigger fake than the snowman, whoever he is."

Billie was getting tired of Joe whining. In many respects, she understood Joe better than he understood himself. She knew Joe was capable of more right now, and it was time for her to let him know it. "Maybe you're right. Maybe you aren't in the game, but I'll tell you where you are, Dr. Doyle. You are stuck in self-pity."

Joe sipped his water and absorbed Billie's words while she continued to chew his butt. "You have to deal with the preacher. He is ruining your life. No, let me correct that. He is ruining *our* lives. And, Joe, I'm not going to sit back and watch it happen."

Joe looked down at the table in disappointment. "You're right, Billie, but I need an opening, a hole in the crease. I need a shot at that jerk."

Billie shook her head and slapped a ticket down for his Thanksgiving dinner. "Well, you aren't going to find the 'net' hiding in your house."

The Singing Patient

J oe left Kelsey's with a new insight. *A confrontation from someone you care about can be motivational.* He picked up the pace of his step and decided to stuff himself into the bowels of the snowman one more time. By eight o'clock, the snowman had talked with several people, and a brief lull in the action would have been nice. However, there would be no break for Joe, not tonight. "Hi, Snowman," the familiar voice said.

"Hello. I'm glad you came. Are you going to sing for me?"

"Yes, I am."

> Jolly old St, Nicholas, Lean your ear this way!
> Don't you tell a single soul, what I'm going to say;
> Christmas Eve is coming soon; Now, you dear old man,
> Whisper what you'll bring to me: Tell me if you can?

"I'm sorry. I still don't know what St. Nicholas is going to bring to you."

"I was hoping you would know by now, Snowman. I guess I'll go home, but thanks for trying."

Joe did not want to lose this patient, not now. "*Wait!* Can you sing other songs?"

"I could try, but I'd need to practice first."

"Okay. When will you come back?"

"Tomorrow night."

"Do you promise?"

"Yes."

Now Joe was committed to one more day as the snowman.

Pushing Back

The day after Billie's motivational speech, Joe went back to the original game plan. *I have to stay visible. Maybe I can make something happen. How does the snowman fit into this mess?* Joe jogged in the park and went to Kelsey's for morning coffee. Billie watched him enter. *She's got to be glad to see me today.* Joe was hoping for a warm smile and an "it's nice to see you." However, with Billie, things didn't always go as Joe expected. Billie raised her left eyebrow and put an unyielding look on her face. "The preacher's back there, Joe."

"I expected as much," Joe said, trying to project confidence.

Billie withheld any visible reaction until after Joe walked around the corner. Then, she tossed back her long brown hair and punched her fist toward the floor. *Yeah, go get him, Joe.*

Joe joined the others at the table and took a seat. "Hi, Joe, it's been a while," Judge said.

"You do come out in the daylight," Trapper said.

"We were talking about the festival, Joe ... until Pastor Dalton arrived," Art said.

"Actually, we were talking about how good the twins look in evening dresses," Tom said.

"Then Pastor Dalton launched into a never-ending lecture about the Virgin Mary. I feel like I'm back at seminary," Father Riley said.

Joe chuckled, and the others joined in. "I've noticed that the pastor finds pleasure in dominating things."

Dalton did not like being the subject of group ridicule, and he liked the challenge hidden in Dr. Joe's comment even less. His face oozed with contempt.

Joe ignored Dalton. "Art, is the manger built?"

"Not completely."

"What do we have to do yet?" With this statement, Joe was making it clear to Dalton that he was stepping out from the shadows.

"What's left on our list, Trapper?"

"Oh, there's plenty to do. The big jobs are to hang lights and move in the public address system from the courthouse."

"The pastor has to be heard," Joe chimed to make certain his intentions were clear. "What time are we starting?"

"Right now if we can pry Art out of his chair," Trapper said.

Joe stood up and left with Trapper. *I have no idea where that little poke at Dalton will take me, but it sure felt good.* Art took one last gulp of coffee and hurried along a few steps behind them.

Surprise Encounters

The men worked through lunch, and when they were finished, Joe went back to Kelsey's for an early supper. "I've been wondering if you would ever show your face around here when I'm working," Bobbi said.

"Hi, Bobbi. Have you got a seat?"

"Give me a minute, Joe. There's a waiting line."

"Sure." Joe turned and smiled at an older woman standing behind him.

The older woman smiled back. "I don't like having to wait for a seat." She scanned the visible seating options. There was one empty table, and that needed to be cleared. There was also an empty stool at the counter. "I hate eating alone."

"I don't like that either."

Bobbi came back to the small gathering of people standing by the door. Using her finger, she motioned for Joe to follow her. "You can sit at that table by the window, but there'll be a chill coming off it."

Joe hesitated before following Bobbi. "That's fine with me, but let me check with my date." Joe looked at the older woman and held out his arm as if to escort her. "Would you care to join me for dinner?"

"My, aren't you the charming one? I would love to."

"In that case, allow me to introduce myself. My name is Joe Doyle."

The woman took Joe's arm. "It's nice to meet you, Joe. My name is Ardis."

Bobbi led the couple to the table and wiped off the tabletop. "You can order from the menu if you like, but I would recommend the buffet. Salads, Swiss steak, ham, mashed potatoes, corn, beans, pie—it's really good."

Ardis looked at Joe. "Shall we take her recommendation?"

"It sounds good to me."

Bobbi filled out a ticket in her pad and tucked it back into her apron. Then she smiled and rushed off to seat other customers. Joe and Ardis stood up again, and Joe helped Ardis take off her coat. "That Bobbi, she is so nice, but her language can be frightful, you know," Ardis said.

"Is that so?" Joe motioned for Ardis to go through the buffet line first. After filling their plates, they returned to their table. Joe stood until Ardis was seated.

"Thank you," Ardis said, settling into her chair. "I'll bet you're the new psychologist I've been hearing so much about."

Joe nodded. "My reputation precedes me?"

"It's a small town. People enjoy talking."

"I've noticed."

"That's enough chitchat about small towns. I just love this table. My husband and I used to sit here and look out the window. Did they teach you anything about love in graduate school, Joe?"

"Very little."

"That's too bad. Love is a good thing to know."

"Actually, I think I'm learning a few things about love here in Dakota City."

Ardis laughed. "Heavens, Joe! What can a man with a PhD in psychology learn about love in a place like this?"

"You might be surprised."

"Oh my, now I'm curious. Tell me more."

"I think love is meeting one special person, a person who expects you to do your best."

"And you have met this special woman since moving to Dakota City?"

"I may have, Ardis."

"Are her parents nice?"

"I can't say for sure. I haven't met her mom yet."

Ardis gazed thoughtfully out the window for a moment.

"What are you thinking about?" Joe asked.

"I was just reminiscing about the night my husband asked my parents for permission to marry me. That meant a lot in those days."

Bobbi came back to check on her customers. "Excuse me. Do you need anything else?"

"No, we're fine," Joe said as Bobbi placed a small black tray with a ticket on it in front of him.

Ardis snatched up the ticket, ran her index finger down the numbers, and scrutinized the tabulation. "My, things are expensive these days." She took a little red coin purse out of her sweater pocket, counted out the exact change needed to pay for the meal, and placed it on the tray.

Joe pulled the tray away from Ardis and politely placed her money in front of her. "Please, allow me. You are my date."

"That's very nice of you." Ardis was getting tired and let out a long sigh. "Thanks for a wonderful time, but I should really be going."

"You're welcome."

"I do have some advice for you before I leave though, Joe. Make sure you meet this woman's parents, especially her mother."

"I'll keep that in mind." Ardis hurried off, and Joe stopped at the cash register to pay Bobbi.

"How was everything?" Bobbi asked.

"Great," Joe said, putting a nice tip into the tin can on the countertop.

Bobbi noticed the tip. "Thank you, Dr. Joe."

"You're welcome."

"Say, Joe?"

"Yes, Bobbi?"

"How did you like our mom?"

Joe gave Bobbi a disgusted look. "You're kidding me, right?"

Bobbi shook her head and laughed. "No, Joe. I'm serious. I hope you were polite."

New Song

After the leisurely supper with Ardis, Joe ran to get to the snowman on time. He was not about to miss an appointment with the singing patient. Joe no more than climbed into the snowman and turned on the lights when he heard a voice.

"Hi, Snowman. It's Billie."

"What are you doing here?"

The lack of enthusiasm in Joe's voice told Billie that she was not uppermost in the snowman's mind right now. "Some greeting I get."

"I'm sorry. I'm expecting a patient, and we have important things to discuss."

"And talking to me is not important?"

"Billie, you're the most important person in my life. I cherish every moment we spend together. I crave your massages. Now, will you tell me what you want and get out of here?"

"That wasn't very convincing."

"Billie—"

"I'm teasing, Joe. I stopped to see if you're still going to help me set up tables tomorrow afternoon?"

"Of course. What time do you want me there?"

"Let me think. We're closing right after lunch, and I need to change clothes. Will one thirty work?"

"I'll see you then.

"Good night, Snowman. I love you."

Billie's silhouette was still fading from Joe's mind when his eyes saw another, now familiar shadow emerge from the darkness.

"I have a new song, Snowman."

"Will you sing it for me?"

"Oh, yes, I want to sing it for you." The voice searched for the correct pitch and sang.

> Oh holy child of Bethlehem, descend on us we pray.
> Cast out our sin and enter in, be born in us today.

The singer caught her breath and asked, "Do you like my new song?"

Joe sat in silence thinking about what the snowman had told him. *Listen to the people. If you listen to them, you'll know what to do.* Joe racked his brain under the pressure of the moment. *What is she trying to tell me?* Suddenly, Joe's jaw dropped. He knew what the girl was saying, and now his heart ached for her.

"Snowman, are you there?"

"Yes. I'm sorry. I was thinking. Your song was very nice."

"Thank you."

"I think I know what St. Nicholas is going to bring you."

"You do?" the fidgeting silhouette asked.

"He's going to bring you a baby, isn't he?"

"Yes, Snowman. Can you help me?"

"Maybe. How old are you?"

"I'm fifteen."

"Does anyone else know you're pregnant?"

"No."

"Who's your baby's father—"

The fidgeting silhouette turned rigid. "No more questions for now, Snowman. I'm scared—really scared. Promise that you'll help me."

"I'll do my best, but I need to know your name."

"I'm too scared to say. Good night."

"Wait. You need to talk to Dr. Joe in the morning!" the snowman shouted. But there was no answer.

Festival Fever

O n festival Saturday, Dr. Joe awoke with improved spirits. *Billie's right. I am helping people. I may not be in the jersey I expected to wear, but when I'm the snowman, I make a difference.* Joe got out of bed and milled around Dakota City. By noon, the town was a flurry of last-minute activity as folks prepared for the evening's celebration. In the afternoon, Joe went to Kelsey's to help Billie set up tables and move chairs.

"Any developments with Dalton?" Billie asked as they were finishing the work.

"No." Joe put the last chair in place and smiled at Billie. "The place looks great. Everyone should have a wonderful time."

Billie nodded. "Thanks for the help. Joe, do you remember the day we met?"

Now why is she asking that? Joe wondered. He envisioned himself on the floor, and the sight of her legs flashed through his vivid imagination. "How could I forget?"

"Joe, I know how you think, and if you want to see my legs, tonight is your night. You're going to regret sitting in that stupid Snowman."

"Billie, *you're* the one who said the snowman has to work. And as much as I hate to say this, he's been doing some very important things."

"I was wrong. You should reconsider."

"I can come to the nativity scene before I sneak off."

"I won't have my dress on until after the potluck."

"How come you dress so late?"

"Dinner is always a mess. We dress later … after we've cleaned up and the moms take the kids home to be with sitters."

"That sounds complicated. Maybe I can come to the dance later."

"I'll say it one more time. You're going to regret not being there." Billie let her hair out of her customary ponytail and gave it a flirtatious toss.

Joe closed his eyes for a moment. The provocative motion of Billie's flirtatious flip; the beautiful, long brown hair; and Billie's lovely face were punishing. "I'm sure I will," he said.

Seeing Joe's agony, Billie stood on her toes and gave him a quick kiss. "Thanks for the help." Joe paused while he savored the flavor of Billie's lips.

On the way home, Joe stopped at the grocery store to pick up a newspaper. He sat down at his kitchen table, read the sports page, and turned back to scan the headline news. *Boring.* After folding the paper in half, he flopped it down on an ever-growing pile of junk mail. *Maybe I can catch a nap before going to the nativity scene.* He crashed out on the couch and had just closed his eyes when the doorbell rang. Joe answered the door, and after his eyes adjusted to the bright sunlight, they nearly popped out. There was Debra in her purple dress, holding a small plate of cookies.

"Hi, Joe. Do you like my dress?" That said, Debra tossed out her arms and turned up the palms of her hands to draw attention to the purple dress. Then, she gently pushed out her right hip to draw attention to the entire package.

"Wow, is that you, Debra?"

"Let's call it dress rehearsal for tonight. What do you think?"

"Debra, I have to say, you surprise me. You look very nice. The pastor will love you in that outfit."

"I've never worn anything like it before, so I expect to get a reaction from him. Wearing it is kind of a—no, wearing it *is* a breakout moment for me."

Debra held out the plate of cookies. "Here, these are for you. Thanks for the piano lesson," she said. Joe took the cookies and stepped into the kitchen. Debra followed close behind. Joe turned his back so he could set the cookies on the countertop. Meanwhile, Debra closed in tight from behind. When Joe turned to face her again, he discovered that he was trapped. Now they now stood face-to-face, Joe with his back against the counter.

"Do you really think I look nice?"

"Debra, I don't—"

By now Debra had slid her hands up Joe's hips and was gently rubbing her index finger over the black lettering on his bright red hockey jersey.

"Debra, what are you doing? I mean, I know what you are doing. Stop it!"

"Joe, the way you touched me at the piano, it was so nice, so gentle and yet so strong. I liked it."

"Debra—" Joe could tell that Debra would not be easily dissuaded. She had already crossed every line on the ice. He pushed her away at the shoulders with both hands and held her firmly at arm's length. "Debra, this isn't right, and you know it. Stop it now."

Debra ignored him, turned her head toward her own shoulder, and started to kiss Joe's fingers.

Joe pushed back harder in an effort to hold her away. Still with both arms on Debra's shoulders, he firmly shook her in hopes that she would come to her senses. "Knock this off, Debra. You've already done things you'll regret."

Being physically shaken and rejected by Joe reminded Debra of life with Dalton. She started to cry. "You're no different than he is."

"Not different than who? What are you talking about?"

Debra was awash in tears and overrun with emotion. "I'm not good enough for him, and I'm not good enough for you, am I, Joe?" Deflated and in her purple dress, Debra dashed across the kitchen and out the door, realizing she had allowed Dalton to drive her to an embarrassing act of desperation.

Joe, still paralyzed by Debra's advance, watched her run out of the kitchen. As she bolted through the door, she tripped going down the outdoor steps. Falling hard and fast, she twisted her ankle, screamed, and smacked onto the ground. Joe ran to the door only to see Debra lying in her beautiful purple dress, holding her ankle in pain, and rolling in a mix of snow, grass, and brown leaves. He rushed out to help her. Stepping behind her, he gently lifted her up and brushed the debris from her dirty face with his fingers. "Are you okay?"

"No, Dr. Joe, I am not okay." Debra hopped around to face Joe and huddled against him in a supportive embrace. "I'm sorry for what just happened, Joe."

Just then, Pastor Dalton stepped around the corner of the house. He scowled at Joe. "Adulterer, you will burn in hell." Dalton looked at Debra. "The purple prostitute has come. Get home where you belong." Dalton turned and gave Joe a fiery stare. "Doyle, you can be thankful it's a weekend. Come Monday morning that ethics committee will see to it that you're finished."

Debra hobbled toward their house. Dalton caught up with her, grabbed her by the upper arm, and jerked her along. The sight of Debra defiantly wearing a tight purple cocktail dress had sent him into another rage. Seeing her in Joe's arms thrust him into insanity. Dalton dragged Debra into their bedroom and closed the door. There, he lost all touch with reality and escaped somewhere into the book of Revelations. "The Red Beast comes, and he carries the Purple Prostitute. You'll be damned for this, wife." Crazed with anger, he grabbed Debra and tore the purple dress off her. He ripped it to shreds and threw it on the floor. Then Dalton seized his wife again, threw her over his knees, and beat her severely. Debra screamed in hopes that Dr. Joe would hear her plea. "Please, somebody, help me!"

On Very Thin Ice

*D*alton's eyes were spitting the flames of hell. *I may not be safe here right now.* Thinking it wise to put some distance between himself and the enraged pastor while things calmed down, Joe sought the tranquility of his favorite bench by the lake. First, he looked across the frozen sheet of ice, and then he looked at his wristwatch. *The nativity scene starts in an hour.*

Billie, who was scurrying about taking care of last-minute details in the restaurant, saw Joe from the front window. His body posture told her that something was terribly wrong. She went to check on him. "You're upset. Is it the preacher?"

"Yes, and now it's Debra too. She just came over to my house wearing a hot purple dress and tried to seduce me."

"Are you serious?"

"I've never been more serious in my life. I had to push her off me. She ran out of my house, tripped on the back steps, and hurt her ankle."

"Oh my gosh."

Joe skipped the details and jumped to his own defense. "I was only helping her get off the ground; I swear. She hugged me and apologized for making the advance. About that time, Dalton came around the corner. I'm sure what he saw didn't look good. This game is over, Billie. Dalton is reporting me to the ethics committee Monday morning."

Billie had not sworn for several days, but the ominous tone in Joe's voice scared her. "Damn it, Joe, don't you give up."

"Give me some space, Billie. I need to think." Joe stood and stared at the thin sheet of ice covering the lake.

"There's got to be something I can do. I want to help."

Joe stepped toward the lake. "Watch while I walk on the ice. Call for help if I fall through."

"Joe, you're scaring me. Stop it."

"Please, Billie, stay here and watch. I know it sounds stupid, but that's what I need you to do."

Billie plopped down on the park bench in resignation. "Go, Joe. Just go."

Joe stepped onto the perilous ice. He needed an idea, and he needed it fast.

The Festival

Inflicting the severe beating upon Debra calmed Dalton's rage, but the pastor's mind remained lost. And it would not return to reason. "I have to go to the festival, you worthless Jezebel." Dalton pointed to the shredded dress that lay on the floor. "Get the devil's cloth from our bedroom." He put on his suit coat and stomped off to the park. Tonight, it was Dalton's job to inspire the community and introduce the arrival of the holy family at the nativity scene.

Christmas lights decorated the entire town, and a thin blanket of white fluffy snow covered the park. The stage was set, the manger lit, and a crowd waited for the cast of players to arrive. The animals and actors were hidden on the opposite side of the courthouse where they waited for Dalton's entrance cue. As Dalton stepped to the podium and turned on the microphone, Trapper turned on the flood lights, drawing everyone's attention to the deranged pastor. "If I could have your attention please, our program is about to begin," Dalton said. He waved his arms apart as if he were Moses parting the Red Sea. Everyone understood what Dalton wanted, and the people split into two long lines extending out from the manager so the cast could parade through a tunnel of spectators. Art, Ardis, Susan, Billie, Dr. Joe, and Tom stood in line together.

"Where's Bobbi?" Art asked.

"She said she's feeling a bit under the weather, but I'll bet she's saving energy for the dance," Billie said.

From his elevated position on the podium, Pastor Dalton passed around paper handouts with the words of a Christmas carol written on it. He waited for the handout to circulate, and then his voice blasted through the loudspeaker system. "Welcome, friends and fellow Christians. Let's begin by singing the first and third verses of 'Oh Little Town of Bethlehem.'" Filled with a crazed sense of zeal, the pastor burst forth in song.

> O little town of Bethlehem! How still we see thee lie;
> Above thy deep and dreamless sleep, the silent stars go by;
> Yet in thy dark streets shineth the everlasting Light;
> The hopes and fears of all the years are met in thee tonight.

At the start of the third verse, Pastor Dalton grew even more zealous. He waved his hands high, encouraging the crowd to sing louder. This was the cue for the cast to parade in. As the procession moved slowly through the lines of people, Dalton rejoined the song. Joe watched. *He's a fanatic.*

> O holy Child of Bethlehem! Descend to us we pray;
> Cast out our sin and enter in, be born in us today,
> We hear the Christmas angels, the great glad tidings tell;
> Oh come to us, abide with us, our Lord Emmanuel.

When Joe heard the words 'O holy Child of Bethlehem!' they exploded in his ears. He grew acutely aware of Bobbi's absence. He looked back at Dalton. His deep blue eyes glowed like beacons through the flood lights. He reheard the sessions with Bobbi and the snowman. "*Shut those ugly eyes off. You aren't stupid, Snowman. Figure it out.*" Joe looked at the processional. Three shepherds herded four sheep. A fourth pulled an old milk cow by its harness. Next, Joseph led a donkey on a rope, and on the donkey sat young Laura Walter. Joe looked back at Dalton. A perverted pleasure radiated from his eyes toward Laura. Suddenly, Joe was sick to his stomach. *Laura has to be my singing patient, and Dalton is her baby's father.*

Dr. Joe broke into a sweat, and his mind swelled with anger. "That sick SOB." A compassionate rage came into Joe's eyes, a rage that matched the evil insanity dwelling in Dalton's eyes. The fresh falling snow quickly melted as it fell against Joe's brow.

Art raised his voice over the singing. "What did Joe say?" he asked Billie.

Billie repeated Joe's remark and shook her head. "But don't ask me what he meant by it."

Restless and uneasy, as if standing behind the gate and waiting to step on the ice before the biggest game of his life, Joe thought, *Do this right.* Of course, in Joe's mind, the by-the-book approach was not necessarily the right way. Like a flash, Joe changed positions and went to stand by Sheriff Tom. "Watch my hands *and* the preacher's hair, Sheriff. Did you hear me, Tom? I'm dead serious. When I give you his hair, preserve the chain of custody."

"What are you talking about?" Tom asked in confusion.

"Don't let the preacher's hair out of your sight. If I'm right, you'll need it for DNA testing."

Adrenaline was surging through Joe's body, his heart pounded. Feverish and with his arms at his side, Joe clinched his fists. He shook them, struggling to relax, and then clinched them again. Taking a deep breath, he stared at Dalton's face and zeroed in on Dalton's nose as if aiming Trapper's rifle. *I don't know how Billie's going to take this.* Joe looked over his shoulder toward Billie and yelled, "I'm taking my shot." With that said, Joe sprang out of the crowd, crashed into Dalton, and plastered him against the manger boards. Joe quickly backed off just enough to punch the shocked preacher. Landing a right hook and catching Dalton's nose and left eye, he followed with a jab to the right eye. Then, he let loose with a low uppercut into Dalton's groin. The pastor rose in the air and fell to the ground without so much as ever raising a fist. "Take that collar off. You degrade it," Joe growled.

Dalton squirmed on the ground, mumbling through bloody lips. "How did you figure it out, beast?"

Fueled by his repulsion, Joe shook his head, leaned over, and jerked out a handful of Dalton's hair. He turned toward Tom, whose large hand already had him by the shoulder. "Here's the hair, Sheriff. Preserve it as evidence in case he gets out of town before this is over." Joe knew what came next, so he quickly wiped Dalton's blood off of his knuckles and onto his blue jeans. He sighed at Tom and put his face toward the manger wall. Hands behind his back, he said, "Okay, Tom, do your thing."

"I see you know the routine, Dr. Joe."

"Save the comments, Tom—and the hair. You're going to need it to charge the preacher."

"Charge the preacher! In case you missed something, Joe, you just assaulted a minster singing a Christmas carol. On top of that, you did it in front of the entire town. I'm taking you in."

$\mathcal{D}$esperation $\mathcal{T}$urns to $\mathcal{D}$oom

Devastated and badly beaten, Debra was in desperate need of someone to talk to, so she weighed her sources of support. Had Millie been alive, she might have gone to her. Billie may have lent a compassionate ear, but after the incident with Joe, she was too embarrassed to seek her out. Through her deliberations, Debra came to the conclusion that she was all alone. There was no one for her to talk to—except for the snowman.

Debra eased her aching body out of bed and stood up in front of their full-length mirror to get dressed. She looked at her throbbing backside in the mirror and grimaced. It was already turning a mottled mess of horrid colors. Blotches of purple, blue, green, and red formed on her delicate flesh. Feeling the need to escape her own home, she put a bathrobe on over her battered body and covered the robe with a heavy parka. Searching out her boots, she was intent on talking with the snowman. *"Stay away from that pagan idol, wife,"*

Dalton's voice reverberated in her mind. Wincing through the pain, Debra pulled the black snow boot on over her swollen ankle. She would ignore Dalton's controlling voice and limp to the snowman as fast as she could. But when she got to his side, something was wrong. Her only hope for a friendly ear was not lit up. In the cold night air and standing all alone by the empty fiberglass shell, Debra's body hurt all the more. Her crushed heart fell to her feet.

But Debra needed to talk. She limped closer to the snowman and looked into his dark eyes. New snow clung like heavy tears to his cheeks as if he felt Debra's pain in the dark. "Yes, Snowman, it hurts. It really hurts." Sobbing, Debra turned her back on the snowman. "Where are you when I need you?" She looked all around and in the direction of the crowd. There was no one near. From a distance, she could see that everyone's attention was on the nativity scene. Debra raised her clothing, revealing her battered legs and buttocks to the snowman. "Can you see, Snowman? Can you see what he did to me?" She paused, hoping for supportive acknowledgment, but there was no answer. "I guess you can't," Debra said with resignation. She let the parka fall. In her mind, she had no place to go but home.

When Dalton returned home from the festival, he discovered Debra lying in bed, dazed, and still wearing her parka. "Where have you been, worthless Jezebel?"

"I stepped out for some fresh air."

"I know you. You've been to that pagan idol to cry at his side and spite me. Haven't I warned you of that? Didn't you learn from my hand?" Dalton's eyes filled with wrath, and his bloody face turned flush. A bulge formed in his black polyester pants.

Debra saw his rising excitement, and fear petrified her so much so that she could not speak. She lay on the bed trembling before Dalton. She loathed the thought of his touch but did not have the strength or the courage to resist him. Dalton closed in. He struck

Debra across the face and yelled, "Jezebel, you will know great pain!" Striking her again with all the force his sick anger could deliver, he forced himself on her. Dalton pushed up her housecoat and violently raped her. Having found sick pleasure in doing so, he shoved his wife aside and got out of bed. "A right punishment for your sins," he snarled.

In Jail

Tom drove Dr. Joe straight to jail without saying a word. He finally spoke just before leaving Joe's cell. "Let me get those handcuffs off, Joe." Dr. Joe held out his hands while Tom's giant fingers fumbled with the lock and key. Then Tom left Joe so both of them could cool down before questioning.

Alone in the cell, Joe thought of Billie. He could use some support right now. *Oh, what I would give for one of her massages.* Joe studied the sterile stainless steel, the thin plastic mattress, and the tight confines of the cell. *What if I'm wrong about Dalton?*

In a few moments, Tom returned with a cup of coffee. "What in blazes was that all about, Joe? Have you lost your mind?"

Joe told his side of story, the whole story from its beginning in Minnesota through his attack on Dalton. Tom listened to the entire story without interrupting. When Joe was finished, he said, "That's quite a story, Joe. I'll have to check it out."

"Have you got the hair, Tom?" Joe asked.

"Yes, Joe, I have the hair."

"Don't let him slip out of town."

"I have to get a statement from Laura before I can bring him in. You remember our talk about accusations, don't you?"

"So what happens to me in the meantime?"

"You'll be staying right here. If your story checks out, I'll let you out. If not, you're going to be locked up for a while. If I were you, I'd plan on spending the night."

"Spend the night!" The thought was more than Joe could bear. Even the mere minutes that Tom had left him alone in the cell passed like weeks. Depleted of all emotional and physical strength, Joe started to shiver. He needed food, but he longed for the energy—no, for the passion that flowed from Billie's tender lips. *But why would she share her life with me? I'm always in trouble.* Joe protested. "Tom—"

Having heard Joe's side of the story and his plea for release, Tom empathized. "Maybe, and I stress maybe, I can have you out of here an hour or two after lunch tomorrow."

"Sheriff—"

"Look, Joe, if Dalton is as sick as you say, you'll be safer in here. Who knows what a crazed man like that will do?"

While Tom questioned Joe, Art was doing his best to console Billie in the restaurant. All of the tables were full, so they found an out-of-the-way place where Art could eat his potluck dinner from a plate on his lap. Billie couldn't eat. "Do you have any idea what set Joe off like that?" Art asked.

"This is a nightmare, Uncle Art. The preacher thinks that Joe is having an affair with Debra."

"I thought Joe was torn between you and Susan."

Billie nodded her head. "Joe and I are together, but everything is a big mess. Somehow Dalton found out about Joe's probationary status and has been using that information to threaten him ever since he saw me kissing Joe during one of our therapy sessions."

Billie got a sheepish look on her face and glanced down at Art's dinner plate.

This information brought Art straight up in his chair. "Joe was kissing you in a session? That dirty—"

Billie nodded. "No, Uncle Art, I kissed him, but he thought I was Bobbi."

"What on earth have you girls been doing?"

"We pulled the switch trick on him. I wanted to spend more time with Joe. You know, to find out if I liked him. I talked Bobbi into signing up for therapy so she could work on her swearing problem. She went to one session, and I went to the next."

Art couldn't believe his ears. Collapsing way down in his chair, arms hanging at his side and legs outstretched, he said, "Billie, you didn't..."

"That was before I knew about his past, Uncle Art."

"So Dalton was threatening Joe ... that probably explains why Joe beat the daylights out of him at the manger."

"I'm not sure about that. Joe might have learned something when he was the snowman."

Art's jaw fell. "When he was what?"

"Joe has been filling in as the snowman."

"Wow!" Art wiped his damp forehead with his shirt sleeve.

"I feel terrible, Uncle Art. I've been encouraging Joe to be a man and stand up to Dalton. You have to help him. There must be something you can do."

"I'll see, but if I know Tom, he'll take his sweet time sorting this mess out."

"But it's festival—"

"Why don't I take you home so you can put on that dress I've been hearing so much about?"

"I'm in no mood for a dance, not with Joe in jail." Billie dried her tears and dabbed her nose with a tissue.

At the Dance

A rt took Billie home, and while she changed into her dress, he updated Ardis on the night's events. Forty minutes later, Billie made her entrance into the living room. "That's a knockout dress, Billie," Art said.

Billie shrugged. "It'll have to do." She turned so her mother could get a better look. "My face is a wreck."

"Two hours of crying will do that," Ardis said. Mother looked intently at daughter. "You love Joe, don't you, Billie?"

Billie started crying again. She nodded her head and choked out the answer. "Yes."

Ardis gave Billie a stern look. "He's a good man. This is no time to give up on him."

Billie hugged her mom. "Thanks." Art took Billie's arm, and the three of them went to the dance. "I'm really not in the mood for this," Billie said as they walked in the front door of Kelsey's. She paused by the cash register, and her tears started to flow again.

"What's wrong now?" Art asked.

"This is where I first met Joe, Uncle Art—right here." Billie pointed to the floor where Joe had fallen.

Art looked at Ardis and smiled. "I remember that, Billie. He took one look at you and fell like a rock." Art tried to pull Billie from the entryway and into the main dining hall. Billie resisted his lead.

"Uncle Art, I can't do this. I'm going to find Bobbi and see if she'll manage things here for the night. After that, can you take me back home?"

"If you are sure that's what you want."

When Billie entered the main dining hall, a hush fell over the crowd. Since everyone was expecting Dr. Joe to be her date and he was in jail, it was no surprise that Billie was the sole center of attention. "This is embarrassing. Help me find Bobbi so I can get out of here." Billie pulled Art along arm in arm through the crowd, pausing to ask only one question, "Where's Bobbi?"

They had just about circled all the way back to the doorway by the cash register when Susan rushed up to Billie. Tonight, Susan was a complete contradiction. Wearing a gorgeous slack outfit she had made, Susan was an astonishing statement of feminine appeal. However, being Trapper's daughter and under the influence of alcohol, she was also more than a little rough around the edges. Susan took a firm grip on Billie's upper arm. "Billie, come with me." Susan tried to pull Billie away from Art. "Oh, and Billie, that's a great dress. You look ready to skin and prime to stretch."

Susan's unusual compliment forced a smile out of Billie. "How many drinks have you had, Susan?"

Susan held up a highball. "Only three." She put down her glass and took on a serious tone of voice. "You and I need to get to the kitchen." Susan pulled harder on Billie's arm. Returning to a more casual tone of voice as she tugged Billie along, she said, "You sure did a nice job of decorating this place, and what a great street fight. I never got to see one in high school. Joe was great."

"Have you seen Bobbi?"

"That's why I'm taking you to the kitchen. Bobbi is in there. She came in here about half an hour ago looking like a road-kill coyote—gray sweat pants, torn T-shirt, hair down, no makeup, and crying her eyes out. I've been back there holding her hand and drinking rum." Art clung tight to Billie.

Normally, Billie would laugh at Susan's graphic way of saying things. But tonight, she was upset. Joe was in jail, and something was bothering her sister. "What's wrong? Did she say?"

Susan's casual mood changed with Billie's serious tone. "I'm not sure. She said she wants to tell you a secret."

This statement got Billie's full attention. If Bobbi wanted to tell a secret, this was serious. Billie knew this was no place for a man, especially not her uncle. "Excuse us, Uncle Art." Art immediately understood and let go of Billie's arm. "Let's go, Susan."

The ladies rushed to a back corner in the kitchen, where Bobbi sat crying on the brown tile floor surrounded by stainless steel appliances. "Here she is, Bobbi. I'll leave you two alone now."

Bobbi knew that the upcoming talk was going to be as hard on Billie as it would be on her. She wanted Susan there for support. "No, Susan, please stay. I want you to hear this. I'm tired of hiding."

Billie reached down and took Bobbi's ice-cold hands. "What's wrong?"

"The snowman said I should tell you my secret. And it's not going to be easy."

"The snowman knows your secret?"

"I told him part of it, but not all of it." Bobbi told Billie and Susan about the two rapes she had suffered at the hands of a then, much younger, Pastor Dalton.

Billie could not believe that Bobbi had kept this a secret. "Why didn't you tell me?"

"You met with Dalton right after I did, remember? He choked me and said it was me or you."

Billie covered her mouth, shocked by what her sister had endured to protect her. "Bobbi, I'm so sorry—"

Susan gently put her hand over Billie's mouth before she could say any more. Desperate to support Bobbi, Billie got an annoyed look on her face and started to push Susan's hand away. Susan quickly cut into the conversation. "You too?" she said with receptionist assertiveness. Susan took her hand from Billie's mouth and sat down on the cold tile floor next to Bobbi. The two women held each other tight momentarily and then slid over. Billie huddled in between them and put one arm around Bobbi and the other around Susan.

Bobbi and Susan talked and talked. "He took a picture of me," Bobbi said.

"I'm glad you didn't get pregnant like me," Susan said.

Meanwhile, Billie cried for both of them, and finally Bobbi gave Billie a soft smile. "I heard Joe was really awesome tonight."

The Ladies Go to Jail

It was well after eleven o'clock when the women came out of the kitchen. Billie hurried through the dance crowd looking for Art. "We're going to the jail, Uncle Art. Will you come along? If Tom's difficult, I might need your help."

Five minutes later Billie, Bobbi, Susan, and Art were at the courthouse knocking on the door to the sheriff's office. Art gently pushed the door open, and Tom motioned them in. He was talking to the state highway patrol. "Look, if these allegations prove to be true, I don't want Dalton getting away. You cover the roads out of town, and I'll bring him in for questioning. If you get here before I pick him up, that's all the better." Tom hung up the phone. He looked at Art and rolled his eyes. "It's been a tough night, Art."

As of yet, the sheriff had failed to acknowledge the ladies. Art extended his arm and motioned in their direction to draw Tom's attention their way. "Sheriff, they all need to talk with you."

Tom assumed that Billie had brought her entourage to rescue Joe. "Ladies, if you have something to say, make it quick."

"Sheriff, I need to report child abuse," Bobbi said.

"Me too," said Susan.

"Who was abused?"

"We were," Bobbi said.

Tom paused for a moment to think. "May I assume this was at the hands of Dalton?"

"Yes," Bobbi said.

"Ladies, I don't mean to put you off, but I need to get down to the Walters' house on an emergency."

Billie looked at Tom and sadly shook her head. "Little Laura too?"

Tom looked at Billie and then at Art. "I'm afraid so." He looked back at Susan and Bobbi. "Can I ask that the two of you please wait? Laura is a minor. After seeing Joe beat up Dalton, she's bound to be pretty darn scared."

"Has she made a statement?" Art asked.

"No, but from the sounds of things, Dr. Joe has put together the pieces of a pretty ugly jigsaw puzzle. Couple that with what the ladies are telling me, and I think I know where this is going."

Billie had done her best to say as little as possible throughout the conversation. Tom looked at her. "You too, Billie?"

"No, I'm here to see Joe, and I'm not leaving until I do."

No longer having much doubt about Dalton's guilt, Tom was willing to let Billie visit Joe. He glanced in Art's direction and raised his right eyebrow. "I'll let you in, if you promise not to get lipstick on the visitation glass."

Billie was annoyed by the sheriff's teasing her at a time like this. "The price of coffee can go up really fast, Tom."

Tom pushed the bill of his cap up and called the night jailer. "Take Billie back to see Joe." Billie left with the jailer. Tom looked at the large round clock hanging on the wall. "Look, folks, time is wasting. I need to visit with Laura, and then I suspect I'll need to deal with Dalton."

A Crucial Statement

As Tom walked out of the courthouse, he heard the sound of a single, muffled ring from the funeral bell hanging in the Redeemer Church. He assumed it was Dalton who had made the noise, but why he would ring the bell at this time of night was anybody's guess. Tom got in his SUV and drove to the Walters' home. He knocked on the door, and Laura's mom let him in. "What's wrong?" Mrs. Walter asked.

"Can I visit with Laura?"

Sheriff Tom, Laura, and her parents sat the kitchen table while Tom softly questioned the teenage girl. "Laura did you tell the snowman that you're pregnant?"

"Yes," Laura said, putting her head down.

"Is that true?"

"Yes."

"How do you know?"

"I've taken three home tests."

"Where did you get the tests?" Laura's mom asked.

"I stole them from the grocery store. Is that why you're here, Sheriff? To take me to jail like that Dr. Joe guy?"

"No, Laura, I'm not taking you to jail. Did you ask the snowman to help you?"

"Yes. Did the snowman send you?"

"Yes, he did, Laura."

"Good," Laura said. "I thought he would help."

"Laura, this is a very important question. Who is your baby's father?"

Laura looked nervously at both her parents and hummed for a moment. "Laura, it's important that you tell us," her mother said.

Laura hung her head. "Pastor Dalton. He's not a very nice man." Laura's mom sat in shock.

Her dad stood up and started swearing. "Have you got him in jail?"

"I can understand you being upset, but no, I haven't picked him up yet. I needed to confirm all of this with Laura first."

Laura looked at Tom. "The snowman figured everything out, didn't he?" Laura asked.

"Yes, with help from Dr. Joe."

"I didn't know Dr. Joe until he beat up Pastor Dalton tonight. If he helped the snowman, I'm glad."

"Laura, would you be willing to take blood tests to help us stop the pastor from hurting other girls?"

"Yes, Sheriff. Can I go to bed now? I'm really tired."

"Yes, Laura, you can go, but I might need to talk to you again tomorrow."

The End of Times

After raping Debra, Dalton ordered her to get out of bed and fix him something to eat. She used the opportunity to sneak out the back door and escape to the church. Dalton saw her leave and simply waved off her departure with both hands. Debra's destination was the church kitchen, and there she took a piece of cutlery from a drawer. With knife in hand, she walked through the dark church and made her way to the bell rope closet. She opened the long narrow closet door and slowly pulled down on the thinner of two ropes. Pulling low with one arm and reaching high with the other, knife in hand, she cut off eight to nine feet of rope. When the rope severed, it released the funeral bell that Tom heard ring just before going to the Walters' home. Debra coiled the rope around her left arm and went to the choir loft. There, she looked for something to stand on. The piano bench would work. She slid the bench next to the loft railing; it would serve as a platform from which to jump.

Debra tied one end of the rope around her neck, kneeled on the bench, and tied the loose end of the rope around the sturdy golden oak rail. Now, she stood, wobbling, only inches away from the balcony edge. With one small jump, she could bring an end to her lone-liness and pain. She could free herself from Dalton's control. Debra sighed. She looked at the perpetual candle glowing to the side of the sermon pulpit and listened one last time for a friendly voice in the dimly lit church. Hearing nothing and without any support, she'd had enough. This was one thing she could control. Debra placed her hands on her womb and bent at the knees in preparation to jump. As she bent, her stomach squeezed gently against her hands, and she felt a spark of life coming from deep within. *I'm going to have a baby.* Debra teetered in prolonged contemplation and, taking the first step toward healing, eased herself down from the bench.

The jailer let Billie in to talk with Joe. She eased up to the visitation window and tapped on the glass to get Joe's attention. Joe got off of the bed and forced a small smile as he walked to the visitation window. Billie turned slowly around one time so Joe could see her new dress. The lace skirt rose slightly and floated back down. "You're lovely," Joe said. "The dress is nice too."

Billie wiped a tear and simply tipped her head to acknowledge the compliment. She looked at Joe's eyes through the safety glass and saw a faraway look. She had seen this look before. It was the same cloudy haze that filled his eyes when he talked of leaving town. "Bobbi told me her secret. You helped her, Joe."

"Good. How's she doing?"

"She and Susan are talking things out, sharing the things they have in common."

Joe shook his head in disgusted surprise. "Are you telling me Dalton was Tony's father?"

"Yes. I never thought I would say this to a man behind bars, but Dr. Joseph Doyle, I am so proud of you."

"Thanks. No one has said that to me in a very long time."

"Joe, I know that look in your eyes. You're planning to leave, aren't you?"

"This game is over, Billie. Who knows what kind of damage Dalton has already done."

"We can fight that now. You've got an opening."

"It's more than just Dalton, Billie. The people here don't trust me, and I've blown the snowman's cover. I can't imagine how angry they are about that. What's left?"

"Me, Joe. I'm left."

"You've got Bobbi and the restaurant to look after. There's nothing for me to do here."

Billie pleaded, "Joe—"

Joe did not want to discuss their future from a jail cell, so he changed the subject. "What about Dalton? Has Tom brought him in yet?"

"No, he's getting a statement from Laura first. Then he plans on going to the parson—" Billie stopped speaking and covered her mouth with one hand.

"What's wrong, Billie?"

"Debra—that's what's wrong. She bought Bobbi's dress so she could wear it to the festival."

"We've talked about that, remember? She got it dirty after throwing herself at me."

"She was so proud of that dress. She would've cleaned it up and snuck down to the dance."

"Dang." Joe hit himself on the forehead. "Let me guess; nobody's seen her all night?"

"I was in the kitchen most of the time, but I never heard a word about her."

"Trust me. If Debra had shown up in that dress, people would have been talking. Find Tom, Billie, and do it now."

Billie ran from Joe's cell and stuck her head out the front door of the courthouse in hopes of seeing the sheriff, but he was still at the

Walters' home with Laura. Billie ran back inside and asked the jai
to call Tom.

"Now what?" Tom asked the jailer in frustration.

"Dr. Joe and Billie are afraid that Debra is in trouble."

Tom remembered hearing the funeral bell. He turned on the
emergency lights. "I'm on my way. Oh, tell Billie that visitation
hours are over. I don't want to set any more precedents than we
already have."

During the time that Debra was contemplating suicide, Dalton had
withdrawn further into Revelations. He went to the bedroom closet,
dug out a twenty-gauge shotgun, and prepared for the end. After
pumping one shell into the chamber and pushing three shells into
the magazine, he went back into the living room. He ceremoniously
lit an incense pot and settled into his favorite easy chair. The rising
smoke from the smudge pot drifted through the room and created
a thick haze as emergency lights flashed through the picture window. *Doyle may be in jail, but the Beast has many heads.* While Dalton
waited for his personal confrontation with the sheriff, a glassy look
covered his deep blue eyes.

The Beast Knocks at the Door

When Tom pulled his SUV to the side of the street and parked, the first thing he saw was a metallic reflection moving toward him on the sidewalk. Now, outside the church, Debra was wobbling his way, a knife in one hand and the loose end of rope in the other. Tom walked cautiously in her direction. "Debra, are you okay?"

Clink! Debra dropped the knife on the pavement and warily took a few steps toward Tom, dragging the bell rope behind her. "Not really," she said, lifting up the loose end of rope as high as her waist.

"Did you try to use that?"

"Yes, Tom, but hopefully I'm beyond that crisis."

"I'm glad to hear that. Debra, I think I understand some of the things that you've been going through."

"I wish I understood things. He beat me pretty badly, Tom."

"Are you willing to press charges?"

"If I can do that, yes."

"Do you know where he is?"

"Sort of... his body's at home, but his mind is lost somewhere in the book of Revelations. He's gone completely mad and is talking like this is the end."

"That's not good. Listen, Debra, I've got to take him in. Does he have any guns in the house?"

"One. That shotgun you helped him buy for pheasant hunting."

Tom shook his head at the irony. "Dang it! Okay, you need to go some place safe. Get in my vehicle, lock the doors, and stay there. If something bad happens to me and you see your husband, get out of here quickly. Go straight to the courthouse."

Debra started walking toward the sheriff's SUV as she had been instructed. Meanwhile, Tom ducked around the south side of the house to survey the situation through a window. For the first time in many years, Debra was not afraid, and she would not leave Tom to face her crazed husband all alone. She changed her course of direction and hurried around the north side of the house. Tom was peeking through the window when Debra slipped in the back door and into the kitchen.

Inside, Debra kept her distance from Dalton and talked to him from the doorway between the kitchen and the living room. "Pastor Derrick, let's go see Tom. He's right outside."

"What's wrong, Jezebel? Is your man in jail?"

"Joe's not like that, Pastor Derrick."

Dalton laughed at Debra. "I saw the two of you at the piano, Jezebel. And you, you enjoyed the adulterer's touch." Dalton jumped up and ran a few steps toward Debra. She retreated into the kitchen. Dalton bolted in pursuit and grabbed her. "Get out of here, whore! Run to the devil's embrace!" Dalton pushed Debra across the room toward the back door.

Tom saw the shove and rushed from the window to the front door. He took a brief moment to gather his thoughts and mumbled, "Well, this has to be done." Then he knocked on the door.

Dalton shifted his attention from Debra to Tom. "Go away, Beast!" he yelled as he returned to the living room.

Tom could see through the door glass that Dalton had stopped his attack on Debra. He knocked a second time.

Dalton sat back into his easy chair, picked up the shotgun again, and placed it on his lap.

Tom pulled his pistol and eased the front door open. "I'm coming in, Pastor."

"God's house is always open. Enter if you wish."

The sheriff stepped into the entryway. "Put the gun down so we can talk."

Dalton pointed his finger at Tom's pistol. "So the Beast has horns." Dalton's shotgun still lay on his lap. He turned it so it pointed in Tom's general direction.

"Let's put our guns down, Pastor, so nobody gets hurt."

Dalton took a tighter hold of his gun as Tom stood his ground. "The end has come, Beast."

Hearing the pastor's deranged words, Tom took a deep breath, trying to stay calm. The thick incense was so strong, it made him cough. The cough forced him to look down and inadvertently step forward. Dalton reacted to the sheriff's advance and used the split second of distraction to lift up the shotgun. It now pointed directly at Tom's chest. "It looks like we have a draw, demon. Tell me, how will it end?"

Debra hovered in the kitchen and listened as her husband's insanity escalated. Understanding her husband's violent ways all too well, she knew that Tom's life was at risk. She picked up a heavy cast iron frying pan from her stove and inched toward Dalton. Tom glanced at her, and Dalton saw the glance. Dalton laughed, dismissing Debra. "So the Jezebel hasn't left yet. No matter, Beast. It's of no consequence. She doesn't give life, and she certainly doesn't have the courage to take it."

Debra was fed up with Dalton's belittling. She moved aggressively in on Dalton from behind with the cast iron pan raised high.

Tom, fearing for Debra when he saw what she was doing, deliberately stepped forward. Dalton jerked the shotgun tight against his shoulder. Debra could see that Tom was in immediate jeopardy, a trigger pull from death. Ignoring the pain in her ankle, she rushed her husband with the frying pan. Dalton heard her coming but kept his eyes on Tom. "Worthless whore!" he yelled just as Debra smashed the cast iron pan on the top of his head. Stunned and slumped over in the chair, Dalton tried to raise the gun, but Debra smacked him again. The pan reverberated in her hands while she watched her husband fall from the chair and onto the smoldering incense pot.

Tom approached Dalton's convulsing body and checked for a pulse. "I think he's dead."

Debra dropped the frying pan and stood over her husband with her arms hanging limp until his body lay still. "It's over, Tom. But what have I done?"

"You saved my life, Debra. That's what you've done."

Closing the Case

Tom recognized that Debra was in the midst of an ever-deepening mental health crisis. He took a short statement from her and wrestled the cell phone from his shirt pocket to call Art. "I need some help, Art."

Art rubbed his eyes and looked at his alarm clock. It was one o'clock in the morning. "That doesn't surprise me. What did you have in mind?"

"Could you take Debra to the women's shelter in Sioux Falls?"

"Possibly. Billie called me and said you were worried about Debra. How is she?"

"Remarkably well, considering that she's been beaten and raped and attempted suicide all in one day."

"That's a tough day. I'll be right over."

"Listen, Art, it gets worse. Debra's convinced that she's pregnant and she had to take Dalton down for me."

"Are you saying she killed him?"

"Yes, with a frying pan and saved my life doing it. Can you get down here right away? I need to take pictures, call the coroner, and wait here until we can get Dalton's body removed. Plus, I have to find out what the state's attorney wants me to do about Joe."

"I'm on the way, but I don't think the shelter is the place for Debra, not on the backside of all that. I'd recommend the psychiatric unit for a day or two first."

Tom walked out of the parsonage at seven thirty on Sunday morning. His next job was to look in on Joe. He found his detainee sound asleep on a plastic mattress. "What time did he go to sleep?" Tom asked the jailer.

"About twenty minutes ago. He insisted on staying awake until he knew that you and Debra were safe."

"Did you tell him what happened?"

"I didn't see much point in leaving him in the dark."

Tom gave Joe a compassionate glance and shook his head. "He doesn't belong in jail if you ask me, but that will be up to the state's attorney. He did assault Dalton, so I'll leave him in there for now. I don't have the heart to wake him up anyway. My guess is that Dr. Joe hasn't had any real sleep in several weeks."

"Speaking about sleep, the commissioner called and asked for you at seven o'clock this morning."

"Great. What did he want?"

"You're supposed to report for a one o'clock session at the table."

"This can't be good. The commissioner doesn't work on the weekend."

"He didn't sound very happy. I can tell you that. Are you going to get some rest between now and then?"

"I wish I could. I'm the president of the Redeemer Church Council, and someone has to be there to guide the congregation through this mess."

Art got back from Sioux Falls just in time to attend church and support Tom, who stepped to the altar carrying a message that tore at innocent hearts.

"Friends, last night, our congregation stepped out from under a dark cloud of physical and sexual abuse. This morning, the perpetrator, Pastor Dalton, lies dead as a result of his sickness. Debra is in Sioux Falls at the hospital and doing okay. As your president, let me say this: all of us could have been more vigilant. As your sheriff, I would say that silence is no weapon with which to protect ourselves against such sickness. I'm here this morning to help deal with this mess as best I can and to answer your questions. But first, we should all pray for Debra, the other victims, and God's guiding touch."

Tom and Art sat with the congregation and answered questions. Two hours later, they dismissed themselves for another meeting.

A Special Meeting

While dancing late into the night, people overwhelmed the commissioner with second- and third-hand reports about the events that took place in his city. By morning, he set about getting the details firsthand. He called Kelsey's as soon as it opened and reserved the table for one o'clock. Next, he called together a select list of attendees. The list included the judge, Father Riley, Trapper, Susan, Bobbi, Tom, Art, and Billie. The assembly formed with Tom and Art being the last to arrive. The commissioner kicked off the discussion. "Art, what's going on with the new guy you hired?"

"Well, he revealed a violent perpetrator who has been victimizing women and children in Dakota City for years."

"And you didn't know this was going on when you were working?" Art took on a guilty look. "No, sir."

"Tom, the next question is yours. Has Dr. Joe done anything illegal in the process of exposing Dalton?"

"That's an interesting question, Commissioner."

Nervous, Billie squirmed in her chair and jumped to Joe's defense. "He thought I was Bobbi when I kissed him."

Art looked at Tom and chuckled, but the commissioner addressed Billie with a firm tone in his voice. "Billie, I'll have some questions for you later. For now, wait your turn."

"Yes, Commissioner."

"Tom, I figured you might say what you did. That's why I invited Judge to this little gathering."

Tom looked at the judge. "He assaulted the pastor, but not without undue provocation from what I understand."

"Is anybody pressing charges?" the judge asked.

"No," Tom said. "I talked to the state's attorney, and he doesn't want to touch it."

The judge nodded his head in agreement. "We consulted, and I agree."

Next, the commissioner looked at Susan. "Susan, people are talking, so please forgive my candor." Susan nodded her head. "Tom, what about Dr. Joe sneaking around with Susan and helping her with a clandestine burial?"

"Ah—"

Susan sat up straight in her chair. "There was no sneaking involved. I have the necessary paperwork right here. Signed and dated by Vickie." Susan slapped the pile of papers on the table.

"May I see them?" the judge asked.

"What about the nature of the burial, Tom?" the commissioner asked.

"Actually, protocol suggests that Susan get permission from the cemetery's caretaker before internment." Trapper looked at Susan and raised his eyebrow.

"I see, and who keeps Bethlehem's cemetery?"

"That would be me," said Trapper as he pushed another paper toward the judge.

The judge examined the document granting Susan consent for burial. "The ink looks dry to me," he said.

"Where are we concerning the two bodies in one grave?" the commissioner asked.

The judge handed the papers back to Susan. "Law recognizes the right of second burial."

"Thank you, Judge. Now, another thing. I understand that Dr. Joe and Snowman are one and the same. Did Joe break any confidentiality laws with Laura?"

"Dr. Joe is a mandatory reporter. He has to report suspected child abuse," Art interjected on Joe's behalf.

"I talked with Laura, and she asked the snowman to help," Tom said for further clarification.

"So, if I'm hearing all of this right, Dr. Joe came to town, and in a few weeks, he exposed a violent perpetrator, led the victims to help, and did it all within the law. It makes me wonder what his predecessor was doing all these years."

Art cleared his throat. "That would be one way to look at what's happened, Commissioner."

"Tom, I'm going to go easy on you. You can just thank the good Lord for Debra saving your hide. What were you thinking when you went in Dalton's house alone? Don't bother answering that now. What I want from you is an immediate update. Where's Dr. Joe right now?"

"He's in jail, Commissioner. The door's been unlocked since I spoke with the state's attorney. I thought he needed to catch up on some sleep."

"How thoughtful of you," the commissioner said. "There's a headline that would catch the reader's attention and sway votes: 'Local Psychologist Jailed for Exposing Sex Offender.'"

Tom shrugged.

"But let's leave him there for the time being," the commissioner said.

"Billie, now it's your turn." The commissioner looked at Billie's trembling hands. "Do you really love this guy?"

"Yes."

"Let me explain something, Billie. Aside from Joe's knack for attracting trouble, I think he's the sort of fellow I would like to keep around. What do you think?"

"I think that would be a wise decision, sir, but I don't think he'll be staying." Billie wiped tears from her eyes.

"If we could change his mind, would you help Susan keep an eye on him for me?"

Billie smiled at Art. "I'd love to do that for you, Commissioner—if we can get him to stay."

"So, you really foresee him leaving?"

"I'm afraid so."

"Do you have any idea what it would take to keep him here?"

"I think *we* need to ask him, and I hate to say this, but the snowman has to go."

"I suspected as much. Billie, thank you."

"Okay, Susan, it's your turn again. Has that new piece of park equipment you ordered arrived?"

"Yes, Commissioner, it has. It's being stored in the maintenance shop."

"Good. Why don't you give Dr. Joe Monday off but tell him to start a victim's support group on Tuesday. From what I've been reading this morning, it's going to take a lot of time and work to help people get through this mess."

"I'll take care of that, Commissioner."

"Good. Folks, I think we can adjourn. Billie, I want to put the matter of retaining Dr. Joe into your hands. Let's put together a plan."

Another Switch

A rt hung around the restaurant until Billie finished her private meeting with the commissioner. She came out of the session with a happy glow on her face and with a key to the back door of the courthouse. Billie swung the key in front of Art's face, knowing that he would recognize it. "Uncle Art, I bet the commissioner a week's worth of coffee that you kept a key to your old office. You aren't going to let me down, are you?"

Art got another guilty look on his face. "I may have kept a key just in case Joe needed my help sometime."

"Good, let's go." Billie drove home, grabbed one of her new ice skates, and took Art to the courthouse. "Open the door, Uncle Art."

"What are we doing?"

"Making another switch, just trust me."

When Art heard the words *trust me* and *switch*, he immediately became nervous. "Relax, Uncle Art, we're only going to do a little loss prevention by trading ice skates, one of mine for one of Joe's. Oh, and we are going to close his window shade too. Don't let me forget that." Once inside the mental health office, Billie picked up one of Joe's skates and tucked it under her arm. She put her skate down in its place and drew the shade. "Okay, we're done. Let's go."

"What do we do now?" Art asked.

"We wait and hope this works."

While Billie and Art made the skate exchange, Sheriff Tom hurried to the jail so he could further delay Dr. Joe's departure. "What's up?" the jailer asked Tom.

"Billie and the commissioner need time to enact a plan." Tom opened the unlocked door and went into Joe's cell.

"Can I get out of here now, Tom?" Joe asked.

Tom went into a stall. "Not quite yet. There have been a few delays."

"Delays? What kind of delays?"

"Nothing serious. I've got to iron out a few procedural matters, that's all. Understand, this is a rather complex case, Joe—child abuse, rape, domestic violence, and a death. After I get the paperwork done, I need to consult with the state's attorney one more time and make sure everything is in order." Tom took a deep breath. "I hate to say this, Joe, but it's Sunday, and he's watching football. I'm going to do my level best to get you out of here before dark."

"Before dark! You said after lunch earlier this morning."

"That was before I knew that I had a meeting with the commissioner. Look, I promise to get you out of here as fast as I can."

"I'd appreciate that, Tom. Stainless steel is not my thing. How's Debra?"

"Art took her to the psychiatric unit in Sioux Falls. I think she's going to be fine, no thanks to Dalton. Oh, Debra said I should tell you, 'Thanks for pushing me away.' Doing that saved what little pride she had left."

"I'm glad to hear that she's surviving this ordeal. I was worried about both of you." Joe paused before changing the subject. "I stretched my luck to the limit, didn't I, Tom?"

"Yes, Joe you did, but something had to be done. If it wasn't for you, who knows how many more people Dalton would have hurt."

"The ladies did the work. I just listened."

"Look, Joe, if I'm going to have you out of here before dark, I need to get busy." The sheriff excused himself, went to his office, closed his door, and leaned back into his soft desk chair for a long nap.

While the Sheriff napped, Susan supervised a project in City Park, and Billie rounded up a good portion of the community and held them captive in Kelsey's until dusk. The ladies kept in contact by cell phone. Susan called Billie as soon as the crew finished their job. Now Billie could set the rest of the retention plan into motion. She called Tom. "Okay, Tom, you can let him out now."

Tom went into the jail. "Joe, before I let you out, I want you to know it's a privilege to work with you."

"It was interesting, wasn't it?"

"Was? You sound like a man ready to quit. What are you going to tell Billie?"

"That's a good question. All that time in jail to think and I still don't have an answer for that one. I need some ice time, Sheriff."

"Well, you've got a little daylight left, and there's ice right out your office door."

Doing It Right

Joe walked out of his cell thinking, *What am I going to tell Billie?* He jogged through the courthouse hallways to his office, grabbed his skates, and went to the lake. The massive sheet of ice that sprawled out before him caused him to think about Art. *At least he wasn't lying when he said they had ice.* Suddenly, the expanding ice cracked, and the crack ran across the lake. Its echo carried conversations with Art back from what now seemed to be the distant past. "Billie is special and deserves to be treated that way. If you can't do that, then leave her alone." *Art's right. This boils down to one simple question. What's best for Billie?*

As soon as Joe left jail, Tom called Billie. "He's going to get his skates."

"Good. Keep your eyes on him, and let me know what he's up to. Bye."

A short time later, Tom called Billie back. "He's out of the office with skates and stick in hand. Billie, he's headed for the lake." Tom kept his eyes on Joe from afar with binoculars.

"So far, so good," Billie said. "What's he doing now?"

"He's sitting on the bench and putting on his right skate. Okay, here we go; he's trying on the left one as I speak."

"Good," Billie said with growing impatience. "What's happening, Tom?"

"He's trying to call somebody on his cell phone."

"Did you make sure his battery was dead?"

"Yes, he left with absolutely no power bars."

"I bet he's trying to call me. Maybe we better hang up just in case." Since Billie's phone didn't ring, she called Tom back. "Is he talking to somebody?"

"I can't tell for sure. No, he just put the phone in his coat pocket."

"Good. If I know Joe, he wants that skate, and he'll be over here to use our phone to call me."

"The skate's off, and he's coming your way, just like you planned. He should be at your door right about…now." Tom closed his cell phone and hustled to the back door of Kelsey's.

Bobbi was standing lookout at the front door, and tonight Ardis had joined her. Both of them wanted to share in these pivotal moments in Billie's life. No matter how things played out, they would be there for her. Joe walked into the restaurant holding Billie's skate. Bobbi greeted him with a naughty smile. "Hi, Joe, didn't you eat in jail?"

Joe held up Billie's skate, shook his head, and snarled. "You're too much like your sister. Say, speaking of Billie, I need to talk to her. Can I borrow your phone?"

Bobbi took Billie's skate from Joe and gave him a cell phone. As he started to dial, she said, "You can talk to her in person if you like. She's in the dining area."

"Why didn't you tell me that right away?"

Bobbi shrugged at Joe and grinned. "You said you wanted to call, and I was practicing biting my lip."

"Not funny." Joe pushed the phone back toward Bobbi and walked around the corner into the main dining hall. His jaw fell. There stood Billie in her cocktail dress, surrounded by a room full of people and looking better than in any of Joe's fantasies. Billie stepped delightfully over to Joe and kissed him. "How do you like the sign?"

"What sign?" Joe asked, having been totally distracted by Billie.

Billie pointed at a ten-foot-by-four-foot paper banner hanging on the wall.

"I'm sorry. I missed it. All I could see was you." Joe took his eyes off Billie's legs and looked up at the large sign: "Please stay, Dr. Joe." With Joe in the room, Billie's hostages got up and circled around the couple. They gave Joe a round of applause and stepped forward to shake his hand.

Joe shook his head. "What's all of this?"

"What do you say, Joe? Will you stay?" Tom asked.

Billie stepped behind Joe and whispered in his ear. "Thank you for helping Bobbi." Then Billie spoke out loud. "Wait a second before you answer Tom's question. I have a surprise for you." Billie took Joe by the arm and led him to the front window. "Look outside," Billie said, trying to contain her excitement.

"What the—" When Joe looked out the window, he saw the snowman loaded in the back of a city dump truck as if nothing other than mere trash. Joe's chest collapsed as an empty sense of sadness drew the air from his lungs. *After what we've been through, they can't just throw him away. He was shelter, helper, and friend.* Fighting hard to hide his grief, Joe gave Billie a smile. *I can't hurt her feelings again. I have to show my appreciation.* Joe shook his head and gave Billie a soft smile. "I suppose you're behind all of this?" he asked Billie.

Billie's answer was all fidgets and grins as she led Joe back into the room full of guests.

"This is quite a sacrifice," Joe said loudly in recognition of the community-wide gesture.

Billie was rightfully proud of what she had done on Joe's behalf. "The commissioner wants the snowman to go. He said the darn thing makes too much trouble for our new psychologist. Joe, won't you please stay? After all you have done, you can't leave."

A hush fell over the crowd as they waited for Joe's reply. Truth be told, his intentions had been decided while trying on Billie's skate, but he didn't want to announce them in a public setting. *Some things are best done in private.* The pressure of the moment made Joe nervous and that faraway look that Billie had seen too often started to cloud his eyes. Billie watched with fear as the distant look deepened. Her heart wept as Joe looked toward the door. She could just see him walking away and never coming back. Life in Dakota City had taken too much out of him.

Joe stood as if paralyzed and unable to speak in the uncomfortable silence that filled the room. The impetuous part of him wanted to rush toward Billie and take her in his embrace. The thoughtful part of him pulled in a different direction. No matter which option Joe chose, he could see that there would be no privacy, not tonight. Dr. Joe had only one option; speak so everyone could hear. "Billie, I appreciate everything you've done—your support, your encouragement, this party, getting dressed up, getting rid of the snowman…everything. But right now, I need to do something." Joe turned his back toward Billie and walked slowly toward the door.

"Joe, please—" In misery, Billie watched through tear-filled eyes as Joe faded into the entryway, where Ardis was frantically trying to tend the cash register and peek around the corner at the same time. Now out of Billie's sight, Joe stepped close to Ardis and put his arm on her shoulder. He whispered in her ear. Hearing what Joe had to say, Ardis smiled and nodded. Joe took her arm and led her into the large dining room where Billie was hovering in dejection.

Heartsick, eyes welled with tears, and surrounded by friends, Billie did not see Joe come back. When Joe asked for everyone's attention, his calming voice surprised her. "Listen, everyone, I appreciate all of this very much. I really do. I know this is your way of asking me to stay, and I want to thank you for that."

The circle of friends separated so Billie could see Joe. Having addressed the audience, Joe turned and spoke directly to Art. "Art, when I came here, I promised to do things right. Truth be told, matters got out of hand, and I'm sorry for that."

"Like I said, it's a complex business. You've done well," Art said.

"Thanks." Now Joe turned his full attention to Billie. He looked deep into her swollen brown eyes. "Billie Kelsey, if there is one thing in my life that I need to do right, it is this." Joe took a deep breath and slowly walked up to face her. He gently took both of her hands in his.

"Joe—"

Joe let go one of Billie's hands and touched his index finger to her delicate lips. Blowing a soft *shh*, he reassured her. Then, he took both of her hands again. "Billie, I wouldn't have survived all of this without you. I was so close to giving up, but you wouldn't let me. Thanks for pushing me, for believing in me, and for expecting more of me."

Billie looked at Joe and whispered, "You're welcome." Her tears flowed like water, and she lifted her hands to cover her flush cheeks.

"Billie, you are absolutely the most beautiful creature on earth, and the way you kiss cannot be described. But before I can make a decision about staying, I need to know two things."

Hearing the word *but*, Billie's frustration and dejection boiled over. Her arms fell to her sides and dangled limp by her hips. She shook her head, held out her lace dress on both sides, and let it fall, showing her complete resignation. As the lace floated downward, she said, "Look at this party, Joe. No, look at me. *Just look at me.*" Waiting until he looked her in the eyes, she asked, "Now, tell me, Joe. What more could you possibly need to know?"

"Billie, I need to know if you will marry me. I can't see my life without you in it."

Billie sprang into Joe's arms and gave him a kiss he would never forget. Laughing through her tears, Billie answered, "Yes, Joe. Yes, I will marry you." Joe set her down softly so her feet were back on the floor. Their friends gave them a round of applause. "You wanted to know something else. What was it?" she asked.

Bobbi had brought Billie's skate into the room. Joe pointed at it. "Would you skate with me at sunrise?"

Aside from a momentary scare, Billie's plan was going better than even she had expected. "I'd love to, but let's meet on the bench by the snowman," Billie suggested.

"Great. I'll see you there." Joe kissed Billie good night and walked home.

Art whispered in Tom's ear. "You know what comes next, don't you?"

"Yes, and it's so like Billie. Are you going to get up at sunrise to see Joe's reaction?" Tom asked Art.

"No, I think they need some time alone."

❄

Billie got up well before sunrise the next morning. Beating Joe to the park was an absolute necessity. She just had to see his reaction to the new park equipment the commissioner had the crew install overnight. Plus, the commissioner had given Billie a message to deliver. When Joe walked around the corner of the courthouse, he stopped dead in his tracks. There was Billie looking gorgeous and waving at him as she leaned against a great big fiberglass Santa Claus. Her red cheeks and spunky smile glowed with the colors of the rising sun. A gentle breeze blew through her long brown hair that flowed like a waterfall from under a red stocking hat. She wore a matching red-and-black coat, and her hands were covered with black gloves. Billie ran to give Joe a kiss. Joe held her at a distance with one arm as a playful look of disgust filled his eyes. With his other hand, he pointed at the fiberglass Santa and, thinking that he had been tricked again, started to swear. "Da—"

Billie quickly covered Joe's mouth with the tips of her fingers to prevent him from cussing. "Bite your lip, Joe. Did you know that you can get therapy to stop swearing?" Billie giggled.

Joe shook his head in frustration and looked closely at the Santa Claus. "No two-way speaker system?"

"No. No speakers. But the commissioner said he'll put them in if you leave town." Billie tugged on Joe's arm and led him to the edge of the lake. "So are you going to teach me how to skate?"

The couple sat down on Joe's favorite bench and pulled on their ice skates. "Wait. I'll help you with your laces," Joe said. Joe cinched his laces first, crouched in front of Billie, and placed her skate firmly in-between his calves. Billie sat on the bench with her legs extended while Joe pulled hard on the long white shoestrings. "They need to be good and tight." Reluctantly setting her leg gently on the ground, he slipped on her skate guards. "There. You're ready." Joe stood and reached for Billie's hands to help her up. Then he pulled Billie forward until his nose gently touched hers. The couple turned, and with arms wrapped tight around each other's waist, they glided onto the ice, and … they skated.

One More Refill

Billie came by the table to refill our coffee cups … again. She looked at me, winked, and scolded her uncle. "This story is getting expensive, Art. Aren't you boys about done?"

Art inched back from the table and held his cup up for Billie's convenience. "Warm it up just a tad."

"Uncle Art, sometimes you make me so mad."

While Billie filled his cup, Art looked at me. "Well, Bob, that's the story of Dr. Joe and the snowman."

"What? That's the end?" I asked.

"That's it."

"But who was the snowman?"

"Who was the snowman?" Art said, taking a thoughtful pause. "Bob, I told you when I started this story, no one really knows for sure. Of course, people make accusations. Some think it was the commissioner. He had keys to all the doors. Even Tom and the judge stand accused from time to time."

"The judge?"

"Yes, he always worked odd hours. Father Riley was a popular suspect when his knee went bad."

"What about you, Art? Your office door was close to one of those tunnels. And, excuse me for saying so, but you told Joe a misleading thing or two. Did anyone ever suspect you?"

Art laughed. "Don't be ridiculous. I loathed the thing. Anyway, it doesn't matter. What does matter is that for a few days in Dakota City, Dr. Joe was the snowman."

"Hmm … I wonder."

Twelve months after Billie accepted Joe's proposal, I addressed the people gathered at the Redeemer Church as their pastor, Pastor Bob Michael. "In the name of the Father and of the Son and of the Holy Ghost, what God has joined together, let no man put asunder. Amen. Ladies and gentlemen, it is my pleasure to introduce to you, Dr. and Mrs. Joseph Doyle."

The bride kissed her husband before my consent, and the couple walked down the aisle greeting friends and family along the way. The wedding party followed. Trapper made an unusual best man, and Father Riley crossed the street to be a groomsman. Susan was a beautiful bridesmaid. And the maid of honor—well, I think Bobbi would make a wonderful bride.

Epilogue

B efore I say farewell, may I remind you, "Dakota City is a good place to live and good people live here." What brought me here? I came to town in pursuit of a career goal: the goal of guiding a congregation through a very traumatic experience. Allow me to say just a bit more. At five years of age, I screamed in fearful protest while my mother was severely beaten. Afterward, and alone but for being with me, Mom turned her back, and, as Debra did with the snowman, shared her pain. So I'm quite certain that when Bobbi erupted in anger and anguish, she buffered no words. She used no alphabetic abbreviations nor left literary pauses to fill in. Was it wrong for me to buffer her harsh words? Are such words good or bad? It may be that Trapper spoke the truth when he said, "right and wrong are a matter of perception." In telling this story, I softened the tone with the understanding that human hearts, like Debra's delicate flesh, are easily bruised. Might some have empathized more had I done otherwise? Maybe, but I hope not. After all, I, like Dr. Joe, came to Dakota City to do things right. For me, as a pastor, to write such harsh words *would be an abuse of professional trust.*

Also by Steve Riedel
A Homestead Holiday

How do you endure when loved ones can't make it home for the holidays?

In Steve Riedel's heartwarming story, *A Homestead Holiday*, James and Faye Hammer face their first empty-nest Christmas. They accept an invitation from strangers Gus and Sophie Frost, hoping that a country getaway will cure their holiday blues. During perilous travel to the Frosts' remote farm, the Hammers encounter a sinister train conductor, who, as it turns out, covets the Frosts' farm and Faye. Gus and Sophie welcome the Hammers with old-fashioned hospitality, but the conductor may not be alone in his deceitful ways. Having grown up in a children's home, James keeps his guard up, and his suspicions run wild when Gus reveals that their children were abducted years ago. The very foundation of the Hammers' marriage is suddenly threatened. Will James's fears be justified, or is the Frosts' invitation a plea for help?

Learn more about Steve Riedel and his books at
http://steveriedel.tateauthor.com